WANT A FREE

Get a free copy of my Victorian novella, *Restoring Miss Hastings*, as a thank you for signing up for my weekly email newsletter.

You're free to subscribe at any time, but if you stick around you'll get updates, freebies, recommendations and exclusive giveaways, plus encouragement and lots of historical fiction fun!

Sign up here:

EdwinaKiernan.com/FreeBook

For Jesus,
whose love covered all my sins

Hatred stirs up strife, But love covers all transgressions.

— PROVERBS 10:12

CONTENTS

CHAPTER 1

A DEEP LONGING

England, 1848

"Is *that* her?"

Grace Stratton turned her head toward the unfamiliar voice.

Not again.

Her gaze roamed fiercely across the gaggle of middle-aged women standing at the other side of the pew. One attended the church regularly, but the other three Grace had never seen before.

One of the strange women glanced away a little too quickly. She grabbed at her cuffs and straightened her sleeves, her head tilted to one side and an affectation of innocence on her taut face. Her showy hat with its splay of bright feathers reminded Grace of a peacock's unfurled tail, and the woman's demeanour left little doubt that she was wont to strut about with just as much pride.

Insufferable busybody.

Grace exhaled forcefully, then glanced at her mother,

Ruby. She was deep in conversation with a newly widowed parishioner, her brow furrowed in sympathy, and the fingers of her right hand fiddled absent-mindedly with the top button at the neck of her pale green dress.

No one would have been able to guess the pain and devastation of Ruby's early life by merely observing her now. But plenty of people knew the story. And Grace was more than tired of the fact that when someone new visited the church, they did not do so in order to hear a rousing sermon by her father, who was parson there, but in the hope of catching a glimpse of his wife.

"Grace, my dear."

Grace turned to see her father, the Reverend Henry Stratton, striding toward her. His dark eyes shimmered with delight, and his grin made her momentarily forget the frustration that had coiled her hands into tight balls at her sides.

"Papa. Another fine sermon."

"Thank you, my dear." He studied her for a moment, his grin slipping away. "Are you all right?"

Grace swallowed hard. Her father could read her better than anyone. "It is nothing."

He gave her a knowing look. "Are you quite sure?"

Grace sighed, shaking her head gently. "Only the usual."

Her father glanced about at the different clusters of people who were chatting and greeting one another now that the meeting was at an end. He drew his lips into a thin line. "Ah. I see."

Grace followed his gaze, which seemed to have fallen upon the group of gossiping ladies at the end of the pew. She looked again at her father, gratitude stirring within her. He was gentle and kind, but a fierce streak of ardent protectiveness lay within him, and her great aunt had told her how daringly and passionately he had defended her mother.

She still found all the stories she'd heard quite hard to believe sometimes, but what was clear was the deep love that each of her parents had for one another, and for God.

A parishioner approached her father, who gave Grace a gentle smile before turning his attention to the man.

"Grace?" Her mother's gentle voice drifted through the air.

Ruby smiled gently as she motioned for Grace to join her. The widowed lady was nowhere to be seen.

"Are you all right, my dear? You seem a little... quiet."

"Am I not usually quiet?"

"You know what I mean. What is the matter?"

There was no annoyance in her mother's tone, no judgement. She was as kind and gentle a woman as Grace had ever met. Another reason why Grace was sick of all the gossip and subterfuge that permeated their everyday lives.

How was she ever to serve God freely in this place when every word and look from judgemental strangers seemed only to forge another link in the chain around her heart?

Maybe God would answer her prayers and call her to go elsewhere.

Or, maybe there was more He had to teach her here, first — a thought she couldn't bear to dwell on at present.

Grace sighed in frustration. "Oh, nothing but small-minded gossipmongers."

A shadow of melancholy passed across her mother's face for a mere second. She smiled and looked down. "Oh, Grace... Not everyone is as kind as your father. You know that."

Grace jutted her jaw outwards. "It simply maddens me, that is all. Treating you as though you are some dangerous, out-of-the-ordinary spectacle. Have they not read their Bibles? Are they unaware that sin has tainted *everyone's* life — including their *own*?"

"Hush, now..." her mother said gently, compassion

shining in her dark eyes that looked so much like Grace's own. "I suppose my story is out-of-the-ordinary as far as most people are concerned. But there is no profit in allowing anyone to judge us or intimidate us concerning it. We ought to leave them and their opinions to God. There is much upon which we can focus that is far more deserving of our time and attention."

Her mother's wise words soothed Grace's heart, as they always did. But still she could not shake off the melancholy that had been a permanent fixture in her heart these past few months.

A restless rumination seemed to occupy her days more and more of late. Secretly, she often imagined going somewhere new, a place where no one knew neither her nor the scandalous circumstances in which her parents had met. A place where she could be her own person — not merely the daughter of a former prostitute and the man who had rescued her from a life of vice.

Her father appeared beside them, a warm grin on his face. "Shall we go?"

Grace looked around, surprised to notice they were the only people left in the little church.

As she followed her parents out to the carriage, she sighed. Guilt nudged her heart. Her home and family were good — idyllic, even.

So why was she filled with such a deep longing to leave them?

CHAPTER 2

DEVASTATING NEWS

David Carbury paced the drawing room floor of his London townhouse.

Dead. Dead!

Augustus Moss, his trusted friend and colleague, stood on the edge of the Axminster rug, his chin tucked low.

David turned to face him. "There must be some mistake, Augustus. I administered the chloroform myself. I—"

"He is dead," Augustus said, shaking his head grimly.

David's blood seemed to drain through him all over again.

No.

He'd been so careful.

There had to be some mistake.

Augustus sighed. "Did you administer the same quantity as always?"

David's stomach tightened as he remembered the pitiable state of his patient. "He was so agitated, Augustus," David said, shaking his head slowly. "His coughing was so violent that I had no hope of administering the opium. Not until he was calmed."

"So... you used more?"

David exhaled a deep, shaky breath. "A little more. But only a *little*, Augustus, and I ensured that it was still within the safe parameters."

Augustus's gaze remained fixed on the floor. "Safe parameters," he scoffed. "Many physicians still consider the wretched stuff to be experimental at best. We knew that. We never should have—" He broke off with a forceful sigh, commencing his own agitated pacing.

David stood still and stared at him, a sickening sensation coiling in his gut. "No. Augustus, you know as well as I do — there are doctors up and down the country who are using it now — for all kinds of conditions — why, plenty of surgeons use far larger doses than I. It is safe. And I gave Mr. Edwards an appropriate dosage, I know I did!"

Augustus turned abruptly and raised his eyes to look at David. "Well, that matters little enough now. The man is gone."

A chill plunged through David's heart. "What do you mean, it matters little enough now? It matters a great deal, Augustus! I administered a safe dosage. It was not the chloroform that ended his life, it was the cholera for which we were treating him, *that* is—"

"You. For which *you* were treating him. Do not drag me into this, Carbury. I never liked the idea of using that terrible liquid." Augustus pointed a trembling finger at David, his teeth clenched as he spoke. "The culpability for his death is squarely upon your own head."

David gaped. "Augustus? What do you—"

"I never wanted to have anything to do with it all in the first place, David. You *knew* that. But you insisted that, soon, the use of this horrid substance would become standard practice. That other physicians would laud us as one of the first to adopt it!" He exhaled bitter contempt. "I only wish I had adhered to my own judgement. Had I done so, he might still be alive."

This cannot be happening.

Not only was his patient dead, but now his medical partner seemed determined to blame him for it.

David swiped his forehead with his palm. "Augustus, you know as well as I—"

"No! No more, Carbury. I am done." He strode toward David, his icy gaze piercing him to the core. "We may both be legally liable if his family chooses to hold us accountable. What say you to that?"

David shook his head. He tried to summon the words, but only a throaty groan met the still air.

"Do not expect any support from me, Carbury. I shall *not* give up everything that I have worked for because of *your* error." Augustus fixed David with a menacing glare, then spun on his heel and was out of the room before David could even try to respond.

The silence that closed around him seemed cavernous.

He'd been careful. He knew he had.

A vast number of cholera patients did not survive, even with a physician's intervention. That was a sombre fact of the profession.

It was not the chloroform's fault.

It was not *his* fault.

Augustus's words rang in David's ears as he turned to stare out of the window, seeing nothing of the morning bustle in the street below.

No more, Carbury. I am done.

So, that was it.

His patient. His partner.

One dead. One done.

Both gone.

CHAPTER 3

AN UNEXPECTED OPPORTUNITY

Grace pushed the mutton on her dinner plate from one side to the other, cutting off a small piece now and then and chewing it absent-mindedly. All day, she'd been trying to shake off the memory of the woman from church inspecting her mother, but resentment and frustration still bubbled within her heart.

"Are you not hungry, my love?"

Grace turned to face her great-aunt Abigail. It was often hard to believe just from looking at her that the woman was in her eighties. Her bright eyes and fresh skin somehow seemed to make her wrinkles and grey hair less noticeable.

"Oh, I... I was just thinking, I suppose." Grace forced a smile, which Aunt Abigail freely returned.

She resumed eating, at a quick pace. Glancing at her parents, she noticed her father's analytical gaze and her mother's compassionate look.

Please do not let him ask anything.

She wished she could slip off the burden that seemed to hang around her shoulders like a lead shawl. There were times when it faded into the background, and times when it weighed so heavily upon her that she found it difficult to move or breathe. The desire for a new life forced an ache into her very bones. Would she ever explore more of the world than the quaint little corner of the country she'd inhabited her whole life?

"I did not see Browne at church today, darling, did you?" her mother asked her father.

"Ah, no. He is ill with a chest cold at present. Jonathan was there, though. He reminded me that it is Browne's birthday next week." Henry shook his head slowly, a fond smile lighting his face. "Can you believe it? Browne will be one hundred years old on Tuesday!"

Ruby gasped and gave a small laugh. "I cannot imagine it! Oh, we must visit him soon and bring a birthday gift."

"Yes, indeed! I do wish he were still living here with us. But Jonathan made it clear that he is very glad to take the opportunity to care for his father in his old age."

Grace smiled gently. She'd heard endless stories from Aunt Abigail and her parents about how noble and faithful a servant Browne had been to the family for so many years. He'd retired in her early childhood, but even though he had not been physically present at Shiloh Hall for the past number of years, he was still very much part of their family life.

After dinner, Aunt Abigail decided to go to bed early. Ruby left the room with her, in order to ensure that Abigail had everything she might need for the night.

Grace crossed to the drawing room and picked up the latest novel that had captured her attention, though her mind and heart were still much too distracted to settle upon reading it properly. How well she could relate to its heroine, Agnes Grey, and her yearning for a different life. A life where she could break free from everyone else's opinions and expectations and be who she really was.

"Grace... Tell me what it is." Her father's voice was deep and gentle.

She looked up at him, opening her mouth to deny that anything was wrong. But as she caught his gaze, she realised it would be an exercise in futility. He knew her too well. She'd never been able to shrug off his inquiries whenever she was feeling low, nor would she be able to do so this time.

Grace sighed. "In truth, Papa, I am not sure *what* to tell you."

Henry sank into the chair opposite her, the firelight illuminating the left side of his face. "I find the truth is often the best thing that one can tell."

Grace shook her head. "No... That is not what—" She exhaled in frustration. "I only mean that I do not even know what the truth *is*. Why it is that I feel so... restless."

"Restless?" Her father leaned forward, his brow crinkled in concern. "What do you mean?"

Grace shrugged, shaking her head. She sighed. "I do not know."

As her father opened his mouth to respond, the door eased open and her mother entered the room, settling on a small settee facing the fire. "Aunt Abigail was asleep before I even left her room," she said, her tone one of quiet concern.

Henry was quiet for a moment. "She has seemed to be rather more tired lately."

Ruby's lips pressed together in sympathetic agreement. She glanced at Grace, then back at her husband. "Is everything all right?"

Henry looked to Grace, indicating that the response ought to be hers.

Grace forced a smile and nodded. "Everything is fine."

She knew from her mother's expression that her reply had not been convincing, but she was at a loss as to what more she could even say on the matter, not fully understanding it all herself.

A few moments passed in silence, then her mother turned to her father. "Oh, Mrs. Marshall gave me a note for you this morning." She strode out of the room, returning a moment later with her reticule. Upon pulling a piece of folded paper from within it, she handed it to him with a gentle smile.

Henry unfolded it, tilting it toward the firelight as his eyes scanned the page. "A friend of hers... an elderly spinster... is seeking a companion. Mrs. Marshall wishes me to announce it next Sunday, unless I—" He glanced up at Grace for less than a second. "Unless I already know of someone who might be suited to the post..."

Hope flickered in Grace's heart. "Where does the lady in question live?"

Henry scanned the letter again. "In a small market town called Lindenfell. I have heard of it... It is around, oh, I would say fifty miles west of here, or thereabouts."

"Lindenfell," Grace repeated quietly, the unfamiliar name resonating in her heart with the wistful longing for one's dearly-missed home.

"Do you know of anyone?" Ruby asked Henry.

He glanced at her, then fixed his gaze on Grace. "Perhaps..."

"You mean... Grace?" Her mother turned to face her. "But would you wish to go?"

Grace looked at each parent, weighing the idea in her heart. "I believe I would."

Ruby's eyebrows lifted. "You do not wish instead to be a governess, as you mentioned before?"

Grace sighed. "I had always assumed that I would be a governess, but... well, a companion may be just as useful, do you not think?"

Her parents were silent for a moment, each appearing deep in thought as they looked in surprise at one another.

"Well, perhaps it would," her mother said slowly.

"Pray about it, Petal," her father said kindly. "Seek only what the Lord would have you do."

Grace smiled gently upon hearing her father's nickname for her. And for the first time in as long as she could remember, a fresh stirring of hope bloomed within her.

"I shall." She stood, kissed them both on the cheek, and headed toward her room.

Lindenfell.

She would pray. Of course she would — she never made a big decision without seeking God's will.

Yet, as she entered her room and sank down on her knees beside her bed, part of her seemed to already sense what the Lord's answer might be.

CHAPTER 4

DREAMS AND NIGHTMARES

David swallowed another sip of his tea and replaced the cup in its saucer with a clink. A beam of morning sunlight illuminated the gold-leaf rim, and he noticed a thin, barely visible crack running all the way down the cup's side through the ornate blue and gold pattern.

Mother would be crestfallen. She loved this tea set.

He smiled grimly, remembering her graceful manner and her elegant smile. It had been five years since his parents had died at sea, and the loss still ached when he permitted himself to think of it.

Five years since he'd inherited the house, the servants, the investments... and this tea set.

His parents had always supported his desire to become a physician. He only wished they could have seen him realise his dreams.

David's butler strode into the dining room, a small silver salver held aloft in his right hand. "For you, sir."

David's throat went dry.

This must be it.

The inevitable letter from Mr. Gibbs, his lawyer, the

anticipation of which had haunted his dreams each night since he'd been informed of Mr. Edwards's death.

David accepted the envelope with a shaking hand, his vision threatening to cloud over. He waited for the butler to leave, then drew a deep breath and opened the seal.

Dear Mr. Carbury,

I regret to inform you that Mr. Edwards's family is determined to see justice carried out to the fullest possible extent of the law, with regard to what they consider to be his untimely death.

Their lawyer, a Mr. Polkinghorne, has informed me that they believe you to be guilty of mortally wounding Mr. Edwards, and they have gone so far as to use the phrase 'murder by poisoning' in their communication.

Their position is that, owing to the wary public opinion of chloroform, the substance is evidently more dangerous than previously thought, and has acted as a poison toward Mr. Edwards rather than serving as a medicinal aid.

Obviously, I have written to their lawyer contesting these charges, but owing to the wide mistrust of the substance even among other physicians, and the high societal standing of Mr. Edwards and his family, I do not expect that our chances of resolving the matter merely via correspondence to be very high.

It pains me to admit this, and I will, of course, do all that I can in order to turn things around for you, but it may be wise for you to prepare yourself for a trial. If found guilty on a charge of manslaughter, you would stand to receive a punishment either of imprisonment or transportation. And, if convicted of murder — though, I am determined to ensure that your innocence be proven beyond a shadow of a doubt — you would be sentenced to death by hanging.

Obviously, I shall do what I can to ensure that the ultimate outcome will be the least damaging to your career and life, but I do not wish to provide any false hope. This is a serious matter, and we have a long and difficult road ahead, which may lead to consequences we would rather avoid.

I shall be in touch in a day or two once I have received a response to the scathing rebuttal which I issued to Mr. Polkinghorne this morning.

Yours faithfully,

Benedict Gibbs

Everything in David's awareness seemed to fall away, save for the rapid beating of his anguished heart.

Imprisonment or transportation — having done nothing wrong — would be bad enough. But, *hanging*?

He could scarcely permit himself to imagine it.

This was all a bad dream. It had to be.

It *had* to be.

But the letter in his trembling hands was real, its sickening truth as clear as the ink in which it had been written.

The government had done away with the death penalty for a lot of crimes over the past few decades.

But not for murder.

Murder!

It was a word he'd never imagined could be associated with himself.

Yet, now it seemed inevitable. He'd met Mr. Edwards's family members numerous times, had seen how vindictive and ruthless they could be — even toward their own kin. How much more against the man they deemed responsible for the family patriarch's death?

David glanced at the letter again. His lawyer intended to do all that he could, but — as he'd said himself — even that might not be enough.

What then? What else might be done to escape this dreadful calamity?

He clenched the letter in his hand and flung it onto the table.

All he'd ever wanted to do was ease the suffering of others. As word had trickled through the medical community over the past few years of chloroform and its uses, he had seen what many others had refused to acknowledge — progress.

And so many of his patients had benefited from its powerful properties.

Of course, he'd heard the stories of other patients who had died, but he'd concurred with other physicians who'd blamed underlying conditions for being the real cause of death in each of those cases.

Never had David imagined that the same calamity would befall his own practice.

His parents had raised him to be a gentleman, to always be calm and careful, and he had.

He'd been so careful.

But, it hadn't been enough to prevent him from facing what he now was.

In agony of thought, he sat frozen to the chair — hardly moving, hardly breathing — for what seemed an age. No matter the avenues his mind travelled, seeking some kind of refuge or remedy, he found none.

His parents may not have lived to see him fulfil his dreams, but at least they'd been spared from watching those dreams turn into the nightmare now unfolding around him.

"What can be done?"

Silence met his barely audible whisper.

A thought seized upon him. A thought he chastised himself for not having sooner.

His mentor.

Of course!

Surely, the man who had invested so much of himself in David's early career would have some valuable insight and advice regarding the predicament in which he now found himself.

Hands still trembling, David hurriedly set about gathering his hat and cloak, picking up the letter and tucking it firmly in his waistcoat pocket.

Surely, Professor Steele would know what to do.

For David certainly did not.

CHAPTER 5

FAREWELL

As the morning breeze swept tendrils of Grace's hair into her eyes, she quickly pushed them away from her face.

The railway platform was more crowded than she'd expected, and an almost tangible metallic smell hovered in the air.

"Will you write to us as soon as you arrive?" Her mother's forehead scrunched in anxious hope.

"Yes, I shall," Grace replied calmly, even though she had lost count of how many times she had already assured her of the fact.

"Oh, I shall miss you so much, my darling!"

Grace melted into her mother's arms. "I shall miss you, too, Mamma." She pulled back, catching sight of her father. "Both of you."

Henry gathered both Grace and Ruby in his arms, encircling them with a firm but gentle embrace. "Shiloh Hall will be so empty without you, dear one." His dark eyes glistened.

Grace forced a light smile. "I am sure to have opportunities to visit every once in a while."

A deafening roar obscured the last few words of her sentence. She turned to see a huge black steam train gliding toward the platform on which they all stood. The scent of grease and metal invaded her nostrils, and the locomotive seemed to loom over her like a menacing shadow, despite her inward excitement at the prospect of boarding it — of discovering a new place and meeting new people.

Ruby pulled Grace into her arms once again, squeezing her even more tightly than she had before. "Do be careful, my love." She kissed Grace's forehead. "I *love* you."

"I love you too, Mamma."

Grace embraced her father, whose comforting scent evoked the realisation that she was soon to be without it. She buried her face deeply into his chest, his thick surtout warming her cheek, his strong heart beating a calming rhythm.

"I love you, darling."

"I love you too, Papa."

As Grace parted from her parents amidst a flurry of the other passengers's swishing skirts and clicking canes, the weight of reality crashed around her. For the first time in her life, she would be away from everyone who knew and loved her, from everyone whom she knew and loved.

A porter gathered up her large leather trunks and two portmanteaus with surprising ease.

"Oh, wait, please!" Grace motioned toward one of the portmanteaus, and the man lowered it back onto the platform. Deftly, Grace scooped *Agnes Grey* out of the leather bag before returning it to the porter with a nod of appreciation.

With the novel in her hand, she walked toward the train, but doubt slowed her steps. As she neared the imposing metal beast that would carry her to an unfamiliar place, she thought of the many calamities that had befallen the heroine of the story on her quest for purpose.

And of the possible calamities that might befall herself.

What if Grace did not like the woman whose companion she was to become? What if the woman did not like her?

What if there was no one her own age in Lindenfell?

As she reached the train's door, she cast a glance back at her parents. They were each smiling bravely, trying to hide their sorrow. Her father's arm encircled her mother in a snug sideways embrace.

Her parents were so close, so in love with one another, even after more than twenty years together.

Sadness tinged Grace's heart.

Would *she* ever find someone with whom to share such a love? Or would her existence in Lindenfell be just as unremarkable as it had been here?

CHAPTER 6

A DESPERATE PLAN

The springtime air cooled David's face as he hurried down the street to the building that housed the Royal College of Physicians. He jogged up the wide steps and strode through the portico of towering columns, hoping that his old mentor would be found sequestered in his office, as he so often had been years before when David had frequented the building.

Twisting and weaving through the familiar corridors, he soon reached his intended target — the office of his former mentor, Professor Steele.

David pounded on the door with a heavy fist, his breathing fast and heavy owing to his atypical exertion.

Silence met him.

He cannot be gone already. He—

"Enter!"

Hope leaped inside David's chest as the familiar voice sounded from within the room. Boldly, David swung the door open.

The rotund man behind the desk glanced up at him, his dark, beady eyes instantly flickering with recognition.

"Carbury, my boy."

David slipped inside, closing the door behind him. "Professor Steele. How do you do?"

Professor Steele folded his hands across his enormous stomach and peered over the rim of his spectacles at David, who was trying not to show surprise that his old mentor remained seated, not making any effort to shake his hand or offer any other kind of decorous greeting.

"Well, now," he said with a chuckle, "I do very well indeed. But that is not why you have come, is it? For if I were to ask you the same question, I would receive a very different response."

David's eyes widened. "How... how did you know that?"

Professor Steele tapped his fingertips together, staring at David all the while. "Well, would you believe me if I said that a little bird whispered it to me?"

"No."

"Mmm. Thought not." Professor Steele hesitated. "As a matter of fact, you are the second one of my past mentees to pay me a visit today."

"The second?"

"Mmm. Funny how years go by without a word and then two of you show up almost at once."

"Augustus."

"Moss, yes. He informed me of your... *predicament*."

Something in Professor Steele's tone made David question his decision to come and seek his help. Nevertheless, he cleared his throat and drew a deep breath. "And?"

"And?"

"What is your view?"

"Well, that would all depend, my boy. Did you ensure that your chloroform was pure, from a reputable apothecary?"

"Yes."

"And you used the appropriate amount?"

"Yes, absolutely."

"And you believe it was Edwards's underlying condition that ultimately led to his death, rather than any... *misadventure* with the substance?"

"I do. He was terribly stricken with cholera. You know how deadly it is. And there have been a great many cases of late. I do believe we are on the precipice of another pandemic."

Professor Steele waved his hand in annoyance. "Irrelevant, my boy. So, you administered a safe dose of chloroform..."

"Yes. I had to increase the dose a little the last time I saw him due to his agitation. But only enough to be able to administer his opium. I was careful to stay within safe parameters."

"But you acted against Moss's wishes, correct?"

"What?"

"He explicitly informed you of his aversion to using chloroform, given that it has somewhat of an... unfounded reputation as a curative agent?"

David frowned. Augustus's words echoed in his mind.

I never wanted to have anything to do with it all in the first place, David. You knew that.

"I... He mentioned it briefly, a long time ago. But then, after Mr. Edwards passed away, he insisted that he had *never* been happy with the idea." David shook his head. "He had plenty of other opportunities in which to inform me of this, yet he took none of them. We have been using chloroform successfully for many months now. On a variety of patients. Never did he—"

"But that is your word against his, is it not?"

David's heart sank. "What?"

"You heard the question, my boy. Now, answer it."

David frowned. "What are you trying to say?"

Professor Steele sighed, an air of experience and impatience seeming to fill the room alongside it. "What you have is an irate former colleague, a dead patient, and what is largely viewed as an experimental treatment. The courts will side with him, my boy. You may be assured of that."

"Side with him? You mean with *Augustus*?"

The room seemed to tilt and sway.

"Indeed. He has a year or two on you, as well. I am sorry to say it, but the whole debacle is not looking very good for you."

"But, no... It is the patient's family intending to pursue legal action against me — not Augustus."

Professor Steele fixed David with a beady stare. "Ah. You have not spoken to him recently, I take it?"

All the air seemed to squeeze from David's lungs. "I spoke with him last week. Why?"

Professor Steele pursed his lips. "He was here this morning. He is very upset by the whole matter. And he intends to do all within his power to ensure that he will not share in your downfall."

Fear raised the volume of David's voice. "Meaning, what?"

"I believe he intends to pursue his own case against you. Or, at least, be a witness for the Edwards lot."

Everything within David seemed to stop, an eerie silence wrapping itself around his mind. "But... But, he..."

"It is a sorry business, my boy. I always believed your skills to be more advanced than his. It is a shame. But Moss seems determined to see that you are out of the way, and to take your place as the more popular physician." Professor Steele levelled a firm nod at him. "If I were you, I would make sure to employ a *very* good lawyer."

David mumbled something in agreement and was out of the room before he even realised it.

He hadn't even said goodbye.

But what was the use?

Of all the blows which had befallen him of late, this was the harshest of all.

Moss seems determined to see that you are out of the way, and to take your place as the more popular physician.

What was he to do now? To whom could he go? His own lawyer held little hope of a favourable outcome. And if the worst came to the worst, he could face the executioner. Surely—

He froze, his steps halting just as he turned away from the building.

No... Surely he could not...

But what if he *could?*

Professor Steele's words circled in his mind.

Moss seems determined to see that you are out of the way... to take your place...

Out of the way...

Take your place...

"Take *his* place," David said, hardly above a breath.

Out of the way...

Perhaps there *was* something he could do after all. Something risky. Yet, something that would buy him time to think.

But could he really go through with it? Would it really... *work?*

As he strode into the biting cold, reviewing in his mind his conversations with Augustus, with Professor Steele, and the letter from his lawyer... He knew what he must do.

He had no other choice.

CHAPTER 7
LINDENFELL

Grace stepped down from the close confines of the train and drew a deep breath.

The air in Lindenfell had a scent of its own — one of warmth and peace. Of hope.

She stood still for a moment, scanning the new landscape. Cheerful blooms in window boxes nestled on every sill in the station, and men and women from all spheres of society dotted the platforms. Some stood, some strolled.

All were strangers.

"Help you, miss?" The porter's eyebrows were raised expectantly, and his arms twitched by his sides in keen anticipation.

"Yes, thank you."

The wiry man snatched up all the pieces of luggage as though they were weightless and followed her as she made her way to the station's exit.

Waiting outside was a gleaming Clarence carriage. A white-haired man dressed in a coachman's garb stood beside it, looking expectantly at each traveller who neared him.

His gaze caught Grace's. He stilled.

He must be waiting for *her*.

Suddenly, the realisation filled her that she wouldn't be going back to Shiloh Hall tonight. Instead, she would travel with a stranger, to meet another stranger, and spend the next number of years living amidst a whole town full of strangers.

They will not always be so. Some may soon become friends, she reassured herself quietly as she approached the coachman.

"Miss Stratton?" he asked, straightening his already tall, stiff posture.

"Yes."

"Ah." He broke into a smile, which seemed to soften his manner considerably. Grace returned it as he continued speaking. "Miss Withers is expecting you." He opened the carriage door and motioned toward it.

"Very good," Grace said, unsure what the customary acknowledgement ought to be in a situation such as this.

The man helped her into the carriage, and as he closed the door, Grace sucked in a nervous breath. Her gaze veered to the window, and the whole new world that lay beyond it.

How beautiful!

Lush green trees lined the road, and buildings bathed in golden light stood proudly side by side. As the carriage rumbled into motion, each new sight stirred Grace's delight afresh.

They trundled along through the centre of the town, where Grace noticed a post office, a milliner's shop, a greengrocer's, and a butcher's, among many other homes and business establishments. Every shop looked quaint and friendly, and she was glad to have come to Lindenfell — if only, at present, for the change of scenery it afforded her.

As the buildings became more scarce, lush beech trees came into view, lining the narrow road like stately sentries.

Grace noticed a huge house out of the carriage's left window, set back from the road and surrounded by bright white metal railings. She wondered for a second if that might be the place where they were going, but the driver showed no signs of slowing.

Farther down the road, the carriage made a sharp turn to the right, veering down a narrow lane set between two enormous stone pillars and a vast pair of already open, wrought-iron gates.

Grace gasped as a majestic house came into view. Miss Withers may have been a spinster, but she was by no means a poor one.

Massive chimneys forked upward from an extensive expanse of roof, crowning a house that was wider than any Grace had ever before encountered. And those windows! Never had she seen so many panes of glass in a single building.

This was where she now would live? Dazed by the realisation, Grace thought of her parents and great-aunt back in Shiloh Hall. Theirs was not a small home, but the spectacle in front of her could easily swallow it up many times over.

The carriage stopped, and Grace's heart picked up speed. This was it.

Careo House.

There was no turning back now.

Grace froze. What was Miss Withers like? Perhaps she would be expecting someone a little more rich or cultured, instead of an unremarkable parson's daughter from the middle of nowhere.

Grace drew a deep breath. She must not worry. God had brought her here, and whomever Miss Withers was anticipating, Grace could only do her best to ensure that she would assist her new employer to the best of her ability.

Her initial hesitations resolved, Grace crept out of the carriage, straightened her posture and prepared to meet the stranger with whom she would now spend most of her time.

As she followed a footman through the front doors, Grace looked upward, in awe of how much taller the house looked the closer one grew to it.

She told herself to keep walking as she entered the hall, but astonishment compelled her to stop and stare.

Never had she seen anything so grand. Seemingly endless corridors branched off from the tallest entrance hall she could have imagined. A magnificent flourish of delicate, far-reaching blooms rested upon a demi-lune table, the skilled arrangement displaying their beauty to the fullest. A gilded chair with cream and gold cushioning sat like a silent guard in front of one of the panelled walls, and a mahogany longcase clock stood in an alcove next to one of the doors. Warm carpets stretched wide across the floor of the hall, and exquisitely ornate brass wall sconces filled it with light throughout. The flickering flames of the candles seemed to sway in a merry dance in celebration of her arrival, and Grace wondered if this was what it must be like to visit a palace.

Realising that the footman had stopped to wait for her, Grace hurriedly resumed her steps, each one now echoing against the expansive polished floor of the wide corridor.

Before she had time to gather her thoughts, he opened a pair of white double doors and ushered Grace inside.

He announced her, then quickly withdrew from the room, just as Grace noticed an elderly lady seated in a dark orange wingback chair next to the fire.

Perfectly coiffed white hair crowned a lined, melancholy face, and the lady's violet silk dress seemed of an older style than the dresses worn by the elderly women Grace saw every week at church.

"Miss Stratton, so lovely to meet you. Will you not sit down?" Miss Withers's wavering voice sounded positively regal.

"Oh yes, of course! Thank you." Grace dashed forward,

seating herself in the armchair opposite. "It is a pleasure to meet you, Miss Withers."

The old lady eyed Grace keenly. "Such a pretty young thing. Why did you decide to become a companion? Most girls of your age are eager to secure a husband, not employment."

Her frankness surprised Grace a little, but she was also glad of it. Too many of the church women danced around saying how things *really* were, not speaking openly or asking honest questions. Grace had always believed that speaking the truth in love ought to more often be practised — especially among those who claimed to obey the Bible's teachings.

She offered Miss Withers an understanding smile. "Indeed. I suppose I am not much like most other girls, in that case. That is, I do wish to marry. Only, I am in no hurry to do so." She cleared her throat, inwardly scolding herself for her stuttering response. "What I mean to say is that, well... I wish to be useful. To help others. And, when I heard that *you* were in need of help, I wished to make myself available. To assist you in whichever way you might have need of it."

"I see." Miss Withers's eyes twinkled. "Well, thank you. I am sure we will do very well together."

Grace relaxed a little. "This is a beautiful home," she said, taking the liberty to glance around at the drawing room and its exquisite furnishings.

Miss Withers nodded slightly. "Thank you. My father was a skilled investor. He did very well for himself. Then he married my mother, who had a fortune of her own. My brother and sister each married, so I inherited this estate after our parents passed away."

"I see." Grace struggled to maintain a neutral expression. The grandeur was overwhelming. She shifted her gaze back to Miss Withers. "Do you see your siblings often?"

"No, not at all. My sister passed away a number of years ago, and my brother lives in Bath. They each had families and interests of their own, none of which ever brought them back to Lindenfell. And I do despise travelling, myself. My brother and I write every so often, but I confess I have not seen him, or either of my nephews, for many years now."

"I am sorry for that," Grace said gently. She paused. "I do not have a brother or sister."

"An only child, and now a companion?" She gave a short, almost bitter laugh. "I am surprised that your parents were not trying harder to steer you toward matrimony, given that they have no other child for whom they might scheme a match."

As she saw the kind faces of her parents in her mind's eye, Grace's heart squeezed with melancholy. She hadn't expected to miss them quite so soon. "They have always encouraged me to follow the Lord's leading about everything, not merely the dictates of society."

Grace hadn't fully seen it first-hand, but she knew that her parents had been subjected to all sorts of accusations and suspicions upon announcing their union, purely because of her mother's unsavoury past. But, as her father often preached — and ardently believed — no one is beyond redemption in the Lord's eyes. No matter what a person has been forced to live through, or indeed has chosen to live like, God can cleanse, heal, and forgive even the most bitter, broken, and stained soul.

"I see. Your father is a parson, you mentioned? In your letter?"

"Yes."

Miss Withers nodded, her gaze drifting from Grace to the fire. "Hmm."

Grace relaxed against the chair's cushions. The rhythmic

fluttering of the dancing flames threatened to lull her to sleep.

A few moments passed in easy silence.

Miss Withers gazed at Grace again. "Are you fatigued? From your travels?"

Grace stifled a yawn. "I must admit, I am a little. But it is no matter, I—"

"I shall have Higgins show you to your room so you can settle in and rest a while before dinner." Miss Withers snatched up a brass hand bell from a side table and waved it daintily. "You may begin your position officially in the morning."

"Thank you," Grace stuttered. "Are you quite sure?"

Miss Withers fixed her with a steely eye. "As you shall soon discover, I never say anything unless I am quite sure of it."

"I see. Well, thank you."

Higgins, the footman who had led Grace to the drawing room upon her arrival, strode back into the room and bowed, then motioned for Grace to follow him.

"I shall see you at dinner, then," Grace said.

Miss Withers nodded in response as she leaned her head back against her chair and closed her eyes.

Grace followed Higgins up a grand wood-panelled staircase, lined in the centre with exotic carpeting which silenced their footsteps. As he swung open the door to her room, she was sure there must be a mistake.

This room was for *her*?

Cheerful floral paper lined the walls. A French-style mahogany bed stood at one side of the room, with a mahogany bedside table placed either side of its head. A washstand, a dressing table with a small, open-backed chair, and a large mahogany wardrobe stood at the other end of the room. Along the other walls were a Davenport writing desk, a chest of drawers, and a fireplace with a chair next to it, an inviting marquise upholstered in a cheerful pattern — the perfect place to curl up with a book. A dressing screen stood in the corner, and even though the room held so much furniture, it wasn't in the least crowded, owing to its vast expanse.

Despite her awe, Grace knew she had a very important task to which she must attend before she could discover if her new reading chair was as comfortable as it looked.

She seated herself at the desk by the window, pleased to discover all the implements she might need — ink, quills, paper, envelopes, and sealing wax. She smoothed a crisp sheet of paper onto the green leather blotting pad and selected a quill.

For a moment, she wasn't quite sure what to say. If she poured out all her raptures about the place, it might only hurt her parents even more, yet if she admitted to missing them already, it would surely cause them needless anxiety.

She opted for a short blend of the two, describing the beauty of Lindenfell and Careo House, and assuring them both that she was precisely where God wanted her to be — and utterly content to be so. She reinforced her intentions to write often, expressing her hope to receive their own letters, too.

Having sealed the missive, she sighed, looking once again around her new dwelling.

Weary from travel, and the emotional upheaval of the past few days, Grace unlaced her boots and slipped them off. She tiptoed toward the bed, then dropped onto it, closing her eyes as relief washed over her.

Everything in Lindenfell seemed so tranquil, so beautiful.

Grace smiled as she closed her eyes and drifted off into a light doze, aware that, tomorrow, the new chapter of her life would fully begin.

CHAPTER 8

NO TURNING BACK

The next morning, David took one last look at his bedroom, the sense of dread and apprehension that had tugged at him all morning now fastening itself tightly around his heart.

What was he thinking?

Surely there had to be some other way. Something else he could do before resorting to... *this*?

As he stuffed one last item into his portmanteau, he gritted his teeth, willing himself to be strong.

This is the only way. It must be done.

Quietly, he slipped out of the safe familiarity of his home and strode through the sleepy streets toward the nearest train station. Newsboys and costermongers hovered around him, but he hardly noticed them, filled as his mind was with questions and worries.

With every step he took, a fierce battle raged within him. Part of him wanted to turn back, to face up to things, maybe even hire a different lawyer — one who was determined to win, no matter what the cost. But the fear of what could go wrong if he were to stay in London compelled him forward.

This was the best way, he told himself, for what must have

been the hundredth time. This way he would have time and space to figure out what to do.

His main qualm was that he still hadn't figured out a way to allow his lawyer to contact him without letting anyone know where he was. He had stayed up for most of the night trying to devise a method for staying informed of everything that was happening in London regarding his impending case, but his limited options were each too risky.

He needed this time away — to think. To come up with some kind of plan to clear his name.

He sighed wearily, his heart heavy from ample stress and little sleep.

Eventually, he reached the train station and slid into the queue for the ticket office. Five men stood between him and the little piece of paper that would carry him away from this frightful situation.

One man walked away, ticket in hand.

David stepped forward.

One part of his plan gave him more pause than the rest. He wasn't truly happy with *any* of it, but there was one piece that could unravel it all if things didn't transpire the way he was counting on.

Another man left the queue, his hand closed around a ticket. He nodded at David.

David returned the man's nod as he stepped forward, ever closer to possessing a ticket of his own.

You must not worry. Everything will go smoothly. Everything will go as planned.

Nothing would unravel. Enough time had passed. As long as he spoke confidently, no one would suspect a thing.

David stepped forward again, taking the place where the customer in front of him had previously stood. In time, two more men walked away holding tickets, leaving David face to face with the cashier.

"Good morning, sir. Where is it you're going?"

David drew a deep, tight breath. "Lindenfell, please."

"One ticket to Lindenfell. Single or return?"

David's stomach wrenched. "Single."

An unsettling thought snaked into his mind. Would he *ever* be able to return? And if so, to *what* would he return — his old life? Prison?

Or worse?

The cashier told him the cost of the ticket, and David retrieved the money from his pockets with trembling fingers. He handed the coins to the man, still questioning if his departure was truly the right course of action.

"Here you are, sir." The cashier handed David a ticket. "Platform two. Next train to Lindenfell arrives at seven twenty-five."

David accepted the ticket from the cashier's hands. "Thank you." His voice was hushed and uncertain.

The cashier nodded to him with all the friendly civility of a man who didn't have a care in the world.

David left the queue, nodding to the man who stepped forward to take his place.

After making his way to the platform, he checked his pocket watch. There were fifteen minutes to pass until the train arrived, but he made no move to sit down on one of the wooden benches lining the station's exterior walls. Instead, he strode back and forth, desperate to walk off some of the nervous energy coursing throughout his body.

He clutched the ticket in his hand more tightly. The plan was afoot. He must see it through.

There would be no unravelling.

There *must* be no unravelling.

After pacing the length of the platform several times, David stopped and listened. A faint hissing and screeching grew louder and louder, and plumes of steam bathed the platform in an ethereal haze.

Slowly, the train broke into view as it eased to a stop beside the platform.

Why must his limbs tremble so much?

Awkwardly, he walked toward one of the dark red railway carriages and stepped up through the open door.

He cast his gaze around the wooden interior. There were plenty of empty seats from which to choose.

But that wasn't why he hesitated.

Still, after all the hours of planning and steeling himself for what he must do, he wasn't certain that he would not yet bolt from the train and give it all up.

The doors closed.

The train rumbled and hissed, then jolted into motion.

David crept toward a seat and gingerly lowered himself onto it.

This was it. It was happening. The train was moving.

No turning back, now.

CHAPTER 9
A NEW FRIEND

"Did you sleep well?" Miss Withers eyed Grace as a servant poured steaming tea into her cup.

Grace swallowed the last bite of her breakfast omelette and dabbed her lips with a napkin. "Yes, very well, thank you." She decided to ask Miss Withers the same question but, before she could, the elderly lady spoke again.

"Good. Our days always flow much more smoothly when we are well rested, do you not think?"

"Indeed," Grace said with a nod. She'd always been a good sleeper, a trait for which she was deeply thankful. And even with the change in her surroundings, she'd been able to rest just as easily as if she'd been tucked up in her room at Shiloh Hall.

"We are to visit a friend of mine today."

"Oh?" Grace waited for more information about the friend, or the visit, but received neither. Miss Withers simply carried on eating her small breakfast, her eyes fixed on her plate as though she had no energy to raise them.

After breakfast, Grace and Miss Withers sat quietly in the drawing room, each occupied with embroidery tasks, which

Miss Withers had assigned in a languid manner. Grace worked deftly, and each time she glanced at her silent employer, it took her a moment to ascertain whether or not the lady had fallen asleep.

A few moments after the clock on the mantel struck ten, Miss Withers, still unmoving, spoke with such unexpected suddenness that Grace accidentally pricked her thumb with her needle.

"We ought to depart now. I asked Higgins to tell Parker to have the carriage ready for ten."

"Very well." Grace tucked her embroidery accoutrements into the basket beside her chair and stood, brushing out her skirts absent-mindedly as she did so.

Miss Withers cranked herself gradually into a standing position and shuffled to a nearby bureau, where she retrieved something from a drawer, then proceeded to change her gloves.

Once they were settled in the carriage, Grace, having grown completely weary of the morning's silence, turned to Miss Withers and smiled. "Who is it that we are to visit?"

"Miss Price," Miss Withers responded, without even turning to look at Grace. "She and I have been friends for quite some years."

"And she lives in town?"

"Yes."

The carriage rumbled into motion. "Alone?"

"With her niece. The girl's parents both died a number of years back, from typhoid fever—"

"Oh, dear..."

"So, Miss Price took her in. She is a very kind lady."

Grace nodded sympathetically.

As they trundled past the enormous house with the white metal railings, Grace quickly pointed out the window. "Pray, who lives there?"

Miss Withers glanced in the same direction, just as the house passed out of view. "Oh, that is the Bennett estate. The Earl of Lindenfell lives there with his daughter."

"*Earl?*" Never had she encountered the nobility back home, nor had she imagined doing so here. "Do you know them well?"

"I see them at various functions. And at church, of course."

"Where is the church? I did not see it on my way in from the station."

"It is across the river. From the station, one would turn left to go to the church, and right to go to the lace mill. Straight on will bring you through the main part of town."

"The lace mill?"

"Oh, yes. Mr. Evans owns it. He is a tough man, but a good one. I believe his daughter is around your age."

Grace's heart stirred with hope as she thought of all the people and places she had yet to encounter in Lindenfell.

"I expect you shall meet a lot of the town's folk at church on Sunday," said Miss Withers as the carriage pulled to a stop. "Here we are, Miss Stratton."

Grace couldn't wait until Sunday. She smiled as she stepped out of the carriage and looked around at the friendly buildings lining either side of the street — houses on one side, shops on the other.

Miss Withers held out her hand to the coachman and he assisted her down the steps of the carriage.

Grace followed Miss Withers as she shuffled toward the pale blue front door of a house situated on the corner, with a narrow lane to its right and another house adjoining it on the left.

A girl around Grace's age, with tumbling strawberry-blonde curls, opened the door, greeting the two of them with a large, genuine smile. "Good morning, Miss Withers. How are you today?"

"I am quite well, Miss Beckwith, thank you."

The girl's gaze moved to Grace. "Good morning," she said, still smiling.

"Good morning."

"This is Miss Grace Stratton — my new companion."

"Oh, how splendid. It is lovely to meet you, Miss Stratton. I am Miss Beatrice Beckwith — Miss Price's niece."

Grace returned Beatrice's warm smile. "It is a pleasure to make your acquaintance, Miss Beckwith."

"Do come in," Beatrice said. "Aunt is expecting you."

She ushered them into a small but pleasant drawing room where a lady — who seemed a little younger and a lot more robust than Miss Withers — sat by the fire knitting.

Beatrice introduced Grace, and everyone greeted one another before Beatrice motioned for Grace and Miss Withers to sit down.

The older ladies instantly began to converse, and Grace fought to keep her eyebrows in their rightful place, surprised by how talkative Miss Withers was compared to earlier that morning, when it had been just the two of them.

Beatrice moved toward a cabinet in the corner of the room. "How do you take your tea, Miss Stratton?"

Grace offered her a thankful smile. "Oh, just a dash of milk, please."

Beatrice smiled and nodded, then set about preparing four cups. She served the older ladies first, then presented Grace with hers.

"Thank you."

Beatrice nodded in response, then seated herself on the small sofa beside Grace. "Have you only just arrived in Lindenfell?"

"I arrived yesterday."

"Did you travel far?"

They chatted for a while about Lindenfell and Shiloh Hall, discovering the many differences and similarities between the two.

Eventually, Beatrice sighed wistfully. "It must be lovely to embark on an adventure. Move somewhere new — see new sights and meet new people."

Grace smiled gently. "It is refreshing, I must admit. I am very keen to explore Lindenfell. Already, I am forming a deep appreciation for its beauty."

"Yes," Beatrice said, her tone growing more serious. "In truth, I cannot complain. It is a lovely place to live."

"Do you have many friends here?"

"Oh, yes. Quite a few. I shall have to introduce you to them after church on Sunday." Beatrice observed her for a moment. "And you have one, at least, now." She smiled. "Me."

Grace smiled in return, her heart buoyed with gratitude. Back home, as much as she loved the place, she'd always lacked company her own age. She'd yearned for a dear friend, someone with whom she could share her deepest hopes and heartaches.

Now, perhaps, she had found her.

Too soon the visit was at an end, and Grace reluctantly stood, draping her shawl back around her shoulders.

"Well, Miss Stratton, you seem to have made fast friends with my dear Beatrice," Miss Price said.

Grace smiled shyly and glanced at Beatrice, who smiled reassuringly at her.

"You are free to visit anytime you please — as long as Miss Withers does not have need of you, mind."

Grace's eyebrows lifted. "Thank you, Miss Price."

"And we are due to visit you both at Careo House on Friday," Beatrice said.

"Splendid," Grace replied. "I shall see you then. Unless, of course, you wish to visit before then. For you would be most welcome anytime, too."

The instant Grace had finished speaking the words, she realised what she had said. Careo House was not her home — she did not have any authority or permission to invite anyone to visit it.

Her cheeks growing warmer, she forced herself to look at Miss Withers.

"In this instance, Miss Stratton is correct," Miss Withers said, addressing Miss Price. "You are always welcome to visit without arranging it beforehand — both of you." She shifted her gaze to Grace. "In future, however, Miss Stratton, please do ask permission before issuing invitations so freely."

Grace nodded quickly. "Of course. Indeed. I am so sorry." Her heart hammered, though the lack of annoyance in Miss Withers's tone brought her a slight measure of relief.

Miss Withers gave her a stately nod and a brief, kind smile, then turned again to Miss Price as she stood and offered her goodbyes.

As Beatrice walked them to the door, she tugged Grace's elbow, pulling her back a few paces. "Do not worry, Miss Stratton. Miss Withers is a gentle soul, underneath all her decorum. I am sure she understood your intentions, and I know that she will not harbour any ill feelings toward you."

"Thank you," Grace said. She sighed. "As soon as I said it..." She shook her head.

Beatrice squeezed her elbow. "There is no need to fret." Her smile was radiant and comforting. Grace returned it gladly.

After bidding Beatrice goodbye, Grace and Miss Withers climbed back into the carriage. The short ride back to Careo House passed in silence, owing to Miss Withers dozing off before the carriage had even moved.

Grace gazed out of the window, drinking in the friendly sights. Her heart thrilled as she remembered Beatrice's words.

For the first time in as long as Grace could remember, she had a friend. And her new friend intended to introduce her to other friends.

Grace smiled.

Perhaps her lonely days were finally at an end.

CHAPTER 10

A SURPRISE VISIT

David stepped off the train onto the platform and read the sign directly in front of him. He was in the right place.

This was it.

No turning back.

He looked around, realising that the last time he'd visited, he'd been only a boy.

Which meant that he had no idea how to get to the place where he intended to go.

Making his way to the station office, he released a shuddering sigh. Somewhere, in the dark recesses of his mind, a note of alarm sounded over and over again.

He tried to silence it.

He'd had no other choice. He would lie low, buy time to think, and figure out how to deal once and for all with the calamity besieging him in London.

"Excuse me," David said to a train attendant as he strode by.

"Yes, sir?" The man looked at David with keen eyes, though his glance occasionally stole toward the train that was preparing to board new passengers.

With an apology in his tone, David asked the man for directions, then swallowed hard as the attendant relayed them. It was too far to walk, especially laden with his heavy portmanteau in one hand and his carpet bag in the other.

"Is there a stage that might convey me there?"

The man, whose gaze had become fixed on the train, held up his hand. Retrieving a long, silver whistle, he blew into it three times in sharp succession before shouting, "All aboard!"

He turned back to David, his concentration now so fixed upon him that he seemed like a completely different man. "Sorry, sir. If you exit the station down this way..." He extended his arm, waving it behind him to the left. "...You will find a cab or two waiting for passengers."

"Thank you."

David bade the man good day, then hurried in the direction he had pointed out. Once outside the station, he spotted a hansom with a man standing idly beside it, kicking the ground with the toes of his boots.

David set toward him. "Excuse me!"

The man looked up, his startled expression transforming into one of relief. His shoulders straightened in hope. "Take you where you're heading, sir?"

"Yes. Please."

The man's countenance brightened and he opened the cab's door before hurrying to take his place at the back.

As David climbed in, he drew a ragged breath.

Not long now.

He told the driver where to take him and settled back as best he could in the small vehicle. Nervous energy coursed through every fibre of his being.

Constantly, the words and voices of others echoed in his mind. Augustus. Gibbs, his lawyer. Professor Steele.

Even Mr. Edwards's uncertain final words and David's own reply seemed to mock and chide him.

"It... is... safe?"

"Absolutely."

David sighed. The more he thought of it, he could hardly blame the man's family for feeling a sense of injustice at his death. Though his condition had been very serious, the suddenness of his death had been somewhat of a surprise.

David had been exceedingly sorrowful the last day he had seen Mr. Edwards, having observed the worsening of the man's symptoms. That day, he'd refused all nourishment — the life-sustaining broth he'd survived on for weeks cast aside, as every other morsel had been long before.

David's confidence regarding his patient's recovery had died that day — a mere few hours before Mr. Edwards himself.

Clearly, the cholera was to blame. Not the chloroform.

"Here we are, sir."

David started. They had arrived at the house *already*?

His throat grew dry as he climbed out of the hansom and called out his thanks to the driver.

The enormous house in front of him only seemed to magnify the dread clutching his heart. He squinted as he studied its form. It had been such a long time since he had been here, he hardly remembered it at all.

Hopefully, its owner wouldn't remember him, either. At least, not too clearly.

With a long exhale, David approached the door, grasped the knocker, and hesitated for just a moment before tapping it firmly three times against its plate.

Stay the course, David. Remember what is at stake.

A footman opened the door, and after David explained who he was and why he had come, the man ushered him inside without further question.

David tried not to gasp as his eyes took in the lavish interior of the house. It looked even more grand from this side of the door — something he wouldn't have thought possible given how imposing and regal it seemed from outside.

"Here we are, sir," said the footman, opening the door to what David presumed must be the drawing room.

His heart hammered faster as he thanked the man and followed him inside.

A beautiful young lady sat engrossed in needlework. Not what David had been expecting to find at all.

She glanced up at him, her brow flickering in surprise. She turned her head away, and as David followed her gaze, he saw her.

Miss Withers.

She was much older now. Much frailer looking, too. And her stooped, stiff shoulders inclined him to believe that she might suffer from a touch of some rheumatic complaint.

"Miss Withers, this gentleman has just arrived for a visit," said the footman.

The woman looked up at him and frowned. "A visit? And you are?" Miss Withers frowned as she studied him. Her regal tone made her clipped words sound even less welcoming.

David stiffened his posture and bowed. "Good afternoon, ma'am. I am your nephew."

He swallowed hard, his heart pounding.

"Mr. John Withers."

CHAPTER 11

THE MYSTERIOUS STRANGER

Grace noticed Miss Withers's eyebrows lift in surprise. "John?"

The young man cleared his throat. "Yes, ma'am."

Shifting her gaze to the stranger, Grace took in his expressive grey eyes and his wavy caramel hair. He had a neatly trimmed moustache and warm, olive skin. He was trim and a little above average in height, though not enough to be described as tall. His hands, and indeed his entire frame, seemed strong and well-built, yet not bulky. He looked every bit a gentleman.

A rather handsome gentleman.

But his pleasant physique was not what had captured Grace's attention at present. Not fully, at least.

What was it that seemed to have him so on edge? He was pale yet flushed at the same time. And the repeated nervous clenching and unclenching of his hands belied the confidence in his voice.

"Why, you have changed so much!" Miss Withers studied him intently. "My, my..."

John smiled, though to Grace it seemed a little forced.

"Well, it has been a long time since I have the delight of your company, Aunt."

"Oh, you always were a flatterer. Come, come. Sit."

He seemed to hesitate for a split-second, then slowly he approached the empty chair opposite them. He lowered himself into it with a measure of cautiousness that made Grace want to laugh.

"Have you travelled far, Mr. Withers?" she asked, glancing at Miss Withers to ascertain whether or not she might have spoken out of place. But Miss Withers only stared at John, her eyebrows raised in anticipation of his reply.

"Yes, I..." He frowned, his eyes darting a little. Suddenly, he visibly regained his composure.

What a curious man.

"I have travelled from the coast. From Scarborough."

"Ah, yes. Your mother mentioned that you had recently moved there in one of her letters. How do you find it?"

A look of surprise seemed to alter his face for a second or two. "Oh, it is... very pleasant." His final inflection made his reply sound more like a question. He nodded, though his brow seemed to twitch in a way that puzzled Grace immensely.

"And you — how are you doing, Aunt?" He briefly glanced at Grace as he spoke, then fixed his attention once more on Miss Withers.

The eye contact she made with him — fleeting, though it was — stirred a flash of self-consciousness within her. She batted away the thought that followed it — that he was handsome indeed.

"Oh, I am ticking along, I suppose. This is Miss Stratton, my new companion. She only arrived yesterday, herself."

"Is that so?" Miss Withers's nephew seemed to have almost discarded whatever had been troubling him before. He fixed his gaze on Grace with a polite smile. "What think you of Lindenfell, Miss Stratton?"

Her name sounded completely different on his tongue than she had ever heard it before. And as she took in the shapes of his face, she almost forgot his question.

"Oh, I... It is beautiful. Though, I have not seen very much of it yet, in truth. But I am very glad to have come." She smiled awkwardly as it grew more and more difficult to hold his gaze.

"It is many years since I was last here. I am almost a stranger to it, myself."

Grace nodded politely. "What brought you back?"

No sooner had Grace asked the question than the blood seemed to drain from the man's face. He squinted, blinking more frequently than was quite normal, and after a few painstaking moments of silence, he cleared his throat and spoke. "I... I merely wished to visit my dear aunt." He transformed his countenance into a smile, though his eyes still held some of the discomfort Grace's question had seemed to awaken within him.

"Flattery again!" Miss Withers said in a jovial tone. "For a moment, I wondered if I might have written the wrong date on the invitations, and you were merely here too early!"

John smiled at her, his posture stiff and uneasy. "Invitations?"

Miss Withers nodded gracefully. "My garden party. Oh, it has been years since I last held one. Too long. But, knowing that Miss Stratton would arrive, I decided that this was just the year to recommence them." She waved a hand, as though the topic interested her little at present. "Where are you staying?" Miss Withers asked, her crisp voice dispersing the gathering silence.

John seemed to flush a little. He shifted in his seat. "Ah, well... I hoped that I might... perhaps, stay *here*... at least, for a few days — until I am able to secure accommodation elsewhere, if that is what you would prefer."

Though he kept a formal posture and countenance, Grace believed she could see a trace of pleading in his eyes as he awaited his aunt's response.

"Nonsense. Of course, you must stay here. We may not be close, but we are family. Why should you rent a room somewhere else when there are many here from which to choose?"

John let out a mix of a laugh and a sigh. "Oh, thank you, Aunt. You are most welcoming, and very kind." He nodded, a sombre relief washing over his face. "Thank you," he repeated, softly this time.

"You must be fatigued from your journey. When did you set out?"

"The morning train."

Grace frowned. She was no scholar, but she couldn't imagine that even a locomotive could have brought him from Scarborough to Lindenfell *that* quickly.

Miss Withers seemed to have the very same thought. "You do not mean *this* morning, do you?"

John paled, straightening in his seat. "Ah..."

"Surely no train in operation could transport one as quickly as all that!" Miss Withers affixed a laugh to the end of her words, which seemed to encourage her nephew to chuckle along, too.

"No, no... I meant that I got the morning train to Lindenfell, though not from the coast. I had to break my journey, to be sure." He nodded as he spoke, though he seemed to refrain from meeting either of their gazes.

"Where?" Grace asked.

He looked at her, his expression blank. "Pardon?"

"Where was it that you broke your journey?"

His fragile smile slipped off his face altogether. He gaped

for a moment before affixing a new one. "Oh, just a little town around halfway betwixt the two places." He quickly shifted his gaze to his aunt. "In truth, I *am* a little tired. Might I... retire to my room for a while?"

Miss Withers nodded. "Of course. You do not wish for some tea first?"

He stood up. "Thank you, but I would prefer to freshen up and re-energise myself somewhat first."

Miss Withers reached for her bell. "Very well. We have plenty of time to become reacquainted, besides." She smiled as she shook the bell, filling the room with its bright tinkling sound.

Higgins reappeared, and Miss Withers instructed him to settle Mr. Withers in the Hartford Suite.

Grace couldn't help her eyebrows lifting. She did not know Careo House had its own array of suites. Her own room was spacious, though it didn't have a fancy name like the one in which Miss Withers was installing her nephew. Still, she had nothing for which to complain, for her room was the most luxurious place she had ever had the pleasure of calling her own.

"Go and rest," Miss Withers said, in the warmest tone Grace had heard her utter thus far.

"Thank you, Aunt." He paused. "It truly is good to see you."

Grace studied him subtly. He appeared to mean what he had just said, but she couldn't shake the feeling that there was something about him that seemed almost... *dishonest*.

He turned to face Grace. "Miss Stratton," he said, bowing. She nodded in return, and almost as quickly as he had unexpectedly appeared, he was gone.

"My, that *is* a surprise," Miss Withers mused. "Do you know... I have not seen him, or his cousin, since they were, oh, they must have been only eight years old or so!"

"Eight?" Grace echoed. "That *is* a long time."

"I am surprised that he has come all this way. I forgot to ask him if his parents are well." Miss Withers waved a hand in the air dismissively. "Ah, well. Plenty of time to ask him that, and more, besides."

"Indeed," Grace said.

Miss Withers rested her head against the back of her chair and closed her eyes, a soft smile resting on her face.

As Grace resumed her needlework, questions about Miss Withers's nephew seemed to multiply in her mind.

She had anticipated nothing so mysterious as the unexpected arrival of a handsome stranger when she'd accepted the position of a companion. But she was certain of one thing entirely.

Handsome as he was, he was definitely hiding something.

CHAPTER 12
SECOND THOUGHTS

David closed the door to his room, pressed his forehead against it, and exhaled, releasing more tension than he'd ever thought it possible to hold.

He hated lying to his aunt. But he'd been able to think of no other way in which he might hide away in order to gain some time to think. His life was very likely on the line.

Surely, that ought to absolve him a little of the guilt that gripped him?

But as he'd sat there across from his aunt and her unsettlingly wise and beautiful companion, pretending to bear his cousin's name, the horror of his deception had only coiled its ugly fingers more tightly around his heart.

He drew a deep, troubled breath, remaining with his forehead pressed against the door as he exhaled again, his eyes squeezed shut.

It was all a nightmare.

Yet, it was real. All too real.

Slowly, David opened his eyes and moved away from the door. Despite the generous dimensions of the room, the walls seemed to close in tightly around him.

He didn't want this. He didn't want any of it. But what could he do?

He exhaled sharply.

That was the question of the hour. Of his *life*.

A sinking sensation flooded him. He shouldn't have come. He shouldn't have fled London. Now, if he was found, the case against him would be ten times as strong.

Only guilty people flee.

He was innocent, he knew he was. But, surely, now his abrupt decision made him seem guiltier than ever.

His breathing sped as beads of sweat trickled down the back of his collar.

No, no, no!

He lunged across the room, leaned his arms on the dresser, and huffed out a frustrated breath. He lifted his head, his reflection staring back at himself from the oval mirror.

David studied his face in the glass, taking in his wavy hair, his grey eyes, his well-kept moustache. He looked *nothing* like John. He never had. Every feature, every colour, it was all a contrast. The only slight resemblance was in their build, but even that had plenty of differences.

It was all a huge mistake. But he'd set it all in motion now.

There was no way out.

He flopped onto a chair by the window and cradled his face in his hands. His head throbbed so violently that he could hardly think.

What have you done?

He froze. His aunt's companion... She had asked such direct questions.

What if she suspected him?

Think, David, think.

She was a companion — surely, her opinion held little sway.

He remembered her curious eyes studying him, the slight tilt of her head. And her questions... Why had she persisted in asking him about his journey? It was hardly her place.

It could only be because his answers had not convinced her of their truth.

And why should they?

They were all lies. All of them.

His name, his journey's starting point, the duration of his travels. All fabrications woven to conceal the truth.

He was a wanted man. Suspected of poisoning — of murder.

David rubbed his temples, attempting in vain to soothe his weary mind and body.

He'd heard dreadful tales of things that had happened to people under severe stress. He silently hoped no ill effect would latch itself onto him. He had enough to deal with at present — the last thing he needed was an ailment or symptom that might render it a necessity to consume laudanum or some other addictive substance that would further cloud his already frazzled mind.

Forcing himself to at least attempt to put it all out of his mind for now, he retrieved his portmanteau from beside the desk, where the footman had placed it, and set it on the end of his bed. Slowly and methodically, he set about stowing its contents in various drawers, placing his items of clothing onto the wardrobe's rail and shelves.

How long would he have to stay?

How long would he be *able* to stay before being found out?

A sickening thought seized him. He'd been banking on the fact that Miss Withers wouldn't be able to tell that he wasn't John, owing to how long it had been since she had seen them. But what if others in the town had a better memory than she? What if, unbeknownst to him, John had visited recently? If *that* were the case, and David ventured into town, everyone would know instantly the ruse he was trying to foist upon them.

What brought you back?

The memory of his aunt's companion's questioning caused his heart to thud. David released a slow breath.

Where was it that you broke your journey? she had asked him, her dark eyes boring right through him.

Come to think of it, perhaps an ailment wasn't the greatest danger to him now, after all.

In truth, the last thing he needed was a handsome young lady determined to ask too many questions.

CHAPTER 13
A DELIGHTFUL DINNER

"This is truly wonderful, Aunt," John said.

Grace glanced at Miss Withers, who smiled across the vast dining table at her nephew as he took a sip of his wine.

"It is a pleasure to have your company to share it, my dear." Miss Withers glanced at Grace. "Both of you." She shook her head slightly. "Funny how one can go from having no real company to speak of, to having two young people with whom to enjoy passing the time."

Grace smiled sympathetically. She had not known Miss Withers for long, but her initial impression of the lady being a willing recluse was being more and more challenged by the warmth she saw her employer direct toward her nephew. She seemed genuinely glad that he had come. It was a heartening sight.

"And arriving on subsequent days!" Miss Withers added, after another bite of dinner.

"Indeed." Grace stole a glance at John. He smiled at his aunt, then looked at Grace, dropping his gaze to the table upon catching eyes with her.

She'd learned from watching her father's keen

observations of others that those who were reluctant to hold eye contact often had something to hide.

John certainly seemed more relaxed this evening compared to when he had first arrived, although Grace still noticed the occasional nervous movement and uncertain waver in his voice.

Another thought seized her mind — one that she instinctively tried to dislodge. His olive skin and grey eyes gave him a suave, sophisticated appearance, and his handsomely cut suit seemed to be perfectly tailored for him. The more she saw him, she could not deny — as much as she wished to — that he really was a handsome gentleman.

"... Am I right, Miss Stratton?"

Grace turned her attention to Miss Withers, trying to conceal her alarm and hide the fact that she hadn't heard a word the woman had said for the past few minutes. "I..."

John chuckled, stroking his moustache thoughtfully. "Now, Aunt. Poor Miss Stratton ought not to be dragged into the politics of Lindenfell's textile industry!"

Miss Withers waved her hand in the air. "Oh, all right. I suppose it would not be becoming for a young lady to entangle her mind with matters that are best left to the men of the town."

"Or matters that might bore a young lady to tears..." John added.

This drew a chuckle from Miss Withers, who quietly consumed another few forkfuls of dinner.

Grace glanced at John and smiled shyly, hoping to convey a sense of how grateful she was that he had come to her aid.

He held her gaze for a few moments, offering a knowing smile in return.

As he looked away, heat crept into Grace's cheeks. She stared at her plate, sighing inwardly as she scolded herself for being so quick to judge him earlier.

What could he possibly be hiding? Lindenfell hardly seemed a magnet for rogues, from what she had seen of it so far. Surely, if he had an underhanded scheme in mind, or was hatching some kind of nefarious plot, he wouldn't have come to a sleepy rural town.

As she set about finishing the rest of her dinner, Grace tried in vain to push away a growing awareness that was both inappropriate, and potentially dangerous.

Miss Withers was not the only lady at the table who was glad that John had come.

CHAPTER 14
ELUSIVE ANSWERS

The next morning, David settled himself in a brown leather chair in his aunt's library, a stack of carefully selected books on the table beside him.

His aunt and her companion had gone into town for the morning, and he was exceedingly glad. Never had he expected that assuming his cousin's identity would be so exhausting. Every word had to be carefully weighed before speaking, every mannerism that he usually expressed without a thought had to be stifled.

But now, with the two ladies absent, he could breathe a little easier.

He picked up the volume on the top of the stack of books and thumbed through it impatiently. His aunt's library was vast, but he'd found only a few bindings concerning law and criminal proceedings.

Surely, there must be something inside one of these that might help me.

Eagerly, his eyes scanned the pages, taking in the headings and titles of various sections.

Nothing.

He cast it to one side and picked up another.

Time ticked steadily by, the clicking rhythm of the clock and the turning of pages the only sounds in the large sombre room, until all the books that David had searched out lay scattered on the floor.

He stood, raking a hand through his hair and clenching his jaw.

What am I to do?

The clock on the mantel chimed, startling David into movement. Hastily, he scooped up the useless volumes and set about returning them to their rightful shelves. He certainly didn't want his aunt or her companion finding any of them, given the subject matter they covered.

Especially not when Miss Stratton was already a little suspicious of him.

He placed the last book on its shelf.

Although, he *had* seen another side of Miss Stratton at dinner last night. A more relaxed, friendly side. He'd quite liked it.

The door opened, and David swivelled around, startled by the unexpected entry.

"Beg pardon, sir. I didn't know anyone was in here. I shall come back presently."

Before David could say anything, the portly maid had retreated, closing the door behind her with a sharp click.

David thought for a moment. It wasn't the sound of the door opening that had startled him. Not really. It was the fact that he'd been standing motionless like a sop as he'd remembered Miss Stratton's pretty smile.

Get a hold of yourself, man. This is no time for distractions.

He sighed, scanning the spines of the books again, willing himself to find a volume he had overlooked before.

But, just like his life at the moment, what he was trying most to find seemed only to elude him completely.

CHAPTER 15

HEROES AND HAPPINESS

Drizzle misted the glass of the tea shop window, but Grace didn't mind. Inside, with a warm cup of tea and an endearing friend, she could easily ignore the weather.

"He is here? In Lindenfell?" Beatrice's voice was a pitch or two higher than usual.

"You remember him?" She hadn't expected that.

Beatrice nodded. "Oh, yes. Very well. The two of them. John, and his cousin, David." She smiled. "They were always as different as night and day!"

Grace took a sip of tea. "How so?"

"Well, David was always very... sombre. Very well put together and matter of fact."

"Even when they were little?" Grace asked.

"Oh, yes!" Beatrice giggled. "Nothing but the best for the Carburys, you know. His mother married very well indeed — I believe his father was the second son of a *baron*. And young David seemed to have been practically born a gentleman!"

Amusement played on Grace's lips. She looked around the quaint, cosy tea room in which she and Beatrice had been sitting for the past hour or so. Miss Withers and Miss Price sat at a table on the opposite side of the room. No sooner had breakfast finished than Beatrice and her aunt had called at Careo House to invite Miss Withers and Grace to accompany them here.

"Such a different fellow from his cousin," Beatrice mused. "John was always a little more... how should I say it? *Spirited.*"

"Spirited?"

"Yes. Always up to mischief."

Grace frowned. So far, her first impressions of John seemed to fit more with Beatrice's description of David. But then, they had only been little the last time anyone had seen them. Young boys were wont to grow up and mature. Even spirited ones.

"I doubt he would remember me," Beatrice said, more to herself than to Grace. She looked up suddenly, addressing her new friend. "Is he to come to church with you both tomorrow?"

Church. For a split second upon hearing the word, Grace anticipated her father's little church, and attending it with Beatrice and Miss Withers in the morning. But she was in Lindenfell now, and there was a new church to discover. Though a pang of sadness plucked at her heart that she would not hear her father's latest impassioned sermon, she could not deny that she was looking forward to attending the church here in town and meeting some of Beatrice's friends.

"I am not quite sure," Grace replied.

Beatrice chuckled. "I am sure if Miss Withers has any say in the matter, he will be there! Why, I do not believe she has missed a service for years! She may not like to go out terribly often, but she never misses church."

Grace glanced over at her employer. She seemed quite animated at present, talking to Miss Price. No doubt she was singing John's praises.

Grace smiled as she turned back to her talkative new friend. "I am quite certain I shall soon be finished reading *Agnes Grey*, and I shall immediately lend it to you once I am. It is truly a gem of a book." She sipped more of her tea.

"I cannot wait to read it." Beatrice chuckled. "Aunt and I often spend the evenings with our noses in various books. And yours comes so highly recommended. I shall enjoy it as much as you have, I am sure of it."

Grace smiled. "I have never related to a character as much as I have related to Agnes. So many details of our lives in common... It is quite surprising. But it has taught me a lot about contentment and making a difference where one can. Listen to this..."

She reached into her reticule and pulled out the novel, which left little room for anything else in her bag. But she didn't mind. She flicked through the pages until she found the one she'd folded the corner down on the night before.

"'No; by His help I will arise and address myself diligently to my appointed duty. If happiness in this world is not for me, I will endeavour to promote the welfare of those around me, and my reward shall be hereafter.'"

Beatrice looked at her thoughtfully. "If happiness in this world is not for me... But, why, Grace — you do not believe that to be true of yourself, do you?"

Grace thought for a moment as she sipped more of her tea. "I do not know..." John's face flashed into her mind, interrupting her train of thought for a moment. "I suppose it stood out to me because of how restless I have been lately. It inspires me to keep trusting God and seeking Him first, above whatever other joys might be found in life."

Beatrice seemed to reflect on that for a moment, then smiled. "And... does the heroine meet a handsome hero?"

Grace tried to suppress a smile. "Perhaps... though, I do not wish to spoil any of the story for you." They both giggled as Grace replaced the small volume in her reticule. The heroine did indeed meet a handsome hero. And, despite her attempts to the contrary, Grace had begun to picture John every time she read of him.

Beatrice nodded contentedly as she polished off her last bite of cake. She closed her eyes for a moment as she savoured it. "Truly the best cake in the entire country," she said.

Grace smiled at her animated and easy manner. She looked at her plate, empty save for a few crumbs. "Indeed, I believe it is."

Beatrice nodded. "That is Mrs. Fearn's handiwork. Aunt says that everything she makes is fit for the Queen herself, and I am quite inclined to agree with her!"

Grace smiled and nodded. "I think you are both right."

Beatrice tilted her head in reflection. "She is a lovely lady. Very friendly and kind, as is her husband. You may meet Mr. Fearn at the next town function, for he is often the master of ceremonies at such things. He is such a jovial fellow. They are a wonderful match."

Grace dipped her head, fixing her gaze on the lace of the tablecloth as Beatrice's words brought to mind the thoughts she had been trying to suppress since dinner.

Happy matches. Husbands and wives. She scolded herself inwardly, shaking her head slightly. She barely even knew John. It was undeniable that he was rather pleasant to look at, but a marriage ought to be based upon more than physical attraction. She knew nothing of him other than a few basic details. Nothing of his character, of his true interests.

Nothing of his faith.

Grace sighed decisively. He could be as handsome as he liked, but unless he shared her faith in Jesus, there was no way she could ever consider a future with him.

Besides, how silly she was to even think of such words as

'future' when he was her employer's relation and they had only just met.

Please do not let me turn into one of those silly girls who loses all sense the moment she sees a handsome gentleman, she prayed silently.

As she tuned back into Beatrice's conversation she smiled, hoping that her new friend hadn't noticed the lull in her attention.

"Oh!" Beatrice said with a laugh. "You ought to ask John about the time he fell in the river! He had been trying to catch a frog and, after many failed attempts, he decided the best thing to do was to lie on the bank and leap out at it. But, of course, he misjudged the distance and ended up toppling right into the water! His mother was none too pleased, I can tell you!"

The air around the two young ladies filled with laughter as Beatrice relived the moment and Grace imagined it.

"Oh, I must ask him, indeed — what a tale!"

"He was always very daring. Full of excitement, and not much sense!" Beatrice chuckled warmly.

"What are his parents like?" Grace asked, hoping to determine whether they had a faith that was deep or merely the shallow one to which most of society often subscribed without fully embracing.

"Well, his father is Miss Withers's brother, as you know. And his mother always seemed a pleasant lady. She had little fortune, like myself, but that did not matter where Mr. Withers was concerned. He was a prosperous merchant with no need of a dowry."

"Are they still alive?"

Beatrice frowned, silent for a moment. "Do you know, I do not know! I cannot remember hearing anything about either of them passing... Nor have I heard anything about where they are now, or what they are doing." She drained the last of her tea. "Where does John live now?"

"Scarborough," Grace told her. "Miss Withers said he moved there quite recently."

"Oh, lovely," Beatrice said. "I have always imagined it would be charming to live by the sea."

"Yes, I am sure it would." Grace scolded herself silently. She must not dare permit herself to conjure any idea of living happily by the sea with John.

"Are you ready, girls?" Miss Price's voice called out as she and Miss Withers bustled into view.

Grace rose quickly, ready to leave behind all her silly thoughts of the man she barely knew. Beatrice joined her, and the two of them followed the older ladies out into the street, thanking a smiling lady with kind eyes — whom Grace surmised must be Mrs. Fearn — on their way.

As they travelled back to Careo House, Grace half-listened to Beatrice's happy chatter, distracted by the image of John trying to catch a frog. How much more reserved he seemed now compared to his youthful exuberance.

As they rolled past the river, Grace suppressed a smile.

She would indeed ask him all about it. And she was very much looking forward to hearing what he might say.

Especially if his eyes danced as they had at dinner the previous night while he'd conversed with his aunt.

CHAPTER 16

OFF TO CHURCH

"Are you feeling better, John?" Miss Withers asked David as soon as she was settled in the carriage.

"Quite, thank you." He firmed his jaw and forced a smile, trying to relax his posture. How odd it was to be addressed with his cousin's name.

Out of the corner of his eye, he noticed Miss Stratton glance at him, then turn to look out the carriage window.

He was not helping himself any, he knew that. He hadn't gone down to dine with the two ladies last night, and he'd been very quiet at breakfast, too.

All will be well, he tried to assure himself. Yet, he couldn't shake the fear that clutched his heart and stomach in an ever-tightening grip.

What if someone recognised him? It had been decades since he'd last been in Lindenfell, but still. He and John had looked different enough as boys that he was sure some older person with a keen eye and sharp memory might figure out the whole masquerade.

They would expose him as a fraud.

In public.

And at church, of all places.

No, he assured himself again. *All will be well.*

"You seem awfully quiet, my dear."

David looked at his aunt, guilt choking his words as the reality that he was deceiving her seemed to fill the carriage, pushing all the air and ease right out of it. He forced another smile. "My apologies, Aunt." He swallowed hard, his heart trembling. "And you — how are you this morning?"

"Ah, a little stiff. But, I cannot complain." She smiled, her gaze dropping to the floor.

David opened his mouth to ask about her symptoms but stopped himself just in time. After all, his cousin wasn't a physician.

He squeezed his eyes shut. Such torture! Having to constantly monitor and measure what one said... How could anyone live like this willingly, or for an extended period?

How long must he endure this agony?

Upon opening his eyes, he noticed Miss Stratton's gaze fixed upon him. Soft tendrils of wavy dark hair framed her face, and he noticed, for the first time, the pleasant lines of her jaw and her dainty gloved hands resting in her lap. He took in her large dark eyes and dewy skin, her well-proportioned nose and elegant neck.

She was beautiful.

A *natural* beauty — nothing like the coquettish girls he'd seen in London. There was nothing false or coy in her manner, nor did she rely on excessive adornments to enhance her appearance.

He forced a smile, terrified that she could somehow see the truth hiding in his eyes, then turned toward the window, carefully drawing a deep breath.

Miss Stratton cleared her throat. "Mr. Withers?"

David forced himself to meet her gaze once again. It was bad enough that the weight of his deception made it difficult for him to think and speak, but when he looked into those disarming eyes of hers, it was almost impossible. "Yes, Miss Stratton?"

She smiled. "I was speaking with my friend yesterday — Miss Beckwith. Do you remember her?"

David gaped for a moment. "Ah... I am afraid that I cannot say that I do."

Grace shook her head gently, her lips parting as her smile grew wider.

David silently released a long, slow breath.

Pay attention, man. Focus on what she is saying, not how she looks.

"Well, she remembers you!" Grace said with a chuckle.

David froze. He knew it.

He had to have known it. How could he have been so naïve?

Of course people would remember him. And now, here he was, hurtling toward the very centre of the town's civilisation, where a whole crowd of people who might remember him would be gathered.

The minute he walked in, the whole pitiful charade would be up.

"She does?" David asked, trying desperately to keep the fear out of his voice. He dabbed his forehead with his handkerchief.

"Yes, indeed!" Grace leaned forward ever so slightly, the whole atmosphere of the carriage seeming to tip David even more off balance. "She told me of a time when you were trying to catch a frog... down by the river." Her eyes danced as she spoke. "She said that you took it upon yourself to lie in wait for it... and then you jumped on it, to try to catch it, but —" She couldn't contain a giggle. "But you lost your balance instead, and you tumbled straight into the river!"

Miss Withers, who had fixed her attention on Miss

Stratton halfway through her tale, opened her mouth in a silent laugh, her wide eyes glittering with surprise.

David stared at Miss Stratton, a wide grin on his face that he hoped she wouldn't notice didn't reach his eyes. "What a lark!" he exclaimed, aiming to avoid a direct answer.

Miss Stratton giggled again. It was a most delightful sound to his ears. "Do you remember it?" she asked.

David swallowed. "Perhaps... There were so many adventures."

Miss Stratton's eyebrows flickered slightly, and her smile faded into an expression of awkward politeness.

David's heart twisted to see her so evidently embarrassed. He cleared his throat, searching for words that might offer some reassurance and comfort, yet finding none.

The carriage rumbled to a halt.

"Well, here we are," said Miss Withers, adjusting her shawl.

The next few moments were a blur of fast heartbeats and slow, dreamlike movements. Too soon they were all assembled at the door of the church.

David pushed the heavy wooden door open, then stood back to allow his aunt and Miss Stratton to pass. The latter glanced up at him on her way past, dropping her gaze almost instantly as a shy-looking smile played on her lips.

Focus...

David straightened his posture, stifling the cries of alarm that rang in his mind, and strode into the church.

The minister was already speaking. Were they late?

As he settled beside his aunt in the family pew he had not occupied since he was a boy, he quietly released a deep, ragged breath.

This was it. The moment of truth. If anyone recognised him, it could mean the end of everything.

Even of his very life, if word got back to London.

CHAPTER 17
MELODIES AND MEMORIES

"Please turn in your hymnals to number four-seven-four and stand with us to sing *Amazing Grace*." The minister's baritone voice was firm and clear.

Grace smiled as she picked up the book beside her and turned its pages. This was her mother's favourite hymn, and her own. It was the hymn after which she had been named. Her mother's conversion to Christ and healing from the darkness of her past had made the concept of grace very precious to her, so when Grace had been born, there'd been no question as to what she ought to be christened.

John and Grace both stood, but Miss Withers remained seated between them. Grace offered a friendly smile to John, but the one he gave her in return seemed distracted and insincere.

"Amazing grace, how sweet the sound, that saved a wretch like me," Grace sang, the precious truth warming her heart. As she drew a deep breath to sing the next line, the familiar musty smell of wooden pews and hymn books reminded her of her father's little country church, which was only about a quarter of the size of this one. Lindenfell must be bigger than she'd first thought.

They often sang *Amazing Grace* in her father's church, too, and as Grace poured forth the familiar words in this new place, she wondered if her father and mother might be singing the same hymn at this very moment.

"I once was lost, but now am found, was blind, but now I see..."

She glanced again at John. His eyes kept darting from the hymnal he held to various corners of the room. He seemed deeply unsettled.

Ah. That is probably why.

Most likely, he was not accustomed to attending church. After all, he was out on his own in the world, living in a vibrant town by the sea.

Grace had travelled to London once with her father on an errand, and though he'd warned her of the worldly lifestyle that paraded so openly in the city, she'd been very surprised by some of the sights she'd seen and words she'd heard.

"'Twas grace that taught my heart to fear, and grace my fears relieved..."

She could still remember how relieved her mother had been when they'd returned. And the worried whispers her parents had shared when they'd thought her to be out of earshot.

A shudder curled down her spine as she remembered the day her father had told her why her mother never went to London, and why they both thought it best that Grace not accompany her father there again in the future.

Her mother's uncle — Millforte, a wicked and cruel man — was the one responsible for all the trauma that her mother had endured all her youth. And though she'd managed to escape his abusive clutches — thanks in part to Henry, and in part to Millforte being apprehended and imprisoned — she still feared what might happen if he were ever released. It was bad enough that he knew where they lived. But the last thing her mother wanted was for him to see Grace walking down a London street on her father's arm, in the man's own corrupt territory. Ruby knew too well the depths of cruelty and revenge of which his mind and hands were capable. Her body — and soul — still bore the scars.

"I do trust that God will protect you — with my whole heart, I know that He will," her mother had told her, smiling bravely with moist eyes. "I also believe that, as your mother, He has charged me with protecting you as much as I am able, and that I am to do my part to prevent you from suffering as I did." Grace had nodded and embraced her mother, whose silent tears had dropped onto her shoulder.

"How precious did that grace appear the hour I first believed..."

There were times, even now, when Grace's father would gaze and smile at his bride, as though they were young dreamers only just married. He'd often tell Grace how blessed he was that God had given him two beautiful ladies to protect and to love — her mother, and herself. The memory brought a smile to her face and, as she sang, she silently thanked God for the faithful parents and loving home she'd always known.

She glanced around at the other congregants, and for the first time since she'd arrived in Lindenfell, her excitement was eclipsed by uncertainty. Would this new place someday feel like home? She was eager to meet new people and make new friends — especially if they were around her own age, given how starved she'd been starved of such company back home. But she hadn't, until now, considered the very real possibility that people were sometimes reluctant to welcome new folk into their existing circle of companions.

What if everyone in Lindenfell was happy to remain as

they were, and had no interest in befriending an interloping stranger?

As her eyes fixed upon Beatrice, Grace's mind relaxed a little. At least there was one person eager to call her a friend. And, the more she looked, the more she noticed that there were people of all ages and stages of life packed into the church. Beatrice had been right — there were plenty of people their own age.

Grace's concerns subsided. As her gaze moved around the room, she looked again at John. At that precise moment, he looked up, inadvertently catching eyes with her.

Grace smiled, dropping her gaze back to her hymnal, her cheeks warming. She hoped he wouldn't think she'd been looking at him the whole time.

The hymn at an end, the minister instructed them all with his deep, rich voice to be seated once more.

"Let us pray. Lord God, we beseech Thee, give us open ears and open hearts to receive Thy word. May we leave this place more in tune with Thee than when we arrived, and may we ever live to praise Thy holy name. Amen."

As Grace settled into her seat, eager to listen to the sermon, she couldn't help but notice John's restless shuffling out of the corner of her eye.

Silently, she prayed for him. For rest in his body and mind, and for a soft heart toward God.

And that God would use her, if required, to accomplish whatever His will for John might be.

CHAPTER 18

PANIC IN THE PEWS

David shifted in his seat yet again and sighed. He wasn't used to church anymore. He'd attended it with his parents as a child, but once he'd grown up and moved to London, he'd been too busy focusing on his career to make time for regular churchgoing. Eventually, he'd given up on the idea altogether.

After all, he was a man of science now. New discoveries arose year by year in the medical field, and it was altogether more exciting to him than sitting in a pew had ever been.

"And it is the chief of all virtues, as the apostle Paul reminds us in verse thirteen. One day, indeed, faith shall be required no longer, for we shall see our Saviour face to face. One day, hope shall be set aside, as we enjoy forever a life — an eternal life — of freedom from all that assails us in this fractured world. But love... Love will endure forever."

At least the minister here was easy to listen to. He wasn't a shouter or a scolder. He was undoubtedly firm, yet he seemed kind and genuine.

Still, if it hadn't meant so much to his aunt for him to accompany her this morning, he would gladly still be in bed.

He hadn't slept properly last night. Nor any night since the bottom had fallen out of his professional life.

Of his life, in general.

He noticed Grace glancing at him and stilled his manoeuvring for a time. The last thing he wanted was to draw attention to himself. It was bad enough that he was here at all.

Scanning the crowd, moving only his eyes, he was relieved to find that everyone looked unfamiliar to him. Perhaps he would be able to slink back out to the carriage as soon as the service was over without anyone recognising him.

After what seemed an age, when the minister finally ended his closing prayer, David straightened in his seat, readying himself to inform his aunt that he would meet she and Miss Stratton back in the carriage. Perhaps, he ought to mention a headache so it wouldn't seem too strange.

But before he could open his mouth, his aunt turned to him, her eyes shining with excitement. "John, I am so glad that you came with us this morning. Could you help me over there?" she asked, pointing toward a pew in the corner. "I wish to introduce you to Mrs. Baker."

David's heart sank. He tried in vain to think of a way to refuse her but could find none that were remotely satisfactory. He helped her stand, taking her arm. "Of course, Aunt," he replied. "But after that, I might—"

"Oh! Is this the wanderer returned?" exclaimed a portly woman who seemed to have bounded toward them out of nowhere.

"It is," replied Miss Withers, with a proud smile. David glanced from his aunt to Grace, who seemed to be regarding the whole exchange with contented amusement. He turned, reluctantly, to face the unknown lady.

"Good morning, ma'am," he said, bowing slightly.

"My, such manners you have learned, my boy!" The rotund woman laughed. "I remember when you were only this high off the ground..." She waved a hand in the air beside her skirts. "You were always a mischievous little fellow, I declare!"

David forced a smile, muscles tensing all over his body. How many others had similar memories of him? Or, rather, of his cousin?

"Do you remember Mrs. Hughes?" asked Miss Withers, looking expectantly at her nephew.

"I am terribly sorry, I am afraid I do not," David said apologetically.

The woman didn't seem fazed. She waved a dismissive hand in the air. "Oh, I did not expect that you would, child! Do give my regards to your mother when you see her next, though."

David's stomach lurched. He forced another smile and tipped his head politely. "Indeed I shall."

His own mother was gone, but John's was very much still living. A fact he ought to remember much sooner the next time someone expressed a similar sentiment.

"Oh, such a gentleman he has become," said Mrs. Hughes, fixing her attention on Miss Withers and grinning like an excited schoolgirl.

"I imagine there are many others here who will have similar reactions to your presence," said a familiar voice.

David turned to face Grace, trying not to show how nervous her words made him. "Yes... I expect so..."

She smiled kindly at him. "You do not see anyone whom you remember?"

"I cannot say that I do..."

She nodded, no hint of surprise on her face. "You were only a child, after all. Much has happened since then, I am sure."

David froze, fearing for a moment that she spoke of his recent misfortunes.

He sighed, instructing himself to relax. Clearly, attention was to be fixed upon him no matter how determined he was to avoid it.

It certainly wouldn't help if anyone noticed any uneasiness in his manner.

"Yes. Much has," he said, forcing a polite smile.

An unfamiliar voice called out nearby. "Oh, Doctor?"

David swirled around, his eyes wide, his hands jutting out by his sides, his fingers stiffening. As though in slow motion, he saw a man with a questioning look approach the minister.

David turned back to Grace, his heart still hammering.

Astonishment lined her brow. "Are you all right, Mr. Withers?" Grace exclaimed.

David's mind reeled. His heart hammered faster than it ever had before. He sucked in a tight breath, his whole body shuddering as he released it. Slowly, he sank down onto the pew, cradling his head in his hand.

"Mr. Withers!"

He was suddenly aware of something light brushing against his arm, and he unwittingly recoiled at the touch. Jerking his head up, he saw Miss Stratton's wide eyes staring at him in shocked disbelief as she withdrew her hand.

She closed her gaping mouth, looked around nervously, then glanced at Miss Withers.

David echoed her movement, just about taking in the awareness that his aunt was deep in conversation with a different lady.

Turning his attention back to Grace, he forced strength into his voice.

"Miss Stratton... Forgive me. I..."

"What happened?" she asked in an urgent whisper.

David once again met her gaze, her concerned eyes not

helping him in his battle to regain composure. She looked so innocent, so...

No. Focus. Do not give the game away.

"You look dreadfully pale. Are you ill?"

He scarcely heard her, his mind instead mocking himself at his previous choice of word. Game? This was no game. One man was dead already, and he could be next, if Augustus and the Edwards family prevailed.

Fragments of the past few weeks scattered through his mind like jagged thorns, wounding his heart more deeply with each passing moment.

"Mr. Withers?"

Focus, man. Answer her!

"I—" David cleared his throat. "I am extremely sorry, Miss Stratton. I do not mean to be rude. I... I slept very little last night, and I... Well, I suppose I am somewhat unsteady this morning as a result."

Concern lingered on Grace's face, but David's heart stilled as he saw suspicion intermingle with it.

"Oh?" She glanced in the minister's direction, then back at David.

Please do not let her ask. Please let her forget it.

"I am sorry to hear that, of course, but..." She hesitated, then dipped her head. "But it appeared you were... disturbed somehow by the man who called out for Dr. Markham."

"Dr. Markham?" David's voice came out in a hoarse croak.

"Yes. The minister." She glanced at the crowd briefly. "Miss Beckwith mentioned his name to me yesterday."

David nodded, every muscle still trembling. "I see..."

Grace said nothing, only looked at him quizzically. Expectantly.

"As I said... I slept very little last night. I simply... dizzied briefly."

Grace observed him for a moment, then nodded politely.

As she stood up again and turned away, David could think of only two things.

He had lied to her.

And she knew it.

CHAPTER 19
INTRODUCTIONS

"Oh, Miss Stratton! Over here!"

Grace turned to see Beatrice standing by a cluster of pews at the side of the church, beckoning Grace toward her with frantic energy.

Grace smiled and approached her, realising as she neared Beatrice that there were two other young ladies their own age beside her, already engrossed in a conversation.

"Miss Stratton," Beatrice said, extending her hands and gripping Grace's own warmly. "It is so good to see you again." She beamed, her smile lighting up her hazel eyes. "I told you that I would introduce you to my friends. Well, here are two of them — Miss Irene Denton and Miss Alice Markham. Ladies, this is Miss Grace Stratton, Miss Withers's new companion."

"How do you do, Miss Stratton?" Miss Denton smiled warmly.

"Beatrice has told us quite a lot about you," said Miss Markham.

Grace nodded and smiled at each lady in turn. "Forgive

me, but… Miss Markham — are you the minister's daughter?"

"I am," replied Miss Markham. "And you may call me Alice whenever you think it appropriate. I do not wish to be bound by propriety when we are among friends." She offered Grace a good-natured smile.

Among friends. Grace's heart leapt. Already, Alice was referring to her as a friend. Was everyone in Lindenfell so welcoming?

"You are a minister's daughter, too, are you not?" asked Alice.

"Yes," said Grace with a smile.

"And how do you find it?"

Grace blinked. "How do I find it? Well, I suppose I have known nothing different… But my father is a wonderful man, with a strong faith. I am truly grateful to be his daughter."

Irene smiled wistfully. "How lovely."

Alice gave a pronounced nod. "Well said."

Beatrice's smile seemed quashed by melancholy, and Grace's heart stung as she remembered that both of Beatrice's parents were dead.

"Is it true that Mr. John Withers has returned?" Alice asked, before Grace could offer any sympathy or apology to Beatrice.

"Oh, yes," replied Grace, slightly disconcerted as she remembered the odd exchange she'd just shared with him.

"My mother always wished for me to marry his brother," Alice whispered. "But I never cared for him. Much too serious. No romantic sensibilities at all."

Beatrice's giggle rang through the air. "Oh, Alice — surely, he was not old enough to even *think* of matrimony the last time you saw him!"

Grace and Irene joined in the pleasant laughter.

Alice glanced around. "Hush! He was old enough for me to tell what kind of zest for life he had." She raised an eyebrow and looked at each of them in turn. "None whatsoever!"

"Well, then. Be glad it is not his brother who has come back to visit."

As the others tossed quips back and forth, Grace observed them all for a moment. Beatrice was glowing, in her element among friends. Alice seemed confident and free-spirited, though without any arrogance or silliness. And Irene seemed quiet and calm. She had one of the most placid smiles Grace had ever seen.

"How do you like Lindenfell so far, Miss Stratton?" Irene asked.

Grace smiled. "Oh, it is beautiful. I like it very much."

"Is it bigger or smaller than the place from which you came?" asked Alice, her keen eyes fixed on Grace again.

"Oh, it is much bigger."

Alice's eyebrows shot up. "*Much* bigger? My, my... I never imagined Lindenfell to be a sprawling metropolis!" she said, a smile playing on her lips.

Grace noticed a blush on Beatrice's cheeks. "Are you all right, Miss Beckwith?"

The two other young ladies immediately examined Beatrice, too.

"Yes, yes, I— I am quite all right, thank you, Miss Stratton." Beatrice's cheeks reddened even more.

"I know that look..." Alice said, a note of teasing in her voice.

Beatrice glanced at Alice, then dipped her head as though trying to escape whatever it was that Alice had evidently surmised.

"Oh, do not tease her so." Irene's gentle voice did little to dissuade Alice.

"Is he here, Beatrice?" Alice glanced around the room before turning back to her friend.

Beatrice's blush was undeniable now. "Do not draw attention to us, Alice."

Grace had never heard someone scold another in such a kind tone.

Catching eyes with an evidently perplexed Grace, Alice smiled and beckoned her closer. Grace leaned in.

"Miss Beckwith has her eyes and heart set on a certain young man who attends the church," Alice said in a hushed yet happy tone. "And, judging by the colour of her cheeks, he is most definitely in attendance this morning." Alice smiled affectionately at Beatrice, who met Grace's gaze with a sheepish shrug of acknowledgment.

Grace couldn't help but smile as she fought the urge to look around the room in anticipation. "What is his name?"

Beatrice blushed all over again. "Mr. Taylor. *Isaac*." She said his Christian name with tender reverence.

"Well, where is he?" Grace asked, stealing a glance over her shoulder.

"Good question." Alice's gaze searched the room.

Beatrice sighed. "He is over there... Talking to..." She frowned as she studied the other person. "I do not know who that man is."

Alice nodded. "I see him now. Though I cannot see enough of his acquaintance to tell whether I recognise him or not."

Grace manoeuvred herself so that she was standing more in line with the others instead of her back remaining turned to the rest of the crowd. She followed Alice's subtle pointing toward a young man with brown hair and a pleasant face, who seemed to be deep in conversation with—

"Mr. Withers!"

Beatrice, Alice and Irene all turned their heads to look at Grace.

"What?"

"No!"

"Truly?"

"That is him, Mr. Taylor, in the green coat and cream cravat? Speaking to the gentleman with the wavy hair?"

"Yes," Beatrice said, a hint of dreaminess in her voice.

Grace nodded. "That is Mr. Withers with whom he is conversing."

"John Withers? Why, it looks nothing like him!" Beatrice exclaimed.

"He is very like his cousin now. Though, he was nothing like him before," Alice remarked.

"I remember neither of Miss Withers's nephews, I am afraid," Irene said.

"He has changed so *much*!" Beatrice shook her head slowly.

"He has?" Grace asked.

"Completely," Alice said. "Why, he looks how I imagine *David* would at this age. It is really *John*?"

A strange sensation crept over Grace. "Yes. It is John."

It had to be John. Surely, Miss Withers would know her own nephews apart. Though, it *had* been a long time since she had seen them.

But why would David say that he was John? What could he possibly gain by trying to convince his aunt and all of Lindenfell that he was really his own cousin?

Grace dismissed the sneaking question before it had time to take root in her mind.

The man on the other side of the room was her employer's nephew, John Withers.

Wasn't he?

CHAPTER 20
AN INVITING CONVERSATION

David kept glancing about nervously at the small clusters of people chatting among themselves in the church, hoping that Isaac Taylor — the friendly young man with whom he was now engaged in conversation — would not think him rude.

"No, my family moved to Lindenfell around ten years ago." Isaac's face fell. "A few years after we lost my sister."

"I am dreadfully sorry to hear that." David frowned in sympathy. "What happened?"

Isaac swallowed, the memory still visibly painful to recall. "Scarlatina. The doctor tried to burn the fever out of her. We learned only recently that a more successful treatment is to cool the afflicted person."

David nodded. "That is true. It was not known until recently, though — you are right about that."

"I only wish we had moved here sooner. Dr. Turner and his apprentice are certainly not typical country doctors. They stay quite up to date with the latest developments and discoveries." Isaac smiled sadly. "Perhaps they might have been able to prevent Emma's death."

"It is impossible to know. Scarlatina is often fatal, even with the best of treatments. I truly am sorry for your loss."

Isaac nodded and exhaled sharply. "Forgive me. We ought to speak of happier things. You have a cousin around our age, do you not?"

"Yes." David stopped himself just as he was about to say John's name. "*David.*"

"What does he do?"

David blinked. He had to be careful to say everything correctly. Which, in this case, meant saying everything incorrectly. "He is a physician. In London."

"Ah," Isaac said. A melancholy smile passed across his features. "And we just spoke of physicians."

"Yes."

"Do you see him much?"

"Not very often. Our individual circumstances keep us quite busy. Life has simply pulled us in different directions."

Isaac nodded. "That is what tends to happen when one grows up."

"And you? Do you have any other siblings or cousins nearby?"

"No. It was just the two of us. And now, just me." He was silent for a moment, then seemed to compose himself. "Do you know many people in Lindenfell? From when you were younger?"

"No... I cannot say that I do." David glanced around. "One or two people have mentioned that they remember seeing me as a boy, but I do not recall any of them, myself."

Isaac chuckled. "It must be strange to come back after so long. But I am sure your aunt is glad to have you."

"Yes." David's smile was easy and relaxed this time. "She has welcomed me so warmly. I did not expect it at all. It is above what I could have hoped."

Isaac smiled. "And she has a new companion, I hear?"

"Yes..." David's smile faltered as he remembered the look Grace had given him after what he had claimed was his dizziness from lack of sleep.

If ever she suspected him of anything, she must now.

David glanced across the room, looking away suddenly as he noticed her standing with a few other young ladies at the other side of the church.

As he fixed his gaze on Isaac again, he noticed the expectant look on his new acquaintance's face.

"Yes, uh... Miss Stratton. She is... very... nice." David nodded awkwardly.

Isaac let out a small laugh. "Is she indeed?" He cast David a knowing look.

David's mouth fell open as he frowned. "No, I did not mean—" He swallowed, so many thoughts and emotions colliding in his mind that he hadn't a notion how he ought to respond.

"I am sorry, Mr. Withers. I meant no harm. Only, you did seem rather... *flustered,* shall we say?"

David sighed. "I am sorry. I... I had a rather strange encounter with her earlier. To tell the truth, I am still a little out of sorts as a result."

"Oh, dear." Isaac's countenance switched from levity to concern. "Nothing that would cause any problems for Miss Withers, I hope?"

"No, no... Not at all. Forgive me... I am not giving you an accurate depiction of her character at all. She is a clergyman's daughter, a very quiet and steady sort of young lady. I have seen nothing wanting in her conduct or conversation. My aunt is very pleased with her."

Isaac nodded thoughtfully. "But you are not?"

"Oh, I am. I... She is very pleasant. Very intelligent."

Isaac looked at David curiously. "But, this strange encounter...?"

David swallowed. "It was more my doing than hers. Forgive me, but I would rather not speak of it at present."

"Of course, of course. I am sorry. I did not mean to pry."

David waved his hand and shook his head, smiling as he did so.

"Say, would you like to join me for a game of whist later?" Isaac asked. "A few friends and I meet up for a spot of chat and a few games — no gambling, mind."

"Yes, I would like that very much."

"Splendid. Do you know where the assembly rooms are in town, above the Horse and Crown inn?"

"I am sure I can find them."

"Excellent. Meet us there at eight o'clock. I must dash now, but I shall look forward to seeing you later."

The two men said their farewells, and David suddenly felt exposed as he stood alone.

He reluctantly walked toward his aunt, catching sight of Grace up ahead, still deep in conversation with the young ladies.

As she glanced at him, he detected an odd uneasiness on her countenance.

An uneasiness that promptly crept into his own heart as she looked away.

CHAPTER 21
A DARING QUESTION

The whole way home from church, Grace studied John covertly at every opportunity, debating whether or not she ought to say something to him when they returned to Careo House.

But by the time they arrived, she had mostly succeeded in talking herself out of it.

She was being silly, suspecting someone who was clearly a gentleman of doing something so dishonourable. And why? Because people who had not seen him for years believed him to look more like his cousin than he had when they were children!

Of all the ridiculous notions she had ever entertained, surely this was one of the worst.

Grace glanced at her employer as they all made their way inside, out of the light shower that had begun to fall almost at the very moment they were exiting the carriage. Miss Withers looked tired after their outing, and would likely require Grace's constant assistance all afternoon. There would hardly be an opportunity to speak to John in private.

And rightly so.

Decorum not only preserved modesty and manners but, in times like these, it was also a strong deterrent against saying something one would later regret.

As they all entered the drawing room, Grace quickly made her way toward her needlework basket, longing for a distraction from her silly speculations of scandal. After retrieving it, she sank down onto her chair and selected a small needle and pale purple thread, praying as she threaded it that her mind would abandon all the questions echoing therein.

"How did you find the service, John?" Miss Withers asked once she was settled in her usual chair next to the fire.

"It was... very good," he said politely, taking the seat opposite his aunt.

"Dr. Markham is a splendid orator, is he not?"

John nodded. "Very skilled."

Upon the mention of the minister's title, Grace glanced at John. Her cheeks pinked to discover that he had mirrored the gesture, and she swiftly returned her attention to her embroidery.

Miss Withers turned her head to look at Grace. "How did you find it, Miss Stratton?"

As Grace looked up at her employer, she saw from the corner of her eye that John had trained his own gaze upon her as well. Resisting the urge to glance at him again, she fixed a smile on her face and nodded at Miss Withers. "It was wonderful. Truly. I found the sermon very encouraging."

"Was it anything like your father's sermons?"

"It was different in style, but similar in content. Dr. Markham seems a very committed man — very devoted." Her father's face came to her mind, softening her heart. "As is my father."

Miss Withers smiled approvingly and turned her attention

back to her nephew. "Did you see anyone whom you recognised?"

John cleared his throat. "I cannot say that I did."

"Oh, I expect not. You were only little when you were here. David might remember more, being a few years your senior."

"Yes, perhaps."

Grace glanced up from her needlework. Something about the uncertain tone in John's voice revived all the suspicions and speculations she had been trying so hard to silence.

The door opened, and Higgins entered. "Dinner is ready."

"Ah, delightful. I am quite ready for it!" Miss Withers said.

They all rose.

"But the cook wishes to ask you a question before you all eat, if that is satisfactory to you, ma'am. Relating to your dinner party tomorrow evening."

"Of course." Miss Withers glanced at John, then Grace. "I shall meet you both in the dining room."

Miss Withers followed Higgins out of the room, leaving John and Grace standing motionless in her absence.

This was it.

This was her chance.

But she could never ask such a thing.

Could she?

John looked at her, his lips turning up in an awkward smile.

Grace's heart hammered too violently for her to return the gesture.

As John moved forward, Grace stepped between him and the door without even thinking, raising her hand in a gesture of entreaty. "Wait..."

He took a step back, a frown of confusion playing on his brow.

She could see his hesitation plainly. Could see how tightly

he swallowed, how much his breathing had stilled. Though, she wasn't sure if it was fear or concern that had altered his expression.

"Forgive me," she said, almost in a whisper.

He observed her for a moment. "Are you all right, Miss Stratton? Are you feeling ill?"

"I..." Grace dropped her gaze to the floor. Her throat was dry, her limbs weak. She stepped back, leaning against the door, allowing its solid surface to support her. "Forgive me, but there is something that I must ask you," she said, releasing a deep, troubled breath.

"Yes?"

His voice sounded smaller, more distant, but she could not stop now that she had begun.

She raised her eyes to meet his, her voice catching in her throat. "Are you truly John Withers?"

His face fell, growing paler by the second. He stared at her as silence stretched out between them.

Finally, he frowned. "What?" he croaked.

Blood thundered in Grace's ears. "I am sorry... I was speaking to Dr. Markham's daughter earlier, and Miss Beckwith, and well, both of them... They each expressed how surprised they were that you were *John*. They... They seemed convinced that you looked more like *David*."

John raised his hand to his face, smoothing his moustache with his fingers, then rubbing his chin. The look of bewilderment on his countenance only made Grace's heart beat even faster.

She'd been so foolish.

How could she have asked him?

With each word she had spoken aloud, she'd heard the folly and impossibility of the question with her own ears.

She squeezed her eyes shut. "Forgive me..."

She wanted to bolt from the room, from the house. What if he told Miss Withers?

"Miss Stratton?"

Reluctantly, Grace opened her eyes. She was surprised to find no hint of anger on his countenance.

"My cousin and I are bound to share similarities. Two of our parents are siblings, after all. We are part of the same family. It has been a long time since either of us has been to Lindenfell. It surely cannot be a surprise to find that we have changed as we have grown."

"No, of course not." Grace barely managed to force the words out.

"Now... My aunt may be wondering what has become of us. Shall we?"

He extended his arm toward her. She tremulously reached out and placed her hand upon the warm, soft fabric of his immaculate coat.

As they moved into the hall, she found her voice. "You are not angry with me?"

His striking grey eyes gazed intently into her own. "Not at all."

His woody, masculine fragrance somehow made her heart ache all the more. How silly he must think her. Or worse — how offensive.

"Miss Stratton... I am sorry for any confusion I might have caused you."

Grace's eyes widened. "*You* are sorry? Oh, but I have been a dolt." She shook her head. "Truly, Mr. Withers, I am so sorry to have questioned you and suspected you. I have nothing to say in my own defence. I can only assure you that I am deeply sorry."

The mournful pity in John's eyes stole Grace's breath away. "All is well. We need mention it no further."

How kind this man was to overlook such an insulting accusation.

How pleasant it was to be standing by his side, her hand on his arm, their faces closer than they had ever been.

Or, at least, how pleasant it *would* have been, had Grace not been so utterly devastated by her own stupidity.

John gave her a gentle smile, then led her to the dining room. Just as they took their seats, Miss Withers shuffled into the room, completely unaware of the exchange which had taken place in her absence.

Miss Withers sat and signalled to the servant. "All is well. Now, shall we eat?"

All is well. There were those words again.

But as Grace nodded and glanced at John, she noticed how pale and withdrawn he seemed.

All was not well.

And it was her fault entirely.

CHAPTER 22

CHILLS

Had one of the townsfolk stopped David on his way to the assembly rooms and asked him what he had consumed for luncheon, he could not have told them.

He remembered nothing of the meal. Nothing of the conversation with his aunt and Miss Stratton.

Only his treachery, his deception.

His intentionally misleading response to an honest question.

As David trudged along the road toward town, every footstep seemed to beat an accusation.

He hadn't had the courage to face them for dinner, so he'd waited until they were settled in the dining room, then slipped out.

He gritted his teeth as memories assailed him. She had asked him — outright, and directly — and he had led her to believe that the answer to her question had been the exact opposite of what it truly was.

All he could see, even now, were her dark eyes looking at him with regret and embarrassment. It was evident she believed herself to have questioned him wrongly and spoken out of turn.

She did not know that her question, her suspicion... it had all been perfectly warranted.

He *was* David. And he was a deceiver.

His heart echoed with guilt as his feet pounded the dirt path.

It was bad enough that he had lied to them from the start. But then, Miss Stratton — a clergyman's daughter, no less! — had asked him for the truth, and he had purposefully withheld it.

More than that...

He'd twisted it.

How low had he fallen that he was now wilfully misleading a bright and beautiful young lady like Miss Stratton? How could he even dare to show his face in Careo House again?

David tugged his collar close against the evening chill.

All afternoon he had lingered in his room, away from Miss Stratton's pure, sorrowful eyes. Away from his aunt's warm compliments. Alone with his thoughts and the few documents he had brought from London with which he was trying to make sense of the charges against him.

David kicked at the ground in frustration, gritting his teeth. He ought to just go back home. Face whatever punishment was doled out to him. What use was it trying to preserve his life and his reputation only to destroy it all in a different way?

It was agony to recall Grace's innocent face.

Had she noticed that he'd barely been able to breathe as he tried to formulate a response to her question? Had she detected the nervous yearning he'd felt when she had placed her hand upon his arm?

How lovely she was, with her dark, gleaming hair and her

wide, expressive eyes. Her smooth skin, her slender arms. Had he been in Lindenfell as himself, and at liberty to speak freely, he would be planning how best to declare his growing attraction to her, and considering a very different kind of life-altering circumstance.

Matrimony would be his focus, not murder charges. He would declare his feelings, not deny his identity.

But everything was backward. Twisted around out of its proper place.

He had lied to her, and she had presented him with an opportunity to correct it — to tell the truth about who he was and why he was really there.

But he'd let it slip past.

Not only that, he'd dug himself even deeper into the pit his deception had initially carved.

And, now, it seemed there was no way out of it. No way that he could right the wrongs without crushing the two people he had come to care about the most since his arrival — his aunt, and the young lady who had captivated his senses.

The young lady, with whom he wished he could share the truth.

And his heart.

CHAPTER 23

A MOMENT OF CLARITY

Grace sat at the writing desk in her room and stared out of the window, seeing nothing.

After dinner, Miss Withers had gone upstairs for a nap, so Grace decided she would use the spare time to write a letter to her parents. She knew her father would be eager to hear what the church in Lindenfell was like, and she had promised her mother that she would keep in regular contact with them.

But for the past while, she'd been unable to focus on anything except what had happened earlier that day.

After they'd finished eating luncheon, John had excused himself with the same excuse he'd given Grace at the church. And he hadn't joined them for dinner.

Perhaps he *hadn't* slept well. Perhaps it *had* affected him more than she realised.

How could she have been so unkind? So suspicious?

So very, very wrong?

Her heart sank all over again to think of it afresh.

She remembered his voice close beside her ear, telling her that all was well. But, throughout luncheon, he'd barely spoken a word except in response to something his aunt had asked. His gaze had scarcely strayed from his plate, and his countenance and posture had been stiff and uneasy.

What was she to do? He'd said there was no need to speak of it again. But all she wanted to do was apologise until he understood how much she truly regretted what she had asked. What she had implied.

A deep sigh worked its way out of her in frustration.

She thought again of what Alice had said, remembering how Beatrice had looked at Isaac. Beatrice would never have done such a thing — she would never have injured Isaac's dignity by asking such a silly question.

Not that Grace felt about John the way that Beatrice—

Or... *did* she?

Was that why her stomach had churned as she'd compelled John to stay in the room with her? Was that why a strange sensation had overpowered her as she'd stood with her hand upon his arm, looking up into his sombre eyes?

Never had she felt that way whilst standing beside anyone else.

Nor could she think of anyone beside whom she would rather stand for the rest of her days.

Grace rested her face in her hands and groaned.

She was being ridiculous again. She didn't even know the man.

And she would never know him, now. She had single-handedly obliterated any hope of any future confidence or connection they might have shared.

She blinked back tears as she lifted her quill to write. What had come over her? At Shiloh Hall, she'd been sensible and logical. Now, after only a few days in Lindenfell, she had become an emotional, impulsive ninny.

After inscribing her greeting, she sat motionless, the quill clutched in her hand, as the memory of her confrontation with John circled in her mind.

She'd seen him out the dining room window as she'd tried to eat some of her dinner. He'd left the house looking as though a heavy yoke had been draped around his shoulders instead of just his coat.

She'd offended him — she knew that much. But what she did not know was what she ought to do about it. How she might set things right.

Or, if doing so was even possible.

Surely, he could never trust her, never see her as anything but the insolent dolt who had wrongly accused him.

Grace stared at the page, lowering the quill a time or two but each time raising it without making any mark on the page.

What *was* this?

Never had anyone caused her to question her judgement or her future. Not like this.

It wasn't easy to admit, but she cared what he thought of her. She wanted him to think well of her.

Not in a general way. Not in any way she had experienced before.

She wanted him... to *love* her.

Time seemed suspended all around her, waiting with bated breath for her to move away from this moment, this realisation.

Grace closed her eyes and forced out a long, steady breath.

Move away from it, she must.

For how could he ever love her in return now?

CHAPTER 24

THE CONFESSION

"I take it you do not play whist very often?"

David looked up at Isaac's friend, Solomon Shaw, then down at the card table. Isaac had won — again.

David couldn't even remember playing his last few cards. His mind still replayed his conversation with Grace earlier that day, and he wondered how she and his aunt had taken the fact that he'd left without a word, not even sending a servant to convey his regrets that he would not be joining them for dinner.

"My apologies," he said, casting his gaze from Solomon, to Isaac, to the other man at the table whose name he couldn't even remember. "Perhaps I ought to sit the next game out."

David glanced again at Isaac, noticing how keenly his new friend was examining him. He looked away. Inside, his heart ached and burned, and he wanted nothing more than to break free from the room's mirthful company, to be alone. And to weep.

Isaac stood. "John, come with me." He motioned with his chin toward the door before turning and approaching it.

David excused himself and followed silently. He couldn't

blame Isaac for asking him to leave. He'd been a dullard all evening, he was sure of it. And he'd drunk more wine than any of the others.

The worst part was, he didn't even care. None of it seemed to matter anymore.

"John..." Isaac eyed him with no trace of disappointment or disdain. Only compassion and concern. "Will you share your burden with me? What is it that troubles you this evening?"

David looked at him, his expression unchanging. A cold, dull weight seemed to have wrapped itself around him. He tried in vain to form a response.

But nothing came.

He sighed, dropping his gaze to the dusty floor. Slowly, briefly, he shook his head.

Isaac placed a warm, friendly hand on his shoulder. Somehow, it seemed only to reinforce the guilt and shame that filled him.

"Come, let us take a walk. Perhaps the air will do you some good."

Silently, David followed, relieved when Isaac removed his hand in order to descend the narrow staircase.

Neither of them spoke until they stepped out of the building into the cool, crisp evening air. Lindenfell was blanketed by an eerie silence — nothing at all like the bustling noises of London's main streets at night.

Isaac strolled slowly down the empty road. "So," he said as he tucked his hands into his trouser pockets. "Tell me. What is it that distracts you this evening?"

David trudged along beside him. "I do not even know how to put it all into words," he muttered.

"Is it a matter of some gravity, then?"

"Yes."

"You are... in some kind of trouble?"

The gentle compassion in Isaac's tone pierced David's heart. Surely, the man would not be so kind if he knew the truth.

Sorrow and desperation overcame David, and he sighed. "A great deal."

Isaac stopped walking and turned to face him, which prompted David to do the same.

"What kind of trouble?" Again, there was no chastisement to be found in Isaac's voice or manner.

David froze. He'd said too much already. "It... it is no matter." He looked around, wary that someone else could hear them, but they had ambled off the main street onto a grassy verge by the riverbank. No one else was in view, nor likely to be in earshot.

Isaac reached out his hand and placed it on David's upper arm. "Clearly, it is. Do not worry, John. You are among friends here. If there is anything that can be done to aid you in any way, I will gladly see to it."

David forced a restless breath out of his nostrils. "I fear that nothing can be done. That is precisely the problem."

"There is always something—"

"No! Not this time. And all that I do only makes it worse." David shook his head as he spoke, the weight of the situation oppressing him again. He gave a bitter laugh. "It is ironic. I came here to gain some time. To think of a way... But, all I... Everything is..." His words trailed off as anguish tore through him. He raised a weary hand and buried his face in it.

"Listen, no matter what has happened, I am sure that if we put our heads together, we can come up with some kind of solution. John, I—"

"I am not John!" David jerked his hand away from his face and waved it in the air as he stared in wild trepidation at Isaac. "I am not John! I am a fraud. An imposter! And she knows it. And... And I made her think that... Oh, I do not even deserve the second chance that I came here to find. I have done nothing but deceive everyone!"

Isaac's expression of concern changed into one of confusion and disbelief as David bellowed his confession into the night and dissolved into tortured sobs. After gaping at him for a few moments, Isaac swallowed. "Who... who are you, then?"

David grappled for composure. He forced a long, slow breath through parted lips. "My name... is David Carbury."

Isaac's frown seemed to lessen a little. "Miss Withers's *other* nephew?"

"Yes."

Isaac dropped onto the grass. "Come," he said gently, motioning for David to sit next to him.

David sank onto his knees, his head hanging heavily. He released a sigh that shuddered throughout every inch of his being.

"Why are you pretending to be John?" Isaac's voice was calm and steady, as though David's revelation of deceit hadn't troubled him.

David's gut tightened, as did his jaw. "Because... I needed to get away from London for a while. To think."

"Think?"

"Of what might be done."

"Regarding the trouble that you are in?"

"Yes."

"And..." Isaac cleared his throat gently. "Why is it that you could not come here under your own name? You *are* Miss Withers's nephew, after all. Why do you feel you must hide who you really are?"

David's voice sounded detached from himself as he spoke. "Because who I really am... is a physician facing legal proceedings... accused of murder by poisoning."

Isaac's lips parted and his eyes widened. Pallor washed

over his face. He blinked, then tucked his chin low. "Murder?" His voice was barely above a gasp.

Why are you telling him this? If he tells the authorities, you are done for!

David sighed. He was done for already. He should never have left London — he ought to have stayed and embraced his dismal fate.

"A patient of mine died. Mr. Edwards. His family blame the chloroform that we used, but it was the cholera, for which we were treating him... that is what killed him." David shook his head and frowned. "It was not the chloroform. I have used it many times, and it is safe." He sighed. "It was not to blame. But his family see things differently. And the other doctor, with whom I worked closely, has turned his back on me. He claims he was never happy to use chloroform in the first place, and he is siding with the patient's family." David's face twisted in anguish. "But he knows! He knows it is safe. I would never have used it had it not been safe!"

For a moment, David's awareness of Isaac's presence was eclipsed by his own despair. Finally Isaac's gentle voice penetrated his awareness.

"Well, it sounds as though you are most definitely not guilty of *murder*. Is there nothing that can be done? Surely, a lawyer—"

"My lawyer indicated that I ought to prepare for imprisonment at best and..." His voice cracked slightly. "And the gallows, at worst."

Isaac's face grew slack. "The *gallows*?"

David firmed his jaw and nodded.

Isaac sucked in a deep breath and released it, shaking his head. "Oh, David..."

David wasn't sure if it was the compassion in Isaac's voice or the fact that someone had addressed him with his true name for the first time in what seemed an age that made him want to weep. He bit his lip, staring at the ground beneath him, yet not even seeing it.

The two men sat in sombre silence as the river trickled by and night birds called from the trees.

"When my sister died, my parents were so full of grief that it almost destroyed them. My father, especially. He does not fully believe in God, much to his own detriment, I fear." Isaac shook his head slowly. "After the initial shock had worn off, his sadness turned to anger, and he wanted nothing more than to ruin the doctor whose wrong advice had contributed to her demise." Isaac stared at his hands as he spoke, twiddling his fingers and thumbs absent-mindedly. "But after a while, he realised... That would not achieve what he truly wanted. It would not bring Emma back." He sighed heavily. "Nothing would."

As David listened silently, his heart ached not only for his own situation, but for the loss and grief that Isaac had suffered. "I am sorry, Isaac. After all that has befallen you, I should not have spoken of my own troubles. Especially when they involve such similarities. A patient's death... a physician's blame..."

"No, but that is what I am trying to tell you. I know how Mr. Edwards's family must be feeling. The loss is profound, especially at first. The pain eventually fades from a sharp thrust to a dull throb, in time, but it never fully goes away. But as grief subsides, rational thought returns. This man... his family... perhaps once they are over the shock of his death, they will understand that your methods did nothing to cause it."

David looked at Isaac, considering his words. Could that really happen? It didn't seem likely, given the fixed public opinion on chloroform and the rather hopeless letter he'd received from his lawyer.

"David... I understand that you are reluctant to reveal your true identity. I understand why. But, please, consider carefully what I am about to ask of you. Dr. Turner is years ahead of his profession — I have no doubt that he would share your views on chloroform and its safety of use. Perhaps, if we were to seek his advice on the matter, he might lead us to some knowledge or circumstance that could work in your favour, legally."

David shook his head, fear overriding his logic. "Isaac..."

"Think about it. Please. I am sure that he could help. Somehow."

David hesitated. "And if he could not help? Could we still trust him to keep the information in his confidence?"

"Yes, I—"

"Or, would he feel duty bound to let the authorities in London know where I am?"

Isaac's lips pushed together. He looked at David, deep in thought. "I believe that unless he would be breaking the law by remaining silent that he would be trustworthy to keep anything we would tell him in the strictest confidence."

David sighed, smoothed his moustache, then propped his chin in his hand. "I do not know, Isaac."

Isaac was silent for a moment. "If not that, then what? It may be your best opportunity to resolve the matter."

David exhaled slowly. Isaac was right. What other option was there but to hide away in Lindenfell and keep lying to everyone? "I shall think about it." David paused. "Thank you."

"And you need not fear — you may trust me. I shall not reveal your secret to anyone."

David studied Isaac with a blend of admiration and disbelief. "Thank you."

Isaac nodded and offered a sympathetic smile. He sighed, shaking his head. "I cannot imagine how difficult it must be for you, having to conceal the truth from your aunt." He frowned. "Did you say something earlier about her knowing? She knows that you are not John?"

David exhaled, guilt crashing around him again. "No... Not my aunt." He cleared his throat. "Miss Stratton."

Isaac's eyebrows shot up. "Miss Stratton knows that you are really David?"

David shook his head, anguish rising in his chest. "She asked me. She asked me if I was truly John..."

"And?"

"And... I misled her." He exhaled bitterly. "I answered in such a way that I denied the truth that she had detected, and I led her to believe the opposite — that I *am* John. That my only similarities with David are there because we are cousins. I lied to her, Isaac. And she trusted my words." He closed his eyes. "I saw the embarrassment on her face. She told me how sorry she was, and I had to stand there and bear it, knowing full well that *she* is not the one in the wrong. I cannot bear it, Isaac, I—" He stopped abruptly, drawing a shuddering breath.

"You *do* have feelings for her?"

David glanced at Isaac, the question catching him off guard. As he allowed the truth to dawn on him, he swallowed hard. He nodded. "But when she finds out the truth... She will hate me."

Isaac sighed. "Well, we must tackle the more severe problem first. It will not do any good whether she loves you or hates you if you are languishing in prison... or worse. We must rectify the legal issues. Then, there will be time enough to deal with matters of the heart."

He and Isaac stood, brushing themselves off.

"And, whatever happens, know that I shall be praying for you," Isaac said, a smile easing the worry from his countenance. "God shall help us, if only we will ask Him. My own life has proven that. He is faithful and true, just as His word says."

David forced a smile, too distracted to fully take in Isaac's words. Two questions kept circling in his mind.

Might Dr. Turner really be able to help him rectify the legal issues?

And, what had he ever done to deserve a friend like Isaac Taylor?

CHAPTER 25

A LONG EVENING

The next evening, Grace smoothed her red silk gown and pinched her cheeks before hurrying downstairs. Miss Withers had invited a couple from the town for dinner, and they were soon to arrive. She'd insisted that Grace and John wear their best clothes and be ready with plenty of time to spare.

"Ah, you look splendid, dear child!"

Grace smiled in response to Miss Withers's compliment. She'd always loved this gown, and part of her wondered if John would like it, too.

But a sick knot in her stomach soon edged out the thought, replacing it with embarrassment at the thought of having to face him.

"Thank you. You look wonderful, Miss Withers."

"Oh, my dear! At my age, one is only glad when one can see the food on one's plate and has an appetite to consume it!"

Grace glanced around the room, wondering if John would even join them. They hadn't seen much of him since luncheon the day before, and she had never been so nervous at the prospect of seeing someone as she was at this moment.

She forced a casual tone into her voice. "Is Mr. Withers joining us?"

"Oh, he shall be along soon, I am sure. I did give him warning, and he never wishes to disappoint me. Such a good young man."

Miss Withers's innocent observation wrenched Grace's guilt more tightly around her heart. She knew how good he was. How gracious he had been to her when she hadn't deserved it.

That's what made it hurt so much.

Before she could fashion a response, footsteps pacing down the stairs stole her breath, and she turned to see John pausing in the hallway.

His grey eyes latched onto hers, and dismay filled her as she noticed the sorrow within them.

He bowed. "Miss Stratton. Aunt."

"Ever the dashing young man, John! Though Miss Stratton and I were beginning to wonder whether or not you would join us after all."

Grace's cheeks burned with embarrassment. She didn't want John to think she had been speaking ill of him to his aunt in his absence.

"My apologies, Aunt. Miss Stratton. A few matters to which I had to attend merely held me up." His gaze flitted between them as he spoke.

Grace wondered what it was that had kept him so busy all day, and whether it might be more of an excuse than an explanation. Perhaps he simply did not want to face her.

Not that she could blame him.

"She looks splendid this evening, does she not, John?" Miss Withers said gaily, waving her hand toward Grace.

Heat crept up Grace's neck into her cheeks, and she glanced at John for a mere second before fixing her gaze squarely upon the floor.

He cleared his throat gently. Agonising seconds ticked by. "Splendid, indeed."

Her heart hammering, she stole another glance at him, expecting to see a stoic expression of polite indifference. Instead, his doleful eyes lingered on her until he caught her gaze. Swiftly, he turned his own attention to the floor.

The doorbell chimed.

"There they are!" Miss Withers said. "Come, both of you, into the drawing room."

Grace hesitated, reluctant to move too quickly and thus end up colliding with him. She glanced up and noticed that he hadn't moved.

"After you, Miss Stratton," he said, then cleared his throat and motioned with his arm toward the drawing room.

"Thank you," she said, her voice weak. She tucked her head downwards and propelled herself into the drawing room.

Silly girl, she chastised herself. *So busy trying not to cause a commotion that you end up causing one anyway!*

She kept her gaze low as John followed her into the room.

A few moments later, Higgins ushered in a woman resplendent in brocade and a suave gentleman with silver streaks throughout his pomaded black hair. Higgins bowed and departed.

"Welcome, welcome!" Miss Withers called out, delight audible in her voice.

The awkwardness saturating the air between herself and John distracted Grace so much that she could hardly concentrate on the introductions. She gathered the guests's names, at least — Mr. and Mrs. Hartley — but she was at a complete loss to recall anything else that Miss Withers had said about them.

Higgins reappeared and beckoned them all to the dining room. Grace glanced at John as he approached her, her heart picking up speed. Abruptly, he turned and bowed at Mrs. Hartley, offering her his arm.

Mr. Hartley had offered his own to Miss Withers, so Grace waited for the others to leave the room first, then duly followed behind.

John glanced over his shoulder briefly, catching her worried gaze. By the time she forced a quick smile, he had already turned forward again.

She sighed inwardly.

Surely, this was going to be a long evening.

CHAPTER 26

DINNER AND DEVASTATION

David dropped his gaze to his half-eaten dinner for what seemed the twentieth time in as many minutes.

The conversation was lively enough — for his aunt and her guests, at least. But this was the last place he wanted to be — his company expected yet barely acknowledged as the evening whiled itself away in frivolous emptiness.

Movement to his left caught his eye, and he glanced covertly at Grace. She seemed as weary as he was, her own company neglected despite its apparent necessity, too.

David cleared his throat, trying to ignore the lead knot in his gut and the quivering irregularities of his heart. "I cannot remember the last time I ate turkey."

Miss Stratton turned, her eyebrows lifting a little.

David glanced away. Why was it such agony to hold her gaze?

He knew why.

What did he expect — that he could deceive an innocent young lady without any consequences, no matter how unseen and internal those consequences were? He was being careful this evening to present a dignified front, but the anguish within him was suffocating.

"I confess, I have never eaten it before," she replied, after taking a sip of wine. "But it is pleasant."

Her jewelled earrings sparkled as they caught the light, and her movements were so... *graceful*. Her name was extremely fitting.

She looked at him, her dark eyes stealing his breath.

David blinked.

Turkey. That's what they were talking about.

"Oh? Never?" he asked, hoping she hadn't noticed his hesitation.

"No."

Drat. She looks embarrassed.

"Well, I believe my aunt has rather ambitious tastes, at times."

His attempt at consolation seemed to miss its mark. Miss Stratton smiled politely, then resumed eating, her head still dipped a little lower than it had been before.

David turned his attention back to the others, but after listening and observing them for quite a few moments, he could find no entry point in which to join their conversation.

He glanced at Miss Stratton again. "You have made some friends in Lindenfell, I gather?"

Grace placed her fork beside her plate and looked up at him. He noticed a hint of surprise in her eyes, and it appeared she hesitated for a moment before responding.

"Yes... Miss Beckwith, mainly. She is Miss Price's niece. And she introduced me to a few of her friends on Sunday. At church."

Upon the mention of church, Grace's gaze darted slightly. She bit her lower lip and seemed at a loss for what to say next.

"Very good." David nodded, shame and regret filling him

as he remembered the episode between them after one of the parishioners had called out Dr. Markham's title.

"Have you made many friends since... since returning here?" Grace asked, her eyes heavy with sorrow.

David's heart lurched as he realised she was most likely chastising herself for their prior exchange.

As he observed her, he was more and more drawn to her beauty — both outward and inward. How noble she had been to be bold enough to ask him such a direct question, despite how cowardly he had been to deny the truth.

His gaze travelled across her eyes, her cheeks, then lingered for a moment on her lips. The buzz of conversation around them dimmed to a low hum. How well the candlelight showed off her clear complexion.

He looked into her eyes again, and his heart stilled. She was gazing at him with an innocent longing in her expression that made his blood thunder in his ears.

He wasn't merely in danger of falling for her, as he had suspected.

It was too late for that.

But now, the danger that remained was the harm he had done by deceiving her.

He might never know what it would be like to caress her cheek, to feel the soft curls of her hair, to press his lips against hers.

And he had only himself to blame.

CHAPTER 27
SECRETS

"Yes, she has settled in remarkably well — haven't you, Miss Stratton?" Miss Withers said, turning to face Grace.

The question cut through the fraught yet beautiful atmosphere hanging in the air between herself and John. Grace reluctantly turned to face Miss Withers, trying to gather the composure required to speak above a whisper. "Yes. Yes..." She noticed the eyes of Mr. and Mrs. Hartley upon her and smiled at them each in turn, nodding politely as she did so.

"Oh, Martha, I have been meaning to tell you..."

As swiftly as the conversation had steered around to include Grace, it swerved away from her again.

Her heart thudded deeply as she turned her attention back to John.

He was looking at her, his lips tilted at a mournful slant, and his eyes so full of depth that Grace imagined she could fall right into them.

He blinked, looked away for a moment, then fixed his gaze on her once more, clearing his throat gently. "Yes... A friend. I... I met Mr. Taylor on Sunday and have been privileged to spend some time with him since. I can honestly say that I have never met a man like him. He is... very kind. Very understanding."

Grace released a deep breath, which she didn't even realise she had been holding. She silently instructed herself to focus on their resuming conversation, rather than how John's eyes seemed to twinkle and glisten in the candlelight.

"Mr. *Isaac* Taylor?" Grace asked.

"Yes." John frowned in confusion. "Do you know him?"

"I..." Grace gaped for a moment, not wanting to reveal Beatrice's secret. "I know of him by name only."

"Oh?" John's eyebrows lifted in pleasant bemusement.

Grace's heart leapt at the levity with which he spoke. Perhaps there was a way past all their awkward dismay after all.

"Well, I..." She smiled. "All I can say is that it is not my secret to tell."

She was taking a risk, confiding in him, talking of secrets after accusing him of having his own. But she silently prayed she was reading him correctly, and that a lighthearted conversation was what he had intended to elicit from her.

"Oh..." He grinned, drawing the word out in a knowing manner. "A secret, eh?" His smile faltered for a second, though he quickly recovered it.

Grace's heart gathered speed.

"Well, then..." he said, some of the lightness gone from his tone, despite how evidently he was trying to maintain it. "Am I right in suspecting that my good friend, Mr. Taylor, has a... secret admirer?"

Grace's heart wrung within her. All this talk of secrets and suspicion... It was too painful after what had passed between them only the day before.

She forced gaiety into her voice. "Well, Mr. Withers, I

regret to inform you that I simply cannot provide any further comment on the matter."

"Indeed?" He smiled, a genuine one this time.

Grace's hope soared. She pursed her lips in mock insistence. "Indeed, sir."

A low, throaty chuckle escaped him, and the sound warmed Grace's soul.

He looked at her, his gaze gaining intensity. "Have you ever had a secret admirer, Miss Stratton?"

Grace almost forgot to breathe. She blinked, her heart hammering. "Well, Mr. Withers..." She forced a smile, praying he wouldn't notice her hands beginning to tremble. "If I *knew* of any admirers, they would hardly be secret, would they?"

His lips curled into a playful smile. "Too true, Miss Stratton. Well played."

Grace sucked in a deep breath, willing the trembling that had overtaken her to subside. A question floated through her mind, and she seized it with all the boldness she could muster. "And what of you, Mr. Withers? Do you have any admirers... secret, or otherwise?"

His eyes softened, fixing intently on her. "I do not know." He paused, then spoke in a hushed, strained tone. "Though, I would very much like to."

Grace's mouth dropped open. The air seemed to squeeze against her, all around her.

"Yes! Why, that is where John lives at present. John, dear — Mr. Hartley is often in Scarborough on matters of business."

John cast Grace a tender glance before shifting his attention to Mr. Hartley. "Is that so?"

Grace sat motionless, her mind and heart racing. Had she understood him correctly? Did he mean that he wished—

No. It was impossible after how she had treated him.

Wasn't it?

As she watched him converse with the guests, she took in his expressive eyes, his well-groomed moustache, his warm complexion. She'd noticed them all before, but it was as though she were seeing them all for the first time.

How handsome he was. But more than that — how forgiving. How kind. To even speak to her after she had called his integrity into question showed how much of a gentleman he really was.

Surely, he could not have meant...

Grace smiled softly.

If he *had* meant what she'd thought — if he wished *her* to be his admirer — surely... he must know.

She already was.

CHAPTER 28
A REVEALING RESOLUTION

The next morning, David joined Miss Withers and Grace in the drawing room. They'd taken breakfast a little later than usual, owing to their late night entertaining the Hartleys.

David glanced at Grace. Had the connection he'd felt with her last night been real? He shouldn't be encouraging any attraction that lay between them. He knew that. Not now. Not until all of his legal trouble was resolved.

But he'd found that he could not resist hinting at his feelings, trying to ascertain whether or not she might share them.

Last night, after the guests had gone and the three residents of Careo House had been bidding one another good night, he'd successfully fought the urge to kiss her hand. He had squeezed it as he'd wished her a pleasant sleep, then he'd hesitated, longing to draw her hand up to his lips. But his aunt had called to him, and he'd dropped Grace's hand rather too quickly.

The look in her eyes had let him know that she knew what he'd been thinking. And he suspected that she would've been glad if he'd carried out his wish.

The door opened, and Higgins entered. "A Mr. Isaac Taylor to see you, Mr. Withers."

David leapt out of his chair just as Isaac strolled into the room, two books tucked under one arm and a hopeful smile on his friendly face. "Isaac!"

"Good morning," came the kind reply. "I thought I might stop by and see if you wished to, uh, read for a while. With me."

David glanced at Grace and his aunt. The latter seemed oblivious to Isaac's awkwardness, but he was sure that Grace would not be long in detecting it — if she hadn't done so already. "Splendid idea! Shall we remove to the library?"

Isaac nodded and gestured for David to lead the way.

As David approached the door, he glanced back at Grace. At the sight of her disappointed smile, he relaxed a little. It appeared she suspected nothing was amiss.

He offered her a tender smile.

Her own expression altered into one of shy contentment, and she dipped her gaze back to her needlework.

"Should I not have come?" Isaac's worried tone broke through David's romantic thoughts once they were both in the corridor.

After closing the drawing room door, he turned to face his new friend and clapped him on the back. "No, of course — I am glad you did."

Once they had shut themselves inside the silence of Careo House's library, Isaac placed his books in David's hands.

"I borrowed these from my father's collection. He..." Isaac trailed off, a sheepish look on his face. "He purchased them after Emma's death, when he was... considering what action he might take, shall we say?"

Sombre sympathy washed through David. "I see." He nodded. "Thank you." This was hopeful. "Have you found anything in them that might help?"

Isaac shook his head, his mouth a grim line. "I only skimmed through them a little. There was nothing that leapt out at me, but I am not familiar with much of the terminology, so I thought I ought to bring them to you, that you might check for yourself."

"Thank you." David flopped into an armchair and motioned for Isaac to do the same. He opened the first book and began perusing it.

Isaac perched on the edge of a chair and peered at David. "How are you today?"

David looked up from the page. How kind Isaac was. There was nothing judgmental in his manner. Only concern. "As well as I can be, living a lie. Deceiving those closest to me." He pressed his lips together.

"Well, hopefully you may not have to for much longer." Isaac motioned toward the book. "Let us see if there is anything in there that might spark an idea."

David returned his attention to the volume in his hands, though he shared little of his friend's optimism.

Still, no stone unturned, and all that...

Time ticked by in silence as David searched through the books and Isaac shuffled around the library, examining various tomes.

With a sigh, David closed the last volume and placed both books on the table next to his chair.

Isaac swirled around to face him. "Anything?"

"No..." David rubbed his forehead with his fingers and thumb.

Isaac stepped closer and sank onto the edge of the chair facing David's own. "What now?" he asked, the hope with which he had arrived evaporating rapidly from his voice and posture.

"If I knew that, I would have taken action already." David

grimaced. "I am sorry..." He sighed. "You tried your best. And for that, I am truly grateful."

Isaac opened his mouth to speak, then hesitated. "Have you considered my other suggestion?"

David looked at him warily. "Dr. Turner?"

Isaac nodded, his lips pressed together sympathetically. "I do believe he would know... *something*. More than we can find out for ourselves. Especially as you are not at liberty to undertake some of the research that you might have carried out under your own name."

David shook his head slightly. Coming to Lindenfell had seemed like a much better idea at the time. But ever since he'd arrived, all he'd done was conceal the truth from those closest to him. Now, it seemed his only option was to tell a complete stranger the whole truth.

David frowned. "There is no guarantee that he will not straightway write to the authorities and hand me over."

"There is no guarantee of anything — only that if you do not even *try* to gain his help, you will remain in this agony indefinitely." Isaac's sigh was as gentle as his tone. "You cannot evade the authorities forever. You cannot go on pretending as though you are John forever. Something must be done, David. And Dr. Turner is the only man in town who might know what that something ought to be."

David released a long, slow breath. "Very well."

"You will ask him?"

"If I must. Which seems to be the case."

Isaac nodded. "You are doing the wise thing."

David almost laughed. Very little of what he had said or done these past few weeks could be described as wise.

But Isaac was right. He must either ask Dr. Turner for help or continue to inflict grief and misery upon himself by living a lie.

He thought of Grace's smile. How could he ever hope for

anything to transpire between them while he was concealing his very identity from her?

David rose, stretching out his back. "Shall we?"

Isaac smiled and nodded in return.

David headed for the door. He must go to Dr. Turner. He must accept whatever assistance the man might be able to offer.

And he must clear his name, in order to reveal it to the young lady whom he increasingly hoped might one day bear it.

CHAPTER 29

A SILENT JOURNEY

As Grace followed Miss Withers into the hall, she saw John and Isaac emerge from the library and stride toward the main front door of Careo House.

"Where are you two going?" Miss Withers asked.

John spun around, his gaze darting from his aunt to Grace. "Ah, we were just intending to go into town on a short... errand."

"Splendid!" Miss Withers turned toward Grace. "Miss Stratton shall accompany you." She turned back to her nephew.

Grace blinked.

John's face looked as though it had paled somewhat. "Ah... Well, you see—"

"I wish for her to undertake an errand of her own. You may all go in the carriage."

"But do you not require her presence *here*... with you?" John asked.

Grace tried to conceal her disappointment. He was acting as though he didn't want her to go with them. Yet, last night his words, and actions, had been so warm.

"I am retiring to my room presently for a rest. I am quite spent after last night's late exertions with the Hartleys. Therefore, Miss Stratton is free to accompany you. It is a short errand, you said?"

"Yes... That is, I believe it will not be a very long one. Although, one never knows, and I would—"

Miss Withers waved her hand dismissively. "John, instruct Parker to prepare the carriage for you all." She turned to Grace. "Miss Stratton, please visit the chemist, a few doors down from the tea room, and ask for some of their opium liniment and a fresh supply of laudanum — Mr. Shaw shall charge it to my account." Miss Withers turned to face Isaac. "A pleasure to see you, Mr. Taylor. Do give my best wishes to your parents."

Isaac nodded, seeming much more at ease than John. "I shall indeed, ma'am. It is a pleasure to see you, too."

Grace watched John as he trudged off to follow his aunt's instructions. Her heart sank. Did he really not want her around?

Miss Withers disappeared upstairs, leaving Grace and Isaac in the hallway.

"Miss Stratton, how do you find Lindenfell?" Isaac asked in a friendly tone.

Grace fought past the hurt weighing on her and forced a cheerfulness into her voice that was entirely manufactured. "It is lovely. I am glad to have come."

Isaac nodded, smiling. He was about to say something else when John strode back into the hallway.

"Parker is bringing the carriage around presently."

Grace turned her head to look at him and caught sight of the worried look he cast Isaac. Immediately, John's gaze shifted to Grace, his expression altering rapidly.

Grace's heart thudded. He didn't want her to come. He truly didn't.

Realisation dawned on her. It must have something to do with Isaac.

Her stomach flipped. Of course. That must be it.

He was ashamed of her.

She was, after all, only a companion. A companion to his aunt.

He didn't want his friend to know that he had been flirting with someone whom he saw as little above a servant. That *must* be it.

Grace's cheeks burned as the carriage rolled into view. She considered bolting — it wasn't too late. She could run up the stairs and not have to face them.

But Miss Withers needed her medicines.

You cannot let her down.

"Shall we?" Isaac asked, his cheerful tone a stark contrast to Grace's hidden misery.

Once they were all in the carriage, Grace sat as close to the window as she could, wishing she could escape right through it. She didn't even want to look at John, or his friend.

Silence stretched throughout the company, and the more time that passed without John saying anything, the more certain Grace was that her suspicions were correct.

Disappointment and sorrow welled within her. She glanced briefly at the two silent men in the seat opposite her. Isaac was eyeing John nervously, and John...

He was sitting rigidly upright, his jaw and fists clenched, his gaze fixed firmly out of the window next to him.

Still, part of her believed that he would say *something* before the carriage pulled to a stop once they'd reached town.

But he did not.

Not once. He hadn't even looked at her. At least, not from what she'd seen from the corner of her eye as she'd tried to avoid looking at *him*.

Silently, the trio stepped out of the carriage onto the cobbles of Lindenfell's main street.

"You are for the chemist then, Miss Stratton?"

Anguish twisted within Grace's heart upon hearing that the voice was Isaac's, not John's.

"Yes."

"Very well," David said. "We shall meet you back here once..."

His voice was strained, and Grace couldn't help turning to face him as his sentence trailed off into silence.

He looked almost green. His jaw was tight, and his shoulders unnaturally stiff. His eyes were downcast, examining the ground as though it were a dangerous creature preparing to lunge at him.

"We shall meet you back here once we have attended to our errand. We should not be very long," Isaac said reassuringly.

He nodded to Grace, then turned and waited for John to follow him.

John flicked his gaze up at Grace for a split second, then turned and walked away at Isaac's side. After they'd walked a few paces, Grace noticed his shoulders heave and shudder, and her disappointment was slowly eclipsed by concern.

Reluctantly, she turned and headed toward the chemist.

As the physical distance between herself and John increased, she feared their burgeoning connection had been pulled apart irrevocably, too.

CHAPTER 30
DR. TURNER

The afternoon sun shone brightly as David and Isaac approached Dr. Turner's premises, situated just off the main street in Lindenfell's busy town centre.

Shortly after Isaac rapped the door, a broad-shouldered man opened it and smiled. "Afternoon, Mr. Taylor. And Mr...?"

David swallowed hard, consciously selecting his cousin's surname. "Withers."

The man nodded in greeting. "Mr. Withers. Of course — my parents dined with you and your aunt last evening."

David noted the man's features, recognising the similarities between his brow and nose and those of the man with whom he'd dined the night before. "Mr. and Mrs. Hartley?"

The man nodded, his good-natured smile almost a replica of his father's. "How might I be of service to you both today?"

"Thank you, Walter," Isaac said. "Is Dr. Turner available? We very much need to speak with him for a few moments."

"You came at just the right time, for he has only returned." Walter looked at David and smiled. "It is not unusual for his morning calls to last *well* into the afternoon!"

David forced a smile and nodded politely. His throat grew dry and his heart hammered as Walter ushered them inside, making small talk with Isaac that David couldn't concentrate enough to participate in.

Almost immediately they came to a dark wooden door, which Walter knocked twice in rapid succession before opening. "Dr. Turner, sir — Mr. Taylor and his friend, Mr. Withers, wish to speak with you for a moment."

"Bring them in, Mr. Hartley," said a rich, deep voice.

David followed Isaac and Mr. Newman into the room. A broad, sturdy desk occupied the space in front of the window, and behind it sat a man with small round spectacles and a rim of grey hair encircling his otherwise bald head.

The solemn atmosphere of the doctor's office was reinforced by decor clearly displaying the man's profession and prominence.

"Dr. Turner, how are you?" Isaac's warm voice showed his familiarity with the man to whom David must divulge his most dangerous secret.

"Mr. Taylor," said the doctor, rising and reaching across the desk to shake Isaac's hand. "Good to see you." His gaze shifted to David. "And you are... Mr. Withers?"

Isaac glanced knowingly at David.

"Uh... yes. Yes," David stuttered, wondering whether Dr. Turner's apprentice would be leaving the room or staying for the duration of their interview.

"Well, have a seat, gentlemen," said the doctor, motioning toward the two wooden chairs facing his enormous desk. "Thank you, Mr. Hartley." He nodded at his apprentice, who returned the gesture and left the room, smiling at David and Isaac before doing so.

"Now, gentlemen — how may I help you?"

Dr. Turner's intense gaze blinked from one to the other, and David looked pleadingly at Isaac, his insides trembling as the reality of the situation fully engulfed him.

Isaac cleared his throat. "Dr. Turner, even though we are not here today as patients, could we beg of you that you will treat this interview with the strictest of confidence?"

Dr. Turner nodded slowly. "Of course."

Isaac nodded, relief softening his expression. He paused, then looked intently at Dr. Turner. "How familiar might you be with chloroform and its medicinal uses?"

Dr. Turner's eyebrows lifted ever so slightly. "Quite familiar." He glanced from Isaac to David and back again. "Why?"

David's breath stilled. The doctor was familiar with the substance in question. That already rendered him more likely to be helpful than most other physicians who refused to even consider it.

"Do you believe it to be safe?" Isaac asked.

"Well, when properly administered, I believe it is one of the safest drugs known to man, and as soon as the majority of physicians are willing to embrace it, I believe it will alter the medical profession enormously. For the better." Dr. Turner studied the two young men in front of him. "Why?"

Isaac drew a deep breath. "Dr. Turner, I persuaded my friend," he said, motioning at David, "to accompany me to see you in the hopes that you might be able to offer him some much-needed advice. He, too, is a physician, you see."

Dr. Turner's gaze switched instantly to David. "Mr. Withers? Forgive me, I thought it was your cousin who was the physician."

David's heart thudded. "It is."

Dr. Turner's brow crinkled slightly.

"That is... My name is not, in fact, Mr. Withers. It is David Carbury." He drew a shaky breath. "Dr. David Carbury."

Dr. Turner's eyes narrowed in thoughtful concentration. "Mr. Hartley introduced you as Mr. Withers, not as Dr. Carbury. And this, in combination with your good friend's questions about chloroform... Would I be correct in assuming that you are in some kind of... legal trouble?"

David gaped. He nodded, unable to voice his surprise.

"A great deal, Dr. Turner," Isaac said, glancing at David with concern. "I was sure that you might know of something that might be done, for it would seem that his very life could be at stake."

Dr. Turner pursed his lips. "I think, perhaps, you had better tell me the whole story, young man."

He folded his hands together as he raised his eyebrows.

"Omitting nothing."

CHAPTER 31

AMONG FRIENDS

"Oh! Miss Stratton!"

Grace turned to see a smiling Beatrice flying toward her across the chemist's shop, which was much more spacious within than it appeared from without.

"Miss Beckwith," Grace said, relieved to see the friendly countenance of someone who was clearly glad to see her.

"What brings you here?" Beatrice looked around the shop. "Are you alone?"

Grace's stomach lurched as she remembered the miserable carriage ride into town. "No... Well, yes, at present. But I came into town with Mr. Withers and Mr. Taylor, to—"

"Mr. Taylor?" Beatrice's cheeks took on a faint blush as she looked around the chemist again.

"He is not here at present," Grace said. "The two of them had some sort of errand in town. They said they would meet me here upon their return, which they assured would not be very long in coming."

"And how long has it been already?"

"I have no idea."

Beatrice frowned. "Are you all right, Miss Stratton? You do not seem quite yourself."

Grace wanted nothing more than to spill her heart to Beatrice. But she was keenly aware of their public placement and of the other customers within earshot. "I… I shall tell you another time, perhaps."

Concern flooded Beatrice's countenance. "Shall we take a walk? We need not venture very far. That way, we could still see Mr. Withers and… and Mr. Taylor when they return." Upon mentioning Isaac's name again, Beatrice's cheeks pinked even more.

Grace hesitated. She had already procured Miss Withers's medicines. The only reason she remained in the chemist was because Mr. Taylor had said they would meet her there.

But they'd been gone longer than she'd expected, and she couldn't deny that some fresh air and fresh company might be just the thing to lift her gloomy spirits. "Very well."

Beatrice nodded contentedly. As they approached the door, it opened from without, and Miss Markham strode in wearing a magnificent purple gown.

"Why, Miss Beckwith, Miss Stratton!"

"Miss Markham! What a stunning gown!" Beatrice examined it with wide eyes and an even wider mouth.

Alice rolled her eyes. "Mamma insisted that I wear it. She despairs of the fabrics I am inclined to choose for my wardrobe and had this one made for me against my will."

Grace's lips tugged into a one-sided smirk. She imagined Miss Markham's will was not something to be trifled with.

"Well, it is beautiful," Beatrice said, uncertainty filling her voice.

"Do *not* tell my mother so, next time you see her."

Beatrice nodded nervously. "Of course."

"So what brings you both into town?" She dropped her

voice into a whisper. "I am come to fetch some more *nerve* pills."

Alice must have noticed Grace's eyebrows shoot up, for she leaned toward her and whispered, "For the gown procurer."

Grace's mouth dropped open as her eyebrows lifted. She hadn't expected that. "Oh... I am sorry."

Alice waved her hand. "Nonsense. Every family has their own share of drama, as I am sure you know, being a fellow clergyman's daughter."

Grace nodded. "That is true. Although, I do not have such first-hand experience as it seems you do."

A vulnerable expression flashed across Alice's face. She quickly recovered her typical vivacious manner, but Grace was suddenly aware of how little she knew about the histories and current realities of her newfound friends. It pained her to think that they faced all manner of troubles and trials of which she hadn't even begun to be aware.

Alice looked from Grace to Beatrice and back again. "So, what is it that brings you both here?"

"Well, we were just about to go for a short stroll."

"If you can wait for me for a moment, I shall accompany you."

"Of course."

Alice swept toward the counter, leaving Grace and Beatrice silently watching as she procured the bottle of pills for which she had come.

She bustled back toward them. "Shall we?"

"Yes. But we must remember to stay close to the chemist," Grace said.

Alice raised her brows. "Whyever is that?"

"I came into town with Mr. Withers and Mr. Taylor. I must meet them here to return to Careo House."

"Mr. Taylor?" Alice asked in a sing-song tone, looking pointedly at Beatrice.

"Now, Alice, be quiet," Beatrice said, clearly not used to being assertive. Not that Grace imagined anyone could be so with much success when it came to Miss Markham.

Alice flashed a knowing grin at Beatrice. "What do you make of Mr. Taylor, Miss Stratton?"

"He seems a very nice young man," Grace replied.

"Do you think he would be a good match for our dear Miss Beckwith?"

"Alice!" Beatrice glanced about rapidly, as though spies might be lurking nearby, eagerly waiting to herald their covertly-gained intelligence back to Isaac himself.

Alice giggled. "Oh, Bea... You must find a way to let him know how *dashing* you believe him to be. How is anything to develop between you if you will not even *talk* to him?"

Grace thought of the carriage ride. Of how John wouldn't talk to her. She was sure it wasn't because he liked her, though. He was ashamed of her. She was only a companion, after all. She sighed.

"Over here," Beatrice said, beckoning Grace and Alice toward the market cross, a weathered stone structure in the middle of the square. "We can easily see the chemist from here," she said, resting against one of its low walls. "Now, do you wish to speak of what troubles you, Miss Stratton? Despite her constant teasing of me, you can trust Miss Markham not to break your confidence."

Alice examined Grace with a curious solemnity. "Indeed. What is the matter, Miss Stratton?"

Grace looked at the compassionate faces of her two new friends. She swallowed hard. "It is nothing. I—"

"I know that look, Grace. It is not nothing."

Upon hearing Alice use her Christian name for the first time, Grace was filled with a newfound sense of affinity with her. She knew that Beatrice spoke the truth. She could trust Alice, just as she could trust Beatrice herself.

Yet her silence was not owing to a lack of trust. Sorrow weighed her down, and she couldn't think of any words that might make any sense of why it did.

"Let me guess... There is someone who has caught *your* eye, too. And you wonder why he is behaving like such an oaf."

Grace stared at Alice in disbelief. How did she know?

Alice smiled gently. "Ah. We have it. Well then, Miss Stratton. Who is he?"

Beatrice smiled encouragingly. "Ooh, who is he? Has anything been spoken?"

Grace glanced at the chemist. No sign of them.

Alice mimicked her movement. She fixed her eyes upon Grace as realisation dawned on her face. "Ah... Mr. Withers, perhaps?"

Grace looked down. Heat crept into her cheeks, and she wondered if this might be how Beatrice always felt when Alice teased her about Mr. Taylor.

"It is!" Alice's eyes danced with glee.

"Oh! Is it?" Beatrice's eyes were wide with surprise.

"I—"

"Has he given you any indication of his own feelings?" Beatrice whispered excitedly.

Grace sighed. "I thought he had..."

Beatrice squealed.

Alice raised an eager eyebrow.

"But then, today, after Mr. Taylor arrived, he seemed... different, somehow. The whole way into town, in the carriage... He did not even speak to me. Not once."

Disappointment washed over Beatrice's features.

Alice frowned. "That *is* odd." She perked up. "Do tell — what did he say that raised your hopes?"

Grace shrugged awkwardly. "It was silly, really... He—"

Beatrice gasped. "There they are!"

Alice sighed. "Just as we were about to hear the interesting part."

Her heart hammering, Grace looked across the square just in time to see Isaac and John disappear inside the chemist's shop. "Oh, they will be looking for me." She smoothed her skirts and rose.

"Come, let us all say hello." Alice cast a knowing smirk at Beatrice.

Biting her lip, Beatrice glanced at Grace.

As they made their way toward the chemist, Grace silently prayed Alice wouldn't say anything to embarrass Beatrice.

Or herself.

CHAPTER 32

GAZES AND GREETINGS

David's eyes roamed the aisles of the chemist's shop as he paced up and down them, looking for Grace.

Bottles and jars of various sizes crammed the shelves. Two middle-aged women peered at the wares, but Grace was nowhere to be seen.

He turned to look at Isaac, shaking his head.

Isaac smiled reassuringly. "I am sure she is not too far away."

As they walked toward the door, David sighed with relief again.

Isaac chuckled. "I knew Dr. Turner would help. Now, all we must do is wait for him to hear from his acquaintance in London, and hopefully, that will set in motion the resolution of this whole affair."

Even though Isaac had clearly been careful to speak in a hushed tone, David couldn't help but glance around nervously. He turned back to Isaac and nodded in agreement.

They reached the door, and just as they exited the building, they came face-to-face with Grace and two of the young ladies David remembered seeing her speaking to at church.

"Ah! There you are." David offered Grace a polite smile.

Grace blinked. "Forgive me, I stayed in the chemist's shop for quite a while, and then bumped into Miss Beckwith and Miss Markham, so we came outside for a little air."

"Of course, of course. Good day, Miss Beckwith, Miss Markham."

"Mr. Withers... I do not suppose you remember me?" Alice's intent gaze was unnerving.

"I am dreadfully sorry, but I cannot say that I do, Miss Markham."

"Mmm..." She looked him up and down as though he were some curiosity, then turned her attention to his companion.

Relief rushed through David to be free from her piercing gaze. He quickly regained his composure. "Miss Stratton, I am sorry that we took a little longer than expected."

Grace gave him an awkward smile. "There is no need for an apology."

She turned back to face the others, and Isaac greeted the ladies. Miss Beckwith blushed as Isaac spoke to her. And, upon second glance, it seemed as though Isaac's cheeks had a little more colour than usual, too.

David felt Grace's gaze upon him, and he hoped she could not see how awkward and uncertain he was. He gave her a polite smile again, then turned to address Isaac. "Well, we should probably head back to the House. My aunt will require her laudanum a few hours before dinner."

"If you do not mind, I shall make my way home from here," said Isaac.

David froze. Now he would be alone with Grace in the carriage. "Of course..."

Isaac clapped his hand on David's shoulder. "I shall call again tomorrow." He dropped his voice to a volume that only

David could hear. "In the meantime, do try not to worry. I am sure Dr. Turner will soon have favourable news."

David clapped a firm hand onto Isaac's back, his own voice hushed as he spoke. "Thank you, my friend."

Grace bade her friends farewell, then David motioned toward the carriage.

"Shall we?"

CHAPTER 33
UNACCOMPANIED

Grace could hardly breathe as John helped her up into the carriage. She thanked him, hoping he would not be able to detect how nervous she was to be so close to him.

She waved a farewell to her smiling friends as the carriage rumbled into motion. Beatrice beamed shyly as she and Alice stood conversing with Mr. Taylor, and Alice gave Grace a knowing smirk as John settled himself into the carriage.

Grace looked down, willing herself not to blush.

As their friends disappeared out of sight, she released an anxious breath.

"Are you all right, Miss Stratton?"

"Yes... Thank you. And you?"

"Yes, I am... well, thank you."

So. He was talking to her again. And, strangely enough, it was only the two of them present. Would he have resumed any discourse with her if Mr. Taylor had been travelling back to Careo House with them? She could not say with any certainty that he would, and it deeply troubled her to admit it.

"Your friend, Miss Markham, does not seem too shy."

Grace smiled gently. "No, indeed. She is very confident, yet very kind, too. A rather unusual combination in my experience."

John nodded thoughtfully. "The other one, Miss...?"

"Beckwith."

"Yes, Miss Beckwith. I cannot recall if I even heard her make a sound. She seems as shy as Miss Markham is assertive."

"Yes. She is lovely. They both are. I am very glad to have met both of them." Grace paused, fearing she sounded vulnerable. She forced a brightness into her tone. "And your Mr. Taylor seems a nice fellow."

John's countenance grew serious. "Yes. He is remarkable. I am truly glad to call him a friend."

Grace frowned a little as she observed John's sombre demeanour. "Did you and he have a pleasant time in town?"

She had expected the question to lighten John's mood, but it seemed that it served only to deepen it.

John released a deep sigh as he nodded. "We... carried out our intended course of action."

Grace raised her eyebrows slightly. He made it sound as though they'd been engaged in some covert military action rather than a simple errand.

But then, she did not know where they'd gone or what they had done. And as much as she'd considered asking, she was all too aware of the last time she'd questioned him. It was certainly not an experience she was in any hurry to repeat.

"Anyway," John said brightly, evidently attempting to brush off his melancholy. "Would I be correct in suspecting that Miss Beckwith... how should I say it... has a slight *tendresse* toward Mr. Taylor?"

"I—" Grace gaped, then briskly recovered her composure. "Why do you ask?"

John chuckled, the low, throaty sound unexpectedly thrilling Grace's heart. "I merely wondered, as I believe I saw... something in her countenance, when he spoke to her. She appeared as though she... admired him."

Admired. The word let loose in her mind the conversation they'd shared at dinner the night before.

"I do believe we previously established that Mr. Taylor has a secret admirer," John continued. "And, after today, I suspect I am correct in believing it to be Miss Beckwith."

He remembered.

He remembered the conversation about admirers — *secret* admirers. Did he remember what he had hinted to her?

Was he aware of how skillfully he seemed to be playing with her emotions? He'd told her he'd wanted an admirer, then shut her out the very next day.

He hadn't spoken a word to her the whole way into town when Mr. Taylor had been with them. But now that they were alone again, he intended to resume his flirtation?

There was only one kind of man who enjoyed playing such games with a lady's heart. And it was not the kind of man whom Grace wished to encourage.

"You are free to believe as you wish, Mr. Withers."

Grace cringed inwardly. She hadn't intended her voice to sound so harsh.

As John looked at her in surprise, she turned and directed her gaze out the carriage window. Though she hardly noticed the view whizzing by.

John cleared his throat gently. "Miss Stratton?"

Grace forced herself to look at him. Her heart panged with guilt as she noticed the forlorn expression in his eyes.

"Forgive me, I do hope I have said nothing that was offensive to you..."

Grace sighed. "No... Not at all." She forced a smile, though she could only imagine how insincere it looked.

John's gaze remained upon her as though he expected her to continue speaking.

Perhaps she had been too hard on him.

She did seem to have a dreadful habit of that.

"Forgive me."

John nodded in acquiescence. He smiled. "So... Am I correct in my understanding?"

Grace tried not to smile. "Do you really expect me to divulge a lady's secret?"

"Ah ha!" John raised a finger and pointed it mirthfully at Grace. "If she had no secret admiration for him, you would not have said such a thing."

Grace sighed, squeezing her eyes closed. As she opened them again, she fixed them intently on John. "You must not say anything. To anyone. Truly, I did not mean to let it slip out." Her brow furrowed earnestly. "I do not wish to betray her confidence."

"I am sorry. It was my wheedling that led you to divulge it. I assure you, I will not tell anyone." He gave her a playful smirk. "Except Mr. Taylor."

Grace gaped as her eyes grew wide. "No, you cannot!"

John laughed, the glad sound leaving Grace with no other option but to smile.

"I am sorry, Miss Stratton. I assure you — I shall keep the matter to myself. You have my word."

Grace sighed, almost fully trusting him. "Thank you."

They were both silent for a moment, though the carriage had gained an atmosphere of ease since they had first entered it.

"What about Mr. Taylor? Does *he* admire Miss Beckwith?" Grace looked at John expectantly, a smile playing on her lips.

John raised his eyebrows, a teasing look on his face. "Do you really expect me to divulge a gentleman's secret?"

Grace's mouth dropped open, and her eyes widened. "He *does?*"

John raised his hands. "Well, in truth, I have no idea. He has never mentioned her to me. It is only... Well, when I saw the two of them talking, I wondered if... Well, he looked a little different, so there may well be a story there. I shall have to do my best to find out."

"*Without* telling him about Miss Beckwith, of course?"

"Of course."

Grace gave a satisfied nod.

"And, uh... What about Miss Beckwith's friend?" John's voice was softer.

Grace looked at him, her eyebrows raised slightly. "Miss Markham?"

"Or... her other friend?"

Grace frowned. "Miss Denton?"

"Miss who?"

"She is another friend of Beatrice's, whom I met at church."

"Ah." John shifted awkwardly in his seat, drawing his shoulders upward a little. "I meant... her *other* friend."

"But, who—"

Grace froze.

No. Surely, he couldn't mean—

"Me?"

John dipped his head a little, still holding her gaze. He nodded.

Grace was exceedingly glad to be already seated. Though, she feared she was still in danger of falling over somehow.

She drew a deep breath, then smirked as a thought came to her. "I am afraid I must tell you that Miss Beckwith's friend is not a secret admirer of Mr. Taylor's."

Looking down, John laughed nervously. "Well played, Miss Stratton." As he looked up at her again, the tenderness in his eyes unnerved her. "Might you be a secret admirer of anyone else?"

Heat crept into Grace's cheeks. Her heart hammered in her chest. "Ought a lady to admit such a thing to a gentleman? Unaccompanied?" She said the words in jest, though she felt them keenly.

John laughed in surprise, then nodded his head. "I believe you are correct, Miss Stratton. Perhaps it is the gentleman who ought to admit to it first."

Grace clutched the edge of the carriage seat, anticipation seizing her heart. "Perhaps."

John's jaw tensed. He examined the floor of the carriage with a fierce intensity. "I can tell you one thing, Miss Stratton."

Grace could hardly think. Or speak. "Yes?"

"You and Mr. Taylor have at least one thing in common."

"Oh?"

"Yes." He looked at her with the most vulnerable expression she had ever seen on his face. "You each have a secret admirer."

Grace could say nothing, could not even make a sound. Was he really telling her what she had been longing to hear?

"His is Miss Beckwith, and yours is—"

The carriage jolted to a stop, jerking John and Grace forward rather abruptly.

"We cannot have arrived already," he murmured.

He looked about him, then fixed a sympathetic gaze on Grace. He reached for her hand, and taking it into his own, squeezed it gently. "Excuse me, Miss Stratton — I must ensure that all is well."

Grace blinked, relishing the warmth of his hand around her own. "Of course..."

He held her gaze, glanced briefly at her lips, then was gone.

And as Grace sat there, alone in the carriage, she couldn't help but smile.

CHAPTER 34
TWO RESOLUTIONS

David was surprised to find that they had indeed already arrived at Careo House. No sooner had his feet hit the ground, than Parker proceeded to ready the carriage steps for Miss Stratton to disembark, too.

David watched, filled with a disappointment he must now endeavour to hide as they returned to his aunt's company.

"Pray, why did the halt seem more abrupt than usual, this time?" David asked the coachman, trying unsuccessfully to keep his frustration from leaking into his voice.

"Horse spooked, sir. Some little critter ran out in front of her just as we were winding up to the house..."

David didn't hear the rest of the man's explanation. All he could do was stare at Miss Stratton as she joined him on the curtilage, dipping her head shyly.

Silence surrounded them.

"Thank you," David said, flustered, as he realised Parker had stopped talking and was eyeing him quizzically.

The coachman nodded and turned back to the carriage.

Grace looked at David, then the ground, and back again in

rapid succession. "We must give your aunt the medicines she sent me to procure."

"Yes," he replied, stifling a groan. "We must."

As they entered Careo House, the moment they had shared in the carriage seemed like an age ago. Almost like a dream.

Had it really occurred?

As David watched Grace remove her bonnet and shawl and hand them graciously to the waiting footman, he smiled.

It *had* occurred.

And, hopefully, it would not be long until another such opportunity presented itself.

One that he would seize, no matter what.

❧

A few days later, David was just finishing his breakfast when the footman entered the room to announce the arrival of an unexpected visitor. "Mr. Taylor to see you, Mr. Withers."

David glanced at his present company. Across the table, Grace delicately dabbed her lips with her napkin. Miss Withers savoured a sip of her tea then replaced her cup onto its saucer with a clink.

"Thank you, Higgins. Could you show him to the library?"

"Of course, sir."

David's stomach tightened. What if there was news from Dr. Turner? Isaac had called the day after their excursion to town and had visited briefly yesterday for luncheon. Perhaps, he was merely showing himself friendly. Still, the question was always at the forefront of David's mind as to when they might find out whether or not their gamble in telling Dr. Turner the truth had paid off.

"Excuse me, ladies," David said, rising to his feet.

Miss Withers nodded, and Grace's lips turned up in a shy smile as she nodded to him in acknowledgement.

His heart warmed. As a smile crept onto his own face in return, his gaze darted momentarily to his aunt. Had she noticed their interaction?

"I shall see you both presently," he said, though his gaze was fixed only upon Grace.

She nodded, unable to keep from smiling more fully, and though it pained him to do so, he turned away from her and headed toward the library.

Isaac turned to face him as he entered, his eyes wide with urgency.

"I have a letter for you from Dr. Turner. He was intending to send it here, to Careo House, but I ran into him in town, so he entrusted it to me in order that it might be conveyed to you sooner."

"I see..." The seriousness of the situation flooded back into David's mind, dispersing his pleasant thoughts of the young lady in the breakfast room he hadn't wanted to leave.

Isaac handed him the missive.

David held it, examining his cousin's name written on the front, glad that Dr. Turner had been considerate enough to address the letter to him under his assumed identity.

With trembling hands, he opened the letter.

Isaac watched him, his feet shuffling restlessly.

Drawing a deep breath, David read its words aloud.

Dear Dr. Carbury,

I do hope this letter finds you well. I have just this morning heard from Mr. Crump, my acquaintance in London, and he informs me that the public interest in your case is at a very low ebb. There has been some speculation by your colleague and your lawyer as to your whereabouts, but it would seem that no scandal has arisen in the wake of your abrupt departure.

Furthermore, Dr. John Snow, a highly-respected physician, has recently published a paper in the London Medical Gazette declaring chloroform's superiority to ether when administered correctly, and explaining the mechanisms of administration and absorption. As I am sure you will agree, this is wonderful news, not only from our own personal viewpoint that chloroform is a revolution in the making, but also because of the credence and support it will lend to your case, as Dr. Snow's instructions align with your own experiences of how you carefully administered it to the late Mr. Edwards.

My acquaintance, Mr. Crump, has undertaken to write to your lawyer, Mr. Gibbs, to share these recent findings with him and to request that the two of them might work together to obtain a legal victory for you, and, if possible, the dismissal of your case entirely.

Crump is extremely hopeful that we shall meet with success in this endeavour, and I must tell you here that he is not a man given to optimistic imaginations. If he believes that a resolution is attainable, then that is, most likely, precisely what will happen.

I shall write to you again once I hear from him, and if you permit me to share your aunt's address with him, he may write to you directly, too. Using your nom de plume, of course.

Yours faithfully,

Dr. Bartholomew Turner

Isaac clapped his hand on David's shoulder, his joyful laugh ringing through the still library air.

David blinked as he read over the words a second time. Was it really true?

"Oh, David! How wonderful! I *knew* Dr. Turner could help."

David said nothing, raising his gaze to Isaac in astonishment.

Isaac chuckled. "This is wonderful news!"

David nodded. "I confess, I cannot quite believe it."

Isaac reached for the letter, his raised eyebrows silently asking permission to do so. David nodded, watching as Isaac slipped the page from his fingers and read it, still smiling.

"I knew he would know a way to help," Isaac said quietly, relief audible in his voice.

David looked at his friend. "I owe you a great deal, you know. Your counsel and support have been invaluable to me. I do not know how I might ever repay you."

Isaac shook his head, still smiling. "You have no need to thank me, my dear friend. I am only glad that your dreadful predicament seems to be heading toward its resolution. A very good resolution."

David released a sigh, and with it some of the tension that had seized him the past few weeks.

A very good resolution. It was more than he'd dared hope.

"Shall you go back to London soon?" Isaac asked.

David's relief was swiftly replaced with reticence. "Back to London?"

"Why, yes. Considering all that Dr. Turner has indicated, surely it would be wise for you to return — to ensure that all is carried out as it ought to be." Isaac's eyebrows flicked up and down in solemnity. "After all, you left rather abruptly. And the last thing you would want is to be seen as someone evading the law. Especially now that a favourable resolution is likely within your grasp."

David looked at Isaac, weighing up everything his friend had just said. He could not deny the truth of his words.

Nor could he alleviate the heaviness that draped over his heart, weighing upon it so profoundly that he almost couldn't breathe.

The truth was he didn't *want* to go back to London. At least, not yet.

Dr. Turner's acquaintance was hopeful, yes, but nothing had been arranged or settled with even a hint of finality. Ending up in the gallows might still be as real a prospect as when David had first arrived in Lindenfell.

Besides, there was another reason he didn't want to leave.

Miss Stratton.

He smiled softly as he remembered their exchange in the carriage a few days ago.

How close he had come to declaring his feelings toward her. How deeply he longed to do so, still.

He clenched his jaw. Isaac was right. He ought to go to London. He should not be evading the law or his accusers, especially when he knew he was innocent of the charges against him.

But he knew he could not leave Careo House without telling Grace the truth about his feelings for her.

And, before he could do that, he must tell her something else.

His real identity.

Panic seized his gut. What if she hated him? After all, she'd guessed before that he was not John Withers. She'd *asked* him.

And he'd said—

But, wait... He hadn't actually said the word 'no'. He hadn't truly lied to her — only steered the conversation in a different direction.

Who are you trying to fool? You deceived her. How could she see it as anything but dishonesty?

Still, he could not leave without telling her. And, the more he considered Isaac's words, he realised — leave, he must.

As Isaac relaxed into an armchair and grinned up at David, resolve firmed itself within David's heart. He would go back to London and fight alongside Mr. Crump and Mr. Gibbs to clear his name.

Just as soon as he had told Grace what his name really was.

CHAPTER 35
AN UNEXPECTED GUEST

The next day, Grace smiled as she re-read the letter from her parents that had arrived earlier that morning. A fresh breeze wafted through her open window, and she looked out wistfully at the clouds wisping through the pale blue sky.

All was well back at Shiloh Hall, and though they missed her dreadfully, they were exceedingly glad to hear how happy and settled she was at Careo House. They asked her to confer their greetings to Miss Withers.

And to John.

Grace had told them about Miss Withers's nephew coming to stay. But she hadn't told them anything of the attachment that seemed to be growing between them.

Or about the surreal moment they'd shared in the carriage a few days earlier, when it seemed that John had been steadying his nerves to make some kind of declaration to her.

Her heart still raced every time she remembered it. The look in his eyes, the weightiness of the atmosphere — it had almost been too much to bear.

If the abruptness of the carriage stopping hadn't

interrupted them, there was no telling what the outcome might have been.

A thought which thrilled and terrified her simultaneously.

She made her way downstairs, an extra urgency in her steps. The grand day had finally arrived.

Grace bustled into the drawing room and glanced at the clock.

"Oh, Miss Stratton, come and see how everything has been arranged — it is all so magnificent!"

Grace smiled softly as she hurried to Miss Withers's side. The lady's elegant tone and flawless grooming often made Grace think that her employer would not be out of place in a palace. She could picture Miss Withers, sitting on an ornate throne, a sparkling crown upon her perfectly coiffed grey hair.

As they walked together through the open French doors, warmth bubbled in Grace's chest. Tables and chairs had been placed in a picturesque and well-ordered fashion on the sprawling grounds of Careo House. She shook her head slowly, mesmerised by the grandeur and scale of the day's entertainment. All of Lindenfell was sure to attend, and there would still be plenty of room to spare.

"Is it not splendid?"

Grace glanced at her elegant employer. "It is beautiful, Miss Withers. Truly." She smiled, giving a short laugh. "You shall be queen for the day!"

"Oh!" Miss Withers waved her hand dismissively, though a contented smile lingered on her lined face. "The guests should begin to arrive anytime now." Miss Withers glanced back inside at the clock that was too far away for either of them to see.

"Indeed. Do you wish to sit outside and wait, or remain indoors for now?" Grace glanced up at the sky. A few grey clouds on the horizon made her question what kind of weather the afternoon might hold. She silently prayed that God would hold the rain at bay.

"Fetch me my shawl, dear — the warm red one — and I shall sit outside. The breeze has no real chill to it."

Grace nodded and stepped back inside to retrieve the shawl, almost colliding with John. "Oh!"

"Oh, excuse me, Miss Stratton!"

Grace smiled, dipping her head. "I did not see you."

"Nor I you." His grey eyes almost danced as he looked at her.

"Excuse me, I must fetch your aunt's shawl."

"Of course, of course."

"Oh, John?" Miss Withers called.

John stepped aside to allow Grace to pass, then walked outside to join his aunt. Glancing back, Grace noticed a hint of disappointment in his expression.

She paused for a moment as she placed her hands around the shawl resting atop Miss Withers's armchair.

Lord, I am certain of nothing when it comes to the attachment I feel toward John. At times, it seems as though he deeply shares it, but other times… Help me to know, Lord. Help me to know the truth of it all. How he really sees me. What, if anything, the future might hold… And help me, above all, to honour You, and not form an attachment too readily with someone for whom You are not first in their affections. Help me to find out more about his faith, instead of focusing only on my feelings.

Drawing a deep breath, Grace nodded to herself solemnly. She lifted the shawl and brought it outside, placing it around Miss Withers's shoulders.

"Thank you, my dear," Miss Withers said, tugging it around her more tightly.

John motioned to the right. "Ah, the first of your guests have arrived, I see."

Unsurprisingly, it was Beatrice and Miss Price who had arrived before anyone else, striding happily toward them across the lawn. Grace waved a greeting at Beatrice who returned it with a grin.

"Shall we?" John asked, extending his left arm to Miss Withers. As she took it, he glanced behind him. Catching eyes with Grace, he extended his right arm.

Grace paused for a moment, not knowing whether she should stay beside Miss Withers or cross behind them and take John's offered arm. As she caught sight of the silent, questioning hope in his eyes, Grace suppressed a smile. She walked in a slow semicircle and placed her hand atop his forearm. A thrill sparked within her as she relished their closeness.

He gave her an appreciative smile before they crossed the lawn and greeted their guests.

More people arrived, and it seemed that for an extended time they all greeted and welcomed one batch of visitors only to immediately greet and welcome another.

Soon, most of the tables had people dotted around them, sipping tea and eating the canapés the cook had been preparing since before dawn.

When they finally sat down, Grace sighed in relief. John remained standing, deep in conversation with Isaac. Despite Beatrice's happy chatter, Grace could not resist glancing at John more frequently than she believed she ought to. Her heart quickened as she noticed he and Isaac walking toward the table.

Beatrice looked everywhere except at Isaac, her cheeks glowing pink. The two had already greeted one another upon the Taylor family's arrival. Clearly, the thought of an actual conversation unnerved Beatrice even more.

Sympathy bloomed in Grace's chest, and as she looked at her friend, then at Isaac, and back again, she truly hoped

John's suspicions were correct that Isaac shared Beatrice's feelings.

"Is this seat occupied?" Isaac asked, his eyebrows lifting.

Beatrice's cheeks grew darker as she noticed it was the seat beside her to which he referred. "N-no," she stuttered. "It is free..."

Isaac smiled and nodded, looking for a moment almost as flustered as she did. He sat down beside her, and John lowered himself into the chair beside Grace.

As Grace smiled at him, her heart hammered. She had expected him to sit next to his aunt, but she was glad he had not.

Initially, at least.

Something was different, somehow. He seemed distracted. Much more quiet than she had expected. A few times he caught her eye and hesitated, before turning away and feigning interest in Isaac and Beatrice's burgeoning conversation.

Grace was at a loss. She was glad to see Beatrice and Isaac coming out of their shells, for if it had been left to her to carry the conversation, she would have failed miserably. Concern crushed out any ease of making polite chit-chat, and though the atmosphere of the party was warm and inviting, a chill had lodged in her heart that she could not explain.

"Grace, dear, could you please nip inside and fetch my laudanum? I forgot to bring it out with me."

Miss Withers's voice almost made Grace jump.

"Of course." Grace stood and mumbled politely to Beatrice, Isaac, and John. "Excuse me..."

Before any of them could respond, she was hurrying toward the house.

Inside, she squeezed her eyes shut and drew a series of deep shaky breaths.

She'd been imagining a pleasant afternoon of lively

conversation. Maybe even more furtive looks or hinted confessions from John.

Instead, he seemed miserable — heavy and quiet, and she had no idea why.

She sighed and inwardly scolded herself as she made her way up to Miss Withers's room and fetched the bottle on her dresser.

With another sigh of frustrated disappointment, Grace left the room and came back downstairs. She poured a glass of water and decanted the laudanum into it in the precise amount Miss Withers had previously instructed her.

She had only stepped outside and walked a few paces when she heard John's voice behind her.

"Miss Stratton?"

He stood in the doorway, his countenance marked with anxiety.

"Forgive me, I... I followed you inside when..." He glanced at the crowd of people who were far enough away not to hear their conversation. He stepped outside fully, closing the distance between himself and Grace.

"Miss Stratton, I must... There is something I *must* speak with you about."

Grace wasn't sure whether his intended discourse might be good or bad, yet her heart ran away with itself in girlish imaginings, despite her unseen efforts to restrain it.

"One moment. I must give your aunt her medicine."

"Of course." John nodded, a twitchy, resigned nod.

Grace's heart sank.

Surely if he wished to declare any feelings of tenderness toward her, he would not appear so ill at ease.

She turned and trudged toward the table, her limbs as heavy as her heart.

"Here you are, Miss Withers."

"Oh, thank you, dear."

As Miss Withers took the glass from Grace's hands, Higgins cleared his throat beside them.

Grace frowned as she noticed the look of confusion on his usually unperturbed face.

"Miss Withers..." he began, the confusion now audible in his voice.

"Yes, Higgins?"

"Another guest has arrived for you, ma'am." He turned and motioned toward a well-dressed young man with a mischievous grin and tousled hair.

The young man bounded toward them.

"Aunt!" he exclaimed, throwing his arms out to each side.

Miss Withers looked at him and smiled. "David!" she said, pushing herself up on the arms of her chair.

Grace helped her stand and nodded politely at her employer's other nephew, noticing for the first time the look of surprised amusement on his face.

"Aunt... It is me — John."

Higgins cleared his throat. "A Mr. John Withers to see you, ma'am." He paused. "*Another* one."

A sick feeling overtook Grace. She glanced at Beatrice, who looked as puzzled as she imagined she did herself.

Isaac stood abruptly.

Grace looked at him, her frown deepening by the second.

Isaac's head turned to the left, his eyes wide and fixed upon—

Grace looked in the same direction, and noticed John, chalk white as he stared at... the *new* John.

"But, John is already here!" Miss Withers exclaimed, each word zipping like an arrow through Grace's heart.

The young man laughed. "*I* am John."

He raised his finger and pointed at the gaping man standing frozen on the lawn.

The man whom Grace and Miss Withers had been addressing as John for the past few weeks.

The man with whom Grace had fallen in love.

"That is *David*."

CHAPTER 36
THE UNRAVELLING

David blinked rapidly, partly to dispel the dark dots swirling in his vision, and partly to ascertain whether or not his eyes were playing tricks on him.

The next thing he knew, Isaac was by his side, his hand reaching out and clamping firmly on David's shoulder.

He said something. But all David could take in was the look he now saw on Grace's face.

Confusion. Shock.

Betrayal.

"David?" Isaac's voice resonated in his ear.

David opened his mouth, but his own voice had plummeted somewhere out of reach.

In, out, in, out — his ragged breaths were all the sound he could make.

John... Why was John here?

A memory slammed into David's awareness with such force that it made him tremble.

For a moment, I wondered if I might have written the wrong date on the invitations and you were merely here too early!

His aunt had spoken those words to him the day he'd arrived.

But only now was he taking in their meaning.

She had invited John to her garden party. All this time, and—

"David, say something!" Isaac's typically calm tone had transformed into anguished concern.

What could he say?

Grace turned away, moving toward Beatrice, whose face showed only pity and confusion.

He must speak with her — tell her everything, as he'd been trying to do all day.

"What are you playing at, cousin?"

David's gaze snapped to John, who now stood before him with a bemused expression. No annoyance, no malice. Simply the intrigue and excitement that had bubbled under the surface ever since he was a boy.

"I—"

"David?"

David squeezed his eyes shut for a second, before opening them and shifting his gaze to his aunt as she shuffled to a stand beside John. "Ah—"

"What is going on? Whyever did you tell us that you were *John*?"

"I... I am sorry..." His voice sounded as strained as it felt to emit it.

John chuckled. "There must be something scandalous going on if *David* wishes to disguise himself... What is it, cousin?"

David shook his head, his gaze drifting back to Grace—

He stiffened. Grace.

She was gone.

Fear replaced the horror that had frozen him to the spot, compelling him into motion.

"Forgive me… I must…"

His voice trailed off as he left his relatives and his closest friend standing bewildered on the lawn.

"Grace…" His voice was an anguished whisper.

He bolted toward the house, almost tripping as he launched himself through the open French doors.

"Grace?" He called out her name, looking wildly around the room.

Movement at the far end of the room caught his eye.

Beatrice turned and regarded him warily. As she stepped aside, he saw a sight even worse than the expression Grace had worn outside.

"Grace…"

He moved toward her, each step quickening.

"Leave me alone!" Her red-rimmed eyes remained downcast as tears rolled down her pale face.

"I must speak with you… Please—"

"You lied to me!" She shook her head mournfully, fresh tears flooding her cheeks.

Nausea rose in David's throat. "Please, Grace, I was going to tell you — I have been trying all afternoon to tell you—"

Her gaze met his, and the pain in her eyes rendered him speechless.

He longed to reach out, to pull her into a firm embrace and explain everything, begging her forgiveness for all his treachery. But he could only stand there, staring in disbelieving horror at the visible consequences of his selfishness.

"I asked you, and you lied to me. You lied to me!" Her dark eyes were full of questions. Of hurt, and confusion.

Trembling overtook David. "I know… I did not wish to… But, please, if you will permit me to explain—"

"Explain? What explanation is there that would justify

lying to me?" Her lower lip and chin shook. "I thought you cared for me..."

All the air seemed to squeeze from David's chest, and he could take none in nor breathe any out. "I do care for you. That is why I have been trying to tell you the truth. I—"

Grace's expression hardened. "The truth? How am I to know whether anything you say is true or not? You have been here *weeks* and have done nothing but lie to us! How long might you have continued to do so if your cousin had not arrived today?" Her voice increased in volume and pitch with each word, ultimately breaking off in a tortured sob.

"Grace..." David stepped toward her.

Instantly, she retreated. "Miss Stratton, to you. Though, I do not wish to hear anything from you ever again, Mr..." Her gaze flew about the room in distress. "I do not even know who you are!"

David swallowed hard, his throat as dry as dust. "I am Dr. David Carbury. And I—"

"No." Grace shook her head rapidly, waving her hands in front of her. "I do not wish to hear it. Any of it. You are a liar. A deceiver." She shook her head slowly.

"Please, you must understand—"

Grace's jaw slackened. "Understand? Do you mean to *defend* what you have done?"

David gaped at her, his brow furrowing. "No... I do not defend it... I truly regret it. But, if you will only permit me to explain—"

Grace breathed out sharply. "No, Dr. Carbury. I shall not."

Before he could protest, she spun away from him, racing out of the room. Beatrice rushed past him, following Grace.

"Miss Beckwith!"

She stopped and turned, regarding him with awkward hesitation.

"Miss Beckwith... Please... I..."

What could he say? What hope was there? He had heard it from her own lips. She would trust nothing that he said. No matter how well he might explain the circumstances that had driven him to do what he had done, she was right — he could never justify his chosen course.

He stared at Beatrice, hopelessness cascading around him as he slowly shook his head.

Beatrice glanced into the hallway, back at David briefly, then turned and hurried out of the room.

He heard a murmur of voices. A warm hand came to rest upon his shoulder. "David? You are shaking..."

Another hand clasped his elbow and guided him backward. He tumbled into an armchair, silence screaming in his ears despite the voices somewhere nearby.

Isaac appeared in front of him. "I did not say anything yet, but if you wish, I can tell your aunt and cousin some of what has brought you here, and why you did not give them your own name. Would that be a help to you at present?"

David nodded slowly. In his mind, he thanked his friend, but his lips remained frozen, his voice absent.

As Isaac left, his words rang in David's ears.

...and why you did not give them your own name.

His stomach churned, his heart aching in his chest. He had hoped to give Grace his own name... had begun to imagine what their future together might look like.

His eyes squeezed shut in anguish as he remembered the look on her face, the tears that he'd longed to wipe away, the agony of soul that he'd seen plainly as he'd looked into her weeping eyes.

He'd been trying so hard to avoid a painful future for himself that he'd ended up breaking Grace's heart.

And his own.

By his own folly.

Even the gallows could not eclipse such agony.

CHAPTER 37

DIVISION

Grace sat on the reading chair in her room, her throat burning.

Beatrice closed the window against the chill that had worked its way into the early evening air. "Oh, Grace, you will make yourself ill if you keep crying so hard." Her pity only intensified Grace's anguish.

"I trusted him, Beatrice. I..." A fresh torrent of weeping overwhelmed her. "I thought I loved him!"

"I know, Grace. I know." Beatrice stroked Grace's hair as she spoke, her soothing tone pricked with emotion.

Of all the possible outcomes of the day that Grace had imagined, never had this one entered into her mind.

He *wasn't* John, after all. He really *was* David.

Just as she'd thought at the start.

All this time, she'd believed she'd been getting to know him, had been falling in love with him, and now...

Now, she realised, she didn't know the first thing about him. She didn't know him at all.

Grief overpowered her again, and such deep sobs broke forth from her that she could hardly breathe.

One thing she knew. He had lied to her. She'd carried around such dismay after asking him his true identity, believing him to be so noble for not holding it against her. But, the whole time, she'd been right.

And he had lied to her — lied to her face.

Anger and anguish fought for dominance within her.

She stood abruptly, swiping the tears from her face in annoyance as she walked a few paces.

Why should she cry over such a man? If he could not be trusted, then surely she was better off without him. Better that she'd discovered the truth now instead of allowing a deeper attachment to form between them.

A soft knock at the door interrupted her thoughts.

Beatrice placed a gentle hand on her shoulder. "Shall I see who it is?"

Grace nodded reluctantly. "I do not wish to speak to him."

Beatrice nodded, then cracked open the door. "Oh, Miss Withers." She glanced back at Grace, her eyebrows raised. Upon seeing Grace's nod, Beatrice opened the door fully, motioning for Grace's employer — that deceiver's aunt — to enter.

Grace drew a deep breath, battling to regain her composure. She tucked a stray hair behind her ear and wiped her cheeks, hoping to erase all evidence of tears. But her eyes burned, and she knew how puffy they must look.

"Grace, dear, are you well? Mr. Taylor saw you and Miss Beckwith leave the drawing room in a hurry, after..." Her regal voice trailed off as Grace met her gaze. "Oh, child! It is all rather a shock, I know, but—" Her expression altered slowly, realisation dawning in her eyes. "Oh... Grace, dear, would I be correct to assume that there was some... understanding between you and my nephew?"

Grace's heart wrung in her chest. "No, Miss Withers. No

understanding. None whatever." She stifled a sob, holding it in her throat until the ache was more than she could bear.

She turned away from Miss Withers, covering her face with her hands.

"There now..." Beatrice's gentle tone washed over Grace as her warm hands came to rest upon her shoulders. "Please, Miss Withers, have a seat."

When Grace finally lowered her hands, she saw Miss Withers sitting on the small chair where she always sat to read her Bible in the mornings. Beatrice stood beside it.

"But, if there was no attachment, then why is it that you are so upset, my dear?" Miss Withers enquired gently, her tone warm with kindness.

Grace clenched her jaw, trying desperately to remain calm. "I do not appreciate being lied to."

"He lied to me, too," Miss Withers said, her expression compassionate.

Grace sighed. "We had no understanding. At least, no formal one."

Miss Withers nodded, pursing her lips slightly. "I see." She paused. "I take it that you and he have spoken this evening?"

Grace's chin trembled. "I do not wish to speak with him at present."

"I see." Miss Withers sighed. "What a party it was, hmm?"

Beatrice smiled sympathetically. "It truly was lovely, Miss Withers. Until..."

Miss Withers nodded. "I believe most of the guests have gone home, to allow us all some privacy. But I am sure Lindenfell shall be abuzz with gossip for quite some time."

Grace groaned inwardly.

"Does Mr. Carbury plan to stay, Miss Withers?" Beatrice asked.

Grace froze, awaiting her employer's response.

"*Dr.* Carbury," Miss Withers said, gently correcting Beatrice.

Instantly, Grace remembered the strange encounter that had happened at church when someone had called out for Dr. Markham without saying his surname. John — or *David,* as she ought to now think of him — had reacted so fearfully to it.

And *that* was why. He was a doctor himself.

He must have assumed that someone had recognised him.

Only they hadn't. He'd succeeded in deceiving every last one of them.

Grace clenched her teeth. *Insufferable man.*

"In truth, I am not sure what his next steps will be," Miss Withers said, continuing to direct her discourse toward Beatrice. "He has rather a lot to consider at the moment."

Miss Withers turned to face her. "Grace, dear, you need not concern yourself with coming down again this evening, unless you wish to. I intend to have a small bite to eat and then retire. And, I am sure my nephews can tend to me until then, if you cannot."

Guilt washed through Grace. How silly she was to permit her emotions to hold her back from doing what she had come here to do. But how kind was Miss Withers's offer. The last thing she wanted was to go downstairs and be forced to listen to David's excuses.

"I shall come down if you wish it," Grace said, her voice unsteadier than she'd expected it to be.

Miss Withers waved her hand. "There is no need. Not tonight. Get some rest, and I shall see you in the morning. Miss Beckwith, you may stay as long as you wish to make sure our dear Grace is all right."

Miss Withers gave each of them a warm smile, and Grace swallowed hard as the sobs rose back into her throat.

Somehow, she managed to maintain her fraying composure until her employer had left the room. Then, she collapsed into Beatrice's arms, sobbing as deeply as she had when she'd first fled to the safety and privacy of her room.

Her mind battled against itself, half of her wanting to be angry at David, and half of her wanting to hear what he had to say, to see if there was any reason he could give for his behaviour that might even make a fraction of sense.

But how could there be?

He was a liar. He'd lied to her face and had allowed her to keep apologising to him for doubting him. Yet, all along, he'd known the truth.

Now that she did, too, she knew without a doubt that she could never trust him. Could share no sort of friendship with him, never mind anything deeper.

So, why did part of her still want to?

CHAPTER 38
A BITTER TRUTH

A chill seemed to fill the drawing room, and not only from the evening air that filtered in through the open French doors.

"Here, this will help you."

David looked up to see Isaac extending a teacup and saucer toward him. He grasped it with both hands, his fingers still trembling as they closed around the saucer's edges. "Thank you."

Isaac sat in the armchair opposite David, leaning forward, his expression revealing his concern.

John flopped down onto the nearby sofa. "My, my! Never did I think I'd see the day when my strait-laced cousin would be in trouble with the law!"

Troubled, David glanced from Isaac to John and back again.

Isaac spoke. "I told your aunt and your cousin about Mr. Edwards. And about the encouraging message you recently received from Dr. Turner."

"Yes..." John's voice grew sober. "Listen, I am sorry,

David. I do not mean to be insensitive. I just always assumed it would be me, one day. Not you."

David focused on his cousin. "Why would it be *you* in trouble with the law? What have you been doing?"

John's brows rose. "Nothing! I only meant that, well... you are the *boring* one. Everyone knows I am rather more adventurous. And it is usually we adventurous folk who tend to be misunderstood by those in an... official capacity." He ended his speech with a proud smirk that did nothing to assure David of his cousin's proclaimed innocence.

"John..." David chided him.

"Well now, cousin." John settled himself comfortably on the sofa and spread his arms across its back. "You have hardly room to talk at present, do you?" Again, he flashed them both a mischievous grin before leaning his head back and closing his eyes.

David sighed.

Isaac observed John in stunned silence, then shifted his gaze to David. He lowered his voice. "I cannot believe the two of you are related." He shook his head slowly.

David nodded wearily. "Night and day, people always said." His chest ached. "Where is my aunt?"

Isaac's gaze shifted. "I believe she went to check on Miss Stratton."

Weakness washed over David. "Have you heard anything about her? How she is?"

"What's this? An illicit romance with Aunt's new servant girl, too? David, my boy!" John cried in a teasing tone, eyeing them both.

David's jaw tensed as he swivelled his head to glare at his cousin. "How dare you? There is *nothing* illicit at hand! And Miss Stratton is not a servant girl. She is Aunt's companion and deserves a great deal more of your respect." He practically spat the words at his cousin.

John's face turned devoid of all humour. "Should I respect her as much as *you* have? Coming here and pretending to be *me*?" He scoffed. "You are a hypocrite, cousin."

David's blood thundered in his ears. John was right. As smug and arrogant as his cousin's words had been, he could not deny their truth.

He turned away from John with a sigh, shifting in his chair. He glared at the fireplace, clenching his jaw again and again.

"I take it that Miss Stratton was rather upset?" Isaac asked, his tone gentle.

David exhaled through his nose. "Extremely."

Isaac sighed. "I am sorry, David." He dropped the volume of his voice again. "I know how much you care for her." He paused. "Did Miss Beckwith say anything to you before she left the room?"

David glanced at his friend. Isaac's head was low, and a nervous twitching seemed to have worked its way into his hands.

"No," David said, sorrow weighing heavily on his heart.

Isaac looked up at him and sighed. "I am sure she will recover. It must have all been quite a shock to her, that is all. She will come around."

"Perhaps." But even as David uttered the word, a sickening sensation deep within him contradicted it.

It was more than a shock to her. More than something that could be easily forgotten.

He had found the one person who'd turned his usually studious thoughts toward matrimony, and his subsequent actions had turned her own thoughts entirely away from it.

He was certain of it, considering the look she'd given him.

Any hope that he and Grace might have shared a future together had been shattered irrevocably.

He was sure of it.

CHAPTER 39

FOUR TORMENTING WORDS

The next morning, when Grace opened her eyes, she wondered for a moment why they seemed so swollen and uncomfortable.

Then, the events of the previous afternoon and evening rushed back to her memory with such vivid force that she squeezed her eyes shut again, trying unsuccessfully to stop the tears from spilling out.

But, whether her eyes were open or closed, all she could see was David.

His pale face upon the real John's arrival. The anguish in his eyes when they'd spoken in the drawing room afterward. And all the smiles and laughs they had shared before that.

How was she supposed to face him now?

As she peeled herself out of bed, she saw her open Bible on the chest of drawers next to it. More memories flooded back.

Beatrice leaving late last night. Grace curling up on her bed, weeping and praying. The verse she had stumbled upon as she'd pleaded for God's help.

She turned away from the Bible, trying to forget what

she'd read as she set about washing her face and selecting a gown.

She caught sight of herself in the mirror and almost gasped. Her puffy, red-rimmed eyes and pale face made her look like some sort of spectre. Her unruly hair and dejected posture only added to the alarming display.

Once she had wrangled her appearance into its usual respectability, she steeled her jaw, staring at herself in the mirror.

I can do this. I must do this — for Miss Withers. She did not employ me to hide away as a heartbroken ninny.

With a sigh, she swept a nervous hand along her skirts, smoothing them out, despite having little care at present whether or not doing so was even necessary.

As she turned the door handle, her heart picked up speed.

How was she supposed to eat any breakfast while her stomach churned and her limbs trembled?

She lifted her chin, flung her bedroom door open and marched through it. Miss Withers was depending on her.

But as she descended the stairs and approached the breakfast room, her courage began to falter.

You are here for Miss Withers. You must not permit that traitor to interfere with your duty.

Emboldening herself once again, Grace walked slowly into the dining room.

"Ah, good morning, my dear!" Miss Withers smiled.

Grace nodded in response, her eyes quickly darting to the table's other occupant.

John.

The *real* John.

David was nowhere in sight.

She was glad. She truly was.

So, why did her heart seem to sink?

"Good morning, Miss Withers. Mr. Withers." Grace forced

a liveliness into her voice that was entirely alien to her at that moment.

"How are you feeling this morning?" Miss Withers's tone was one of utter kindness.

Grace sat down opposite her. "I am well, thank you. And you? I trust you are not too fatigued after... the party..."

And all the drama that broke loose during it.

"And what a party it was, eh?" John winked playfully at Grace.

She gaped at him in horror. Clearly, his cousin's deception meant nothing to him. Yet it had ruined everything for her.

As Grace opened her mouth to answer him — without being fully aware of what she might say — the door opened.

Grace's blood ran cold. She sat frozen, staring at the table before her, afraid to lift her eyes in order to have her suspicions confirmed.

"Ah, here he is... the man of mystery!" John's voice was low, but he punctuated his words with a loud chuckle.

"John, do not make such jest of it all," Miss Withers whispered, scolding him as though he were still the eight-year-old boy she'd spoken of before.

"Good morning, Aunt. John." A pause. "Miss Stratton."

His voice sounded more strained upon saying her name in comparison to the others, but still Grace could not move, or speak, or look at him.

The Bible verse she'd read late last night circled in her mind.

She pushed it away. Or, tried to, at least.

"Come, Grace. Greet David."

Grace looked up at her employer, devastated by the woman's gentle plea.

"Good morning."

There. That was all she could manage. And it was more than he deserved.

She heard David's chair scrape lightly against the floor as he sat down.

Never had her heart hammered so violently.

How was she to make it through a whole meal with him — a whole day? What folly it had been to imagine a whole life with him.

"So, are we to expect any further surprises from you today, cousin?"

"John..."

John chuckled in response to his aunt's reproof. "Oh, Aunt. Do you really expect me to say nothing when he has *finally* done something worth talking about?" John leaned toward Grace. "David the Dull — that's what my friends and I used to call him."

Grace's heart thundered even more as she sat, still avoiding lifting her gaze in David's direction. This was agony — on all fronts. John and his flippant comments, Miss Withers urging her to greet her betrayer. Even David's silent presence was unbearable.

She shuffled in her seat, welcoming the sight of the food which was now being placed on the table. The sooner she had finished eating, the sooner she could get out of this room.

"I was John the Joker. Infinitely preferable, don't you think?"

"I always believed that jokes were supposed to be funny." The words shot out of Grace's lips before she could reconsider them.

John's mouth hung open, offence written on his face. Miss Withers seemed to be covering her mouth with a napkin. Was that a hint of a smile on her lips?

Bracing herself, Grace glanced at David, completely unprepared for the sight that she beheld. He stared vacantly at his plate, his lips drawn tightly together, a heavy burden almost visible on his shoulders. His face was wan, and the dark circles under his eyes matched her own.

Grace dipped her head, clenching her hands. He looked every bit as miserable as she was.

Anger swept through her.

Rightly so. He should be miserable.

The Bible verse she'd been trying hard not to dwell upon confronted her mind again.

Grace sighed, squirming in her chair, longing to escape what she knew she could not.

Herself.

Her own transgressions.

David had lied to her, had deceived her into thinking he was really someone else. How was that worse than her own sins throughout the years? Besides, Jesus called His followers to love one another. Wouldn't that make her just as much of a hypocrite as David if she failed to do so?

As John and Miss Withers exchanged small talk, Grace silently prayed.

Lord, I do not understand. He has wronged me. Surely, I cannot turn a blind eye to that. And how am I to trust him? He has sinned against You by lying, too. It is really You that he needs to be forgiven by — not me.

Her heart thundered with a deep conviction that she was willfully withholding the very thing she'd been named after.

Grace.

But, Lord, he does not deserve to be forgiven. Not yet.

Yet who was there upon the earth who *deserved* forgiveness? All had gone astray. All had turned their backs on God and disobeyed Him. That was why Jesus had come — why He'd had to die.

Mercy. Grace.

Forgiveness.

A new kind of trembling overtook her as she quietly

attempted to surrender her hurts to God, and as she asked Him for help to live out the truth of the Bible verse that had been plaguing her all morning.

Hatred stirreth up strifes: but love covereth all sins.

She remembered her father telling her how deeply a verse from the New Testament had impacted him with regards to her mother's past, urging its reader to keep loving with fervent love, that would cover a multitude of sins.

The one circling in her mind was disconcertingly similar. And if her father had loved her mother enough that he hadn't stirred up anything from her long, tainted past, then surely she could show the same grace to David.

But, her mother's past had been decided for her — against her will.

No one had forced David to lie. He'd been free to make his own decisions, and he'd chosen to do the dishonourable thing. He'd deceived her — and Miss Withers.

Willingly.

Still, the words plucked at her mind.

Hatred stirreth up strifes: but love covereth all sins.

It was those last four words that tormented her most of all.

Wasn't it love that had brought her into all this hurt in the first place? She'd fallen in love with David, but he had broken her trust — and her heart.

Love was the *problem*.

So, how could it be the solution?

CHAPTER 40

PREPARATIONS

David eased himself into the library after breakfast, closing the door quietly behind him.

He hoped John hadn't seen him come this direction. The last thing he needed was his giddy cousin bursting in and lobbing more hurtful jibes at him.

He'd been so grateful his aunt had kept John in conversation for much of breakfast. It had been difficult enough to be so close to Grace, yet with an almost tangible distance between them. He'd only stolen a glance or two at her, but she looked just as pitiful as she had the evening before.

David raked a hand across his forehead. What now?

The door creaked open.

David closed his eyes in dismay, steeling himself to hear his cousin's obnoxious laugh.

"David?"

He turned at the familiar — and welcome — voice.

"Isaac!"

"David, another letter has arrived for you. From Mr. Crump."

Isaac strode toward him and handed him the envelope, a serious yet hopeful look on his face.

David drew a deep breath. He opened the letter and scanned its contents.

"He is calling upon me to return to London. Immediately. He has arranged for a hearing, and I must be present for it to proceed."

Isaac's brow lifted. "Oh? Surely, that is good news?"

Fear and hope fought within him. "I do not know."

Isaac nodded, seemingly deep in thought. "When shall you leave?"

David glanced at the letter again. "As soon as possible, it would seem. Perhaps... today."

Anguish twisted in his heart as he thought of leaving Grace. Even though she clearly had no wish to speak to him, the yearning to tell her how sorry he was still burned within him. As did his desire to tell her that he loved her.

"I shall come with you."

Isaac's voice brought David crashing back to his surroundings.

"What?"

"I shall come with you. To London."

"Isaac..."

"Unless you do not wish it. But if I can be of any help to you there, I will gladly come."

David swallowed, desperate to rid himself of the lump in his throat, but to no avail. "You are much too kind, Isaac."

Isaac smiled and gave David a firm nod. "That is settled. So, we leave today?"

A measure of relief stirred within David, knowing that he would not be facing all that awaited him in London alone. "Yes, I suppose we must."

"I shall go and pack a few things for the journey. Shall I meet you here, or at the station?"

It was all becoming much too real. David lurched toward an armchair, lowered himself into it, and buried his face in his hands.

"David, are you quite well?"

"Yes, yes. It has been a rather difficult day and night. I hardly slept a wink..."

"Have you spoken to Miss Stratton?"

David shook his head wearily. "She still does her best to avoid me. My aunt compelled her to say 'good morning' to me at breakfast. That is all the communication we have had since last evening." He exhaled a deep, shaky sigh. "And, now that you and I are to leave... it is all the communication I am likely to have with her ever again."

"You never know. Perhaps, once you have everything settled in London, enough time will have passed that she will be ready to speak to you again."

David shook his head, firming his lips together. "I sincerely doubt it."

"Well... Perhaps you ought to write her a letter before we leave. And, it will be there for her to read in her own time."

David looked up at his friend. "Write her a letter? Yes..."

His gaze dropped to his hands, and he nodded.

"Yes, I believe I shall."

CHAPTER 41
GOODBYE

"Could you fetch my shawl, Grace, dear?" Miss Withers asked, leaning her head back against the armchair she always occupied in the drawing room. "I think I must have caught a chill yesterday, even though the weather was quite pleasant."

"Of course," Grace said.

As she placed the warm shawl across Miss Withers's shoulders, concern filled Grace. Her employer's posture was more hunched than usual, and her face seemed uncharacteristically pale. "Would you like some more tea? That would warm you, too."

"Oh, yes please." Miss Withers gave her a weary but pleasant smile. "You are so good to me."

Grace smiled and set about preparing the tea tray. She glanced at the clock on the mantelpiece. Beatrice had mentioned last night that she would call this morning. Perhaps Grace could ask her for some advice. She'd never tended the sick, and she remembered Beatrice telling her once about the time she nursed her aunt through a dreadful fever. Perhaps—

A thought struck her.

David was a doctor. Surely, if anyone could advise her, it would be—

No.

She busied herself gathering an extra pillow for Miss Withers.

"There you are. Are you comfortable? Do you need any of your medicine?"

"Perhaps I should."

"I shall fetch it for you now."

After glancing at Miss Withers warily as she approached the doorway, Grace hurried through it and up the stairs, heading straight for her employer's chamber.

Inside, she snatched the bottle of laudanum from the dresser and rushed — as fast as she could without being indecorous — back down to the drawing room.

She hurried through the doorway. "Now, you—"

Every flurry of activity within Grace's mind and manner stopped abruptly. David was holding his aunt's wrist, looking sombrely at his pocket watch.

He glanced up, and for the first time since their exchange in this very room the previous evening, their eyes met.

Swallowing hard, Grace dropped her gaze to the floor, but not before she'd noticed the sorrowful apprehension in David's own.

"All is well, Aunt," he said. "Only make sure that you keep warm and maintain your regular schedule of laudanum."

Grace's heart stuttered in her chest. His voice... How could such a beautiful sound elicit such agony?

"Thank you, my dear," Miss Withers said.

David sighed, such a heaviness within it that Grace's stomach tensed.

"Aunt... I am terribly sorry, especially in light of everything that happened yesterday, but—" He cleared his throat quietly. "I must return to London. At once."

"So soon?" Surprise and disappointment mingled in Miss Withers's voice.

Grace listened, frozen to the spot, reluctant to raise her head to look at him despite how compelled she was to do so.

"Yes. There is an associate of Dr. Turner's who has kindly agreed to help me. And there is a hearing that I must attend, in connection with... with the case against me."

Grace's heart turned over within her. Hearing? Case? Was he in some kind of legal trouble?

Shame crept up her neck, heating her cheeks. For all she knew, he was in some sort of danger. But she hadn't even given him the chance to explain.

The sting of betrayal sparked fresh anger coursing through her, firming her jaw and stiffening her limbs.

He'd had plenty of time to explain everything to them. To ask them for help, even. But he'd chosen to deceive them instead.

It was good news that he was going back to London.

Good riddance.

"Well, I do hope that all will go well for you, my dear. You will write to us, will you not? And let us know the outcome?"

"Of course, Aunt. And... Thank you, for all of your kindness these past few weeks. I have deserved none of it."

Grace scoffed under her breath. He was right about *that*, at least. It was probably the only truth he'd uttered the whole time he'd been in Lindenfell.

Guilt nudged her heart again. Had *she* always done and said only what was honourable? She knew the answer without even thinking.

Cautiously, she glanced at him, moving her head very little so as not to invite his attention.

Sympathy squeezed her heart. He looked... wretched. Like a man who hadn't slept properly for years, before whom lay some unpleasant event of serious magnitude.

She could hardly breathe.

Deep down, loath as she was to admit it, she didn't want him to leave. And she hated seeing him in such distress.

She stared at the floor again, squeezing her eyes shut. Such torturous agony this whole ordeal was. Never had so many emotions assailed her at the same time.

Never had sorrow and indignation held such equal space in her heart.

"Miss Stratton?" His voice was closer now.

Grace opened her eyes to see David standing just a few paces in front of her. She could only hold his gaze for a few seconds at a time.

He cleared his throat, his head dipped low. "Miss Stratton, I am truly sorry for... for everything."

Grace opened her mouth to speak, to tell him to stop talking. She readied herself to bolt from the room again. But she could do neither. Her limbs refused to budge, and her voice was locked in a haze of overwhelming emotion.

"I understand that you do not wish for us to speak. Please, all I ask is that you permit me to give you this."

He reached into his waistcoat pocket and pulled out a small envelope, then extended it toward her, his hand trembling.

"Please read it, whenever you might be ready to do so."

Almost involuntarily, Grace slowly reached out and took the envelope from his grasp.

He glanced up at her, a pitiable look in his eyes that she knew she could never forget, no matter how much she might try.

"Goodbye, Miss Stratton."

The atmosphere reminded Grace of the moment in the carriage where they'd seemed on the cusp of a whole new life. Only this time, pain had replaced the pleasantness, and the future stretching before them seemed to promise devastation rather than delight.

Grace squeezed her jaw tightly shut, desperate to stave off the trembling that sought to overpower her chin. A lump in her throat seemed as though it might burst, and the sharp barb of grief that pierced her heart compounded each sensation into unbearable agony.

Silently, she watched as David walked toward the drawing room door. Upon reaching it, he turned slowly, giving her one last lingering look of sorrowful longing.

Then, he was gone.

CHAPTER 42
THE ADVOCATE

David watched the Lindenfell station sign slip slowly out of sight, the afternoon glow of sunlight seeming to rest upon the station roof. He turned to face Isaac, who sat opposite him in the railway carriage, flicking through a broadside.

Leaning his head against the edge of the straight back of the seat, all he could think of was Grace. She'd accepted the letter, at least — that had been a pleasant surprise. Though he wasn't certain whether she'd read it or burn it or tear it into tiny pieces.

She might even do all three.

And he would never know.

The train had picked up speed now, hurtling him back to London to face, what — the end of his career? Of his life?

Yet, somehow, stinging deeper than all that, was the memory of how Grace had looked at him when she'd discovered his dishonesty.

He'd wanted no one to be hurt by any of it.

Least of all, himself, if he were being truthful.

He'd gone to Lindenfell trying to preserve his life, without a second thought of the possibility that his actions might ruin that of another.

He didn't deserve Grace. Or her forgiveness. But it was what he longed for, even more than a favourable outcome in the hearing that Mr. Crump had arranged.

"Chin up, old chap."

Isaac's calm voice drifted into David's awareness. He looked at his friend, still touched that he had followed through on his offer to accompany him to London.

"Thank you again for—"

"David!" Isaac laughed. "You have thanked me countless times — there is no need!" His tone and expression grew serious. "I am only too glad to help, in whatever way I can." He paused. "Did you write a letter for Miss Stratton?"

David sighed, then nodded slowly. "Yes."

"Did she read it?"

David paused, willing the grief in his chest to dissipate enough for him to talk without hindrance. "I do not know. She took it, at least. I asked her to read it whenever she is able." He shrugged slightly. "She may never be."

"I cannot imagine that she would put off reading it indefinitely. Perhaps, even in a day or two—"

"There is little to be gained by speculating."

David hoped his words had not seemed too harsh. It was agony to think of Grace. Agony to speak of her. He longed for something that might dull the pain, that might stop the incessant stream of guilt and sorrow that flowed through his heart and soul.

"Well... We can pray, at least. For her, and for the hearing."

Isaac had mentioned God a few times in David's presence, but, today, he found the topic almost unbearable. Who was he to think that God might listen to his prayers after all that he had done?

"David, I know that you are surrounded by troubles on all sides at present—"

"Please, Isaac, I cannot speak of God now. I very much doubt He would be too happy with me after all that has transpired."

"Oh?"

David looked at Isaac incredulously. "You disagree?"

Isaac shifted in his seat. "No... In fact, I know that He is not. I was only surprised to hear you admit it."

Guilt compounded in David's heart as Isaac's words sank in.

"But, perhaps, you have the wrong thing in mind, as to why He is not happy with you," Isaac continued.

David looked at his friend questioningly, still at a loss for words.

"You probably think that He is disappointed in you for your actions of late. Running away, pretending to be someone you're not."

David folded his arms. "Devastating everyone that matters to me, yes."

Isaac nodded, a kind smile on his face. "But that is not your biggest problem, David. Your biggest problem is not all the wrong that you have done, but the fact that you are trying to atone for it by yourself."

"You make no sense, Isaac."

"We have all done wrong, David. You are not the only person who has ever lied. Or been selfish. Or hurt others. We all have. We have all missed the mark."

"Mark?"

"Perfection."

David rolled his eyes. "I am not talking about perfection, Isaac — I know I am nowhere close to that! But I have sunk so far below common decency that—"

"But that is what I am trying to tell you, David. There is

no such thing as common decency. At least, not apart from God. We *need* Him, David. We cannot be good on our own, because only God is good. All of us have gone our own way and, frankly, made a dreadful mess of things."

David sighed, relaxing a fraction as Isaac's words began to make a little more sense.

"Each of us has a problem worse than any of the mistakes we've made. We've broken God's law." Isaac leaned forward. "Why is it that we are going to London? For a hearing. A trial, perhaps. In order to work out the legal consequences of your actions regarding Mr. Edwards, yes?"

David's stomach lurched. "Yes..."

"Yes. And there is a heavenly court, David, where one day God will sit as judge and preside over *all* of our cases. All of our wrongdoings will be laid bare before Him."

The very thought filled David with a new kind of terror, greater than when he'd imagined himself awaiting the fatal drop in the gallows.

"And just as you have Mr. Crump fighting on your side, we all need Jesus to advocate for us on that last day. Because only He can forgive us entirely, owing to the atonement that His death and resurrection accomplished for us. We are all weak and helpless, David. Just as you are now, considering everything that has happened. But just as you asked Dr. Turner for his help, and you permitted Mr. Crump to represent you, you must ask Jesus for *His* help — for His forgiveness — and submit yourself to Him. Allow Him to represent you in that heavenly court we will all one day face."

David stared at Isaac in amazement. He'd never heard Jesus described as a mediator before. He knew God was a judge — he'd heard enough of Dr. Markham's preaching on Sunday to gather that. But listening to how Isaac had explained everything, it was as though David were hearing the truth for the very first time.

Silence settled over the two friends, and as David turned his gaze to stare out of the velvet-curtained window, he silently asked Jesus to plead his case before God, thirsty for His mercy and forgiveness.

For His grace.

CHAPTER 43
CORDELIA

The next day, Grace sighed as she tucked the eiderdown around Miss Withers, whose suspected chill had developed into a full-blown cold.

Miss Withers half-sat, half-reclined in her bed, sipping the warming blend of ginger, lemon, and honey that Grace had prepared for her. She hadn't eaten anything for breakfast or luncheon, but she was still consuming liquids, at least.

"I do wish you would permit me to send for Dr. Turner," Grace said, levelling a serious gaze at her employer.

Despite her weakness, Miss Withers responded in her typical fashion. Waving her hand, she shook her head. "I am quite all right. It is only a, a—" Miss Withers sneezed with such force that it reignited the coughing fit from which she had just recovered.

"Indeed you are not!" Grace chided gently. "Will you not permit me to put both our minds at ease and send for the doctor?"

"David said that as long as I rested, all would be well."

"David said a great deal of things. They were not all

accurate, though, were they?" Grace instantly regretted voicing her bitter thoughts.

"Oh, Grace..." The congestion in Miss Withers's voice did nothing to obscure the notes of pity in which she spoke.

"I am sorry, Miss Withers. I do not mean to disrespect you or your family."

Even though he thought nothing of disrespecting us.

A few silent moments passed, and Grace believed Miss Withers to be falling into a sleep until her weary voice poked the air. "Grace, dear?"

"Yes?"

"Have you... read his letter yet?"

Grace stilled for a moment. She smoothed her skirts absent-mindedly. "I have not, as yet."

"But you do... *plan* to... do you not?"

Grace found herself giving Miss Withers the same response she had given to Beatrice the day before, when she'd arrived shortly after David's departure to find a sullen Grace agonising over whether to even keep the letter or not. "There is little to be gained from going over old history."

"Ah, but that is where you are wrong, my dear."

Grace looked quizzically at Miss Withers, but the old lady only smiled weakly and pointed toward her bureau.

"Could you fetch something for me, my dear?"

"Of course. Is it more of your medicine?"

"No!" Miss Withers gave a strange, grim laugh. "In fact, it is one of the most bitter pills in existence."

The woman was making little sense. Perhaps she had a fever.

Oh, if only she would permit a visit from Dr. Turner.

Miss Withers pointed again. "In the bottom compartment of the jewellery box."

Grace opened the lid of the shiny rosewood box, inlaid with delicate swirls and patterns around each of its edges.

She carefully moved aside compartments full of sparkling jewels until she could see the bottom tray inside. Deftly, she reached in and retrieved an old piece of paper, folded and bearing a red wax seal.

Time had made its presence known within the darkened edges and creases of the page, and Grace was almost afraid to hold it a moment longer than necessary, lest she damage it irreparably.

Gingerly, she handed it to Miss Withers, then took her seat again on the side of the bed.

Miss Withers sighed. "Grace, dear..." She paused, a mournful air seeming to wash over her. "This letter ought to have changed my life. I can only hope that after I have shared it with you, that you will allow it to change yours."

Bewilderment filled Grace. How could an antique letter written by someone she didn't even know change the course of her very existence?

Miss Withers reverently unfolded the letter, her eyes dancing across the lines inside. She rested her head back on the pillow behind her, closing her eyes with a melancholy sigh.

"Miss Withers?"

Grace stared in amazement at the single tear rolling down the lady's cheek, which was as creased and timeworn as the page in her hands.

"Read this, Grace," she said, her red-rimmed eyes fixed on her. "Then, you will understand."

"Very well..."

Grace took the letter that Miss Withers offered to her and drew a deep breath.

"*Dear Cordelia...* Cordelia, that is a lovely name," Grace said, interrupting herself.

Miss Withers smiled and nodded, motioning with her hand for Grace to continue.

Grace read aloud.

Dear Cordelia,

I can bear it no longer. We love one another, and my only desire is to share my future with you.

My father still insists upon my marrying one of the Delacourt sisters, but I have told him, time and again, that the only young lady I will marry is you.

Of course, he still refuses to acquiesce, and has tried many times to manipulate me into giving you up, but I cannot.

Promise me that you will not give me up, either. I know your parents are as set against us as mine, but they do not know our hearts. You and I were made for one another, Cordelia. I ache with loneliness when I am not with you.

If you feel as ardently about our future as I do, then meet me at the station next Thursday at noon. If our parents will not permit us to be man and wife here, then we shall away to a place where no one can stop us from binding our lives together, just as my heart is irrevocably bound to yours.

Come with me, Cordelia. Be my wife, and we shall live in peace and harmony for the rest of our days.

Forever yours,

Samuel

She turned to look at Miss Withers, whose face bore an expression with which Grace was all too familiar, of late.

Sorrow.

"Who is Samuel?"

Miss Withers sighed. "He was the young man who loved me. The young man whom I loved. Our parents refused our pleas to permit us to marry. Samuel's father had arranged a match with a wealthy heiress, and my father always wanted me to marry the son of his closest friend, but…" Her voice trailed off as she shook her head gently.

"Did you go away with Samuel?"

Regret and resignation washed over Miss Withers's face. "No."

"What happened?"

"He wrote that letter to me, and I wondered for days what to do. One day, I decided to go. To leave everything behind and run away with him, never to return. But then, I questioned myself, wondering if I might have been blinded by the folly of infatuation. I questioned if our love was real, if it was a love that could endure." Her chin quivered. "In the end, I did not go. He wrote to me again, telling me how devastated he was, and begging me to meet him at the same place the following week. He was determined to give me another chance."

Grace listened in captivated silence.

Miss Withers exhaled a shaky sigh. "But I was too much of a coward again. And on the second meeting day, as he waited for me, a highwayman came upon him. Samuel had gathered a fair bit of money for us — money that we would need for building our life together." She swallowed hard. "There was a struggle… and they took it from him. I heard he was badly beaten, but I never saw him again. His parents moved away, and I…" She shook her head, her face crumpling.

Deep compassion inundated Grace. "Oh, Miss Withers."

Regaining her composure with evident effort, Miss Withers dabbed her eyes with a handkerchief, then fixed her eyes on Grace with alarming intensity. "I know that David did wrong. But if you love him, and he loves you, then permit nothing to stand in your way. Every day, I regret not meeting Samuel that first day he'd arranged for us to elope. Every day. I do not wish either of you to live with such agony."

Blood thundered in Grace's ears as she took in Miss

Withers's words. Was that really what awaited her, if she was to disregard David's letter? A life of regret and sorrow?

No. Samuel had never lied to Miss Withers. But, David? He had deceived them all.

It was not the same thing.

Miss Withers had suffered a tragedy.

The only tragedy Grace had endured was meeting David in the first place.

CHAPTER 44

MR. CRUMP

David looked around at the imposing rows of leather-bound spines standing as straight as soldiers on the numerous bookshelves. Mr. Crump's office looked more like that of a scholar than a surgeon.

The heavy wooden door opened, and a man completely opposite to the one David had imagined shuffled in. What was left of his hair was white and wispy, and his protruding abdomen and slow gait gave David the impression of a reluctant man who had been called upon to walk somewhere after ingesting a heavy meal.

The man reached his desk chair and dropped into it, its wood groaning under his weight. "Dr. Carbury, a pleasure to meet you at last." He nodded. "And this is?"

David cleared his throat. "This is my good friend, Mr. Isaac Taylor. And it is a pleasure to meet you, too, Mr. Crump. Though, perhaps, not under these circumstances."

Isaac and Mr. Crump exchanged greetings.

Mr. Crump grunted. "I assure you, Dr. Carbury, I have met many others in much worse." The man's voice was gruff, and when he pushed his lips together after speaking, his nasal exhalation was remarkably loud and long-lasting. "Dr. Turner informed me that he conveyed my hopefulness for a positive resolution of this case. That still stands. The hearing now upon us is a short one, but it will determine whether or not you are to stand trial. It may come to that, depending on who presides over you today. But even if it does go to trial, do not be dismayed. There is more evidence to assure the judge of your innocence than of any negligible or intentional wrongdoing."

David swallowed, his tight throat growing more dry by the second. "If the evidence is so favourable, then why is it that the case may still go to trial?"

"Formality and favour, more than anything." Mr. Crump leaned forward with visible effort. "Some magistrates imagine themselves to have a certain reputation to uphold. Snider, for instance, is known as one of the meanest men ever to walk London's streets — no matter how obvious your innocence, he'll send you to the judge just because he can. Norris is rather more lenient. Too much so, if you ask me. I am quite convinced he overlooked key evidence that led to a murderer walking free last year. Milborough is somewhere in the middle, depending on his mood. If any of us could deduce what made his mind swing so wildly, we might be able to stop it from doing so." He shook his head, rolling his eyes. "There are others, all with their own unique quirks and foibles, as every man in England is wont to possess."

"And who is hearing my case today?" David glanced nervously at Isaac.

"We shall find out when we enter the meeting room." He scooped a gold pocket watch out of his waistcoat and squinted at it. "We ought to make our way there now," he said, hauling himself to his feet. He gestured to the door. "Gentlemen."

In a sombre procession, David followed Mr. Crump. Isaac

was close behind him — a comforting presence. As they wound their way through the chilly corridors, David's heart beat swiftly, echoing an anxious rhythm with his footsteps as he traversed the black and white chequered floor.

Finally, they stopped outside large double doors. Mr. Crump placed his large hands on the doorknobs, and swung the doors open to reveal a humourless room, all straight lines and symmetry.

Mr. Gibbs was already present, as were two men whom David had never seen before. One of them bore a striking resemblance to Mr. Edwards — a sight for which David was thoroughly unprepared. His blood ran cold. *That must be his son...*

Memories of his own father skimmed through his mind. Sympathy buckled his heart. He knew what it was to lose a father. Only, in his case, he was in no doubt of the circumstances surrounding his father's demise. He knew there was no one to blame. For Mr. Edwards's son, however...

A warm, firm hand clamped down on David's shoulder.

"Pray, David. God will help you through this."

Isaac's encouragement brought his earlier words on the train back to David's remembrance, which seemed to alter the whole atmosphere of the room.

David nodded, a calm resolve settling in his heart.

God was with him.

Silently, he prayed for strength, and that God would guide everything that would be said and decided in this influential room.

David, Isaac, and Mr. Crump all sat down, and a trim, tall man strode in behind them, settling himself at the desk which had been laid out facing their own. His jet-black hair was perfectly styled, and his piercing eyes glanced at each of them in turn before lowering to the papers that lay upon his desk.

“Which one is he?” David asked in a whisper, leaning closer to Mr. Crump.

Mr. Crump glanced at David out of the corner of his eye and sighed.

“Snider.”

CHAPTER 45

UNFOLDING THE TRUTH

Grace stared at the still unopened letter from David that she'd tucked behind the clock on the mantelpiece in her room last week.

Perhaps, she ought to read it. What harm could it do?

But as she turned away in anguish, she chided herself. She knew exactly what harm it might do — it could very well reignite the tenderness toward him that she'd succeeded in burying under duty and distraction as she'd tended to Miss Withers during her illness.

Now that her employer's symptoms were improving, Grace had a little more time to herself in the afternoon, during Miss Withers's restorative naps.

Picking up her Bible and trying to force the letter's presence from her mind, Grace settled into the bright, cosy armchair in front of the fire and flipped through its well-worn pages.

She read a short psalm, then skipped to a different portion.

After a few minutes, she sighed. No matter which book or chapter she scanned, one word kept confronting her.

Love.

Her gaze drifted to the letter, its silent presence growing louder and louder in her heart with each passing second.

Ever since Miss Withers had shown her the letter from Samuel — and so vividly expressed her own regrets — Grace had been growing more and more aware of how deep her feelings for David truly ran.

In a flash, she left her chair, dashed toward the fireplace, and snatched the letter up. Her finger stroked David's handwriting on the envelope, her heart stirring as she stared at her name written in his own careful script.

After only a second's hesitation, she cracked open the seal and gently tugged out the page from within the envelope.

Her pulse quickened. She could never unread it once she had consumed its message. Was she really prepared to live with the knowledge it contained, whether good or ill?

With trembling hands, she unfolded the letter. Three pages of scrawled words stared back at her.

Drawing in a long breath, she began to read.

Dearest Grace,

I have searched in vain for words to convey my message with the depth of solemn regret that fills me. Permit me instead to relay to you first the facts — the events which led me to Lindenfell. And to you.

My friend (or former friend, as he is now), Augustus Moss, and I are both physicians in London. We work together, sharing patients. Or, at least, we did.

One of our patients, a Mr. Edwards, came to us initially for what he believed to be a minor complaint, but which turned out to be quite serious indeed. I shall not expound upon every medical detail, but the end of the matter was a tragic one. He died, even though his condition was one that I had treated previously (though with a relatively high death rate, all the same).

One of the ways in which I assisted Mr. Edwards was using chloroform as a sedative, in conjunction with his other medications, and indeed, in order that he would have the ability to consume the other ones at all. Chloroform, though slowly coming into common use as a calming agent and as an anaesthetic for surgery, is a substance of which most physicians still disapprove, owing to questions and debates regarding its safety. Mr. Edwards agreed to its use but, owing to his untimely death, his family hold me squarely responsible, believing the chloroform to have poisoned him in his already precarious state of health.

Augustus then betrayed me, taking the family's side, severing our practice and our friendship.

The Edwards family have employed a lawyer and are seeking to charge me with Mr. Edwards's death.

I know the whole matter is alarming, but I assure you, Miss Stratton, that I am not to blame for his death at all. He was not in good health, and his body was simply not strong enough to endure the effects of the cholera from which he suffered.

The chloroform was not to blame.

I was not to blame.

No doubt, you may struggle to believe me after everything that unfolded on the day of my aunt's garden party, but I can only hope that you will discern that I am telling the truth.

Facing such serious charges — which could carry fatal consequences, depending on the conviction, if any, that I receive — I fled from London, taking refuge in Lindenfell under my cousin's name, purely to gain time to think of how I might prove my innocence in the matter of Mr. Edwards's death.

Instead, I became truly guilty of a horrendous charge — lying to you. I did not expect to find you in my aunt's home, and your early suspicions caused me no end of distress. I am truly sorry for leading you to believe that you had been in error when you asked if I was, in fact, David. I longed to tell you the truth, and I have nothing to plead in my defence in that regard.

I should have been honest with you, and with my aunt, from the very beginning.

You may notice that I called you Grace at the beginning of this letter. I do not wish to offend you by taking such a liberty, for I know decorum bids me address you as Miss Stratton, but I wish for you to know how deeply embedded you are within my heart.

I made so many mistakes during my time in Lindenfell. So much of what I did was wrong and hurtful.

And the worst of all, to me, is the fact that I hurt you. It was never my intention to do so, because — as you may have surmised during our conversation in the carriage — I love you, Grace.

I admire you, no longer secretly, but openly, and unendingly.

It is agony to me that the best and the worst of Lindenfell is you — the best, because I never expected to encounter such a gem, and the worst, because I did not treat you as I ought to have.

Truly, I am sorry, Grace. I am sorry for all of it. All of the deception, and the pain and sorrow it has caused you. I do not deserve to even ask for your forgiveness.

All I can hope for is that you will understand these two things — that I deeply regret my actions, and that I love you more than I can say.

I know not what awaits me in London. Depending on the outcome of the hearing and possible subsequent trial, my name and reputation may be restored, my life may meet its end, or something betwixt the two extremes may occur.

Whatever happens, please know that if I could return in time to my first arrival in Lindenfell, I would have told you and my aunt everything, throwing myself upon your mercy.

And I would have lingered in the carriage on that fine Tuesday afternoon, relishing the sound of your voice and your laughter, confessing my love for you in person.

I am sorry, Grace. I cannot find adequate words to express precisely how sorry I am.

And, I love you. I only wish I had chosen the right path, for how wonderful our lives — nay, our life, together — might have been if I had. Oh, how bitterly I have wept at the thought.

I am deeply sorry, my sweet, precious Grace.

Yours in truth and admiration,

David Carbury

Grace sank slowly onto the armchair, holding the letter in both hands as though it were made of thin, fragile glass.

So many revelations. So many words she had never expected to find within its pages.

He was sorry. He truly was.

And he was in danger — wrongly accused. It could cost him his life.

And he loved her. Had loved her for some time — maybe even as long as she had loved him.

Tears of distress blurred her vision and rolled down her cheeks.

She wiped her eyes and glanced at the top right corner of the letter.

It was there — his address in London.

She must write to him. At once.

She blinked away the tears as she sped to her desk, fumbling for the accoutrements required to prepare a letter of her own.

Her heart wrenched. What a fool she had been! Judging him without knowing all the facts. Holding a grudge against a man whose very life could be at stake.

Why had he returned to London, given the danger awaiting him there?

Grace gasped. The hearing. Hadn't he mentioned a hearing to Miss Withers the day he told them he was leaving?

Trembling overtook her. He'd been gone for five days now.

The hearing... had it already taken place? Had all been decided?

Clutching her quill with a shaky hand, she smoothed the already flat page and touched it with the freshly inked nib.

Dear David...

David. How much better his real name suited him than the name John. And how accurate Beatrice's description had been of her memory of them as children — David, the more serious and demure of the two, and John, the merry-making popinjay.

What might Grace have said, if David *had* told her the truth? Would she have doubted his innocence? Or would his honesty have deepened her bond toward him?

She remembered the look in his eyes as he'd handed her the letter. Such resigned grief, yet such burning anguish. Her heart ached at the thought of it.

...love covereth all sins.

How wrong she had been — expecting perfection from him, when he didn't even profess to know the Lord.

She paused, staring at the page on which she had written his name.

He didn't profess to know or obey God... but she did.

And she'd done a dreadful job of representing Him.

David had seen from her only anger and offence, only self-focused hurt and steely, distant silence. Yet how had God treated *her*? With compassion and understanding, with selfless love and glad, joyful closeness.

Grace buried her face in her hands as she asked God for forgiveness. A forgiveness she knew He offered freely and fully to all who would ask it of Him.

Even those who'd asked for it many times before.

Pain pricked at her head. The fervour that had seized her upon reading the letter had transformed, settling into a deep-seated resolve.

She sighed, weariness and sorrow mingled together within it.

Her mother could always detect Grace's precise mood just by hearing her sigh. She'd told her once that it was one of the blessings that had come about through the pain of her earlier life. God had brought Ruby's own years of sighing to an end, and now she could empathise with others as they endured the various trials and tribulations of life.

How Grace wished her mother — and father — were here with her now. They always advised her wisely, always operated with compassion and justice.

Justice.

A chill washed over Grace as she remembered David's words.

...my life may meet its end.

Fear clutched her heart at the thought.

"No... Please, Lord, do not let him be convicted, not of this. Please convict him only of his need for You. And please... give me wisdom regarding what I ought to say in my letter."

She lifted her quill, and issued a long, deep breath.

Dear David,

Thank you for your letter. I am terribly sorry to hear of all your difficulties, and I want you to know that I am sorry, too, for how I treated you when I discovered your true identity. I failed to live up to my name, and for that I am truly sorry.

Please know that I forgive you, and that I do not hold any of it against you in any way.

I pray that you will turn to Jesus, and that He will help you through this terrible ordeal.

She paused, conflicting thoughts stirring within her as she wondered how to respond to his declaration of love.

Her father had cautioned her multiple times against forming an attachment with someone who did not share her faith.

"How can you truly become one with a person if you are not walking in agreement regarding the most important aspect of your life?"

That's what her father had said.

And she knew he was right.

Besides, Scripture said so, itself. And Grace had always held strong convictions that she could never marry someone for whom God was not their ultimate priority.

Yet, could she really say that she had been living as though the very same thing were true about *herself* of late?

No.

It hadn't been. She knew that now.

But she also knew that she wanted it to be.

Maybe that's what had been missing lately — the real reason she'd been so restless and discontent. She had allowed other things to creep in and take the place in her heart that ought to be reserved only for God.

After praying further, she stared at the letter, torn between doing what she knew was right and what she wished was right.

She loved David.

As much as she had tried to deny it and forget it, she loved him.

But she could offer him no hope on that front. Not now.

More pressing than his wish to love Grace was his need to love the Lord.

She must encourage the latter before she could, in good conscience, address the former.

I pray that He will spare you, and that the resolution of all these proceedings will require nothing that might take away your life, or even your profession.

I cannot even imagine all the dreadful thoughts that must be engulfing your mind at present, and indeed have no wish to heap further distress upon you, but I would not be acting in your best interests if I neglected to warn you of the gravest danger in which you stand.

We all need forgiveness for the wrong that we have done. And it is to be found only in Jesus — in His sacrifice on the cross, upon which He bore our sins and cancelled them, and in His resurrection, which procured eternal life for us when He defeated death once and for all. I may not be explaining it all too well, but I urge you to find a Bible, and to read about it all in the gospel of Luke.

The man who wrote that account was a physician himself, and therein he presents a very clear and orderly account of the most important events in history — events which, depending on how we respond to them in the present, shall impact the future state of our souls for all eternity.

Peace settled deep in her heart, though her turmoiled thoughts constantly attempted to uproot it.

That was enough to say for now. She could offer nothing more at present.

I am praying for you, and I would be grateful if you could find any time to write to me and let me know the outcome of your hearing.

Yours with Christian love,

Grace

She briefly read over all that she had written, then set about addressing an envelope and nestling the letter within it.

As she grasped the letter with both hands, she wept and prayed once more, her heart declaring the words she'd restrained herself from writing.

I love you, too.

CHAPTER 46

THAT WHICH IS BEST

David wearily climbed the freshly swept steps of his townhouse, unlocked the door and trudged inside.

Isaac followed him. "David, this is a splendid home!"

Home. Somehow, the word didn't seem suitable anymore. The well-known furnishings were still in their familiar arrangement, but a decidedly unfamiliar sensation resonated within him.

Mere weeks before, this had been a place of comfort and ease. Now, it held neither.

Andrews, his butler, was not there to greet them. Just before leaving for Lindenfell, he'd put the faithful servant on paid leave. But the sharp metallic clang of a kettle from belowstairs indicated the rest of the servants were tending to their usual duties.

David shuffled toward the mustard armchair and flopped onto it, covering his face with his hands.

Isaac settled himself in a chair opposite. "I am sorry, David. I had hoped that today would have put an end to it all."

David sighed, lowered his hands, and leaned his head back against the top of the armchair. "As had I."

"Mr. Crump still seems certain that you will avoid the worst, though. That is encouraging, at least."

"He also said that he thought the case would not even go to trial."

"Depending on the magistrate."

David sighed. "I suppose."

Mr. Crump had been right about Mr. Snider. David only hoped the man's assurances of optimism regarding the final outcome of this whole sorry ordeal were not misplaced.

"Have you heard anything from Miss Stratton yet?"

David's heart plummeted. "No. In truth, I do not expect that I shall. She was rather clear, even without words, in conveying to me how deeply I had betrayed her."

"I am sorry, David."

David shrugged, hoping his friend wouldn't realise how devastated he truly was. "She deserves better, anyway."

"What do you mean?"

David snorted. "Could you really picture her caring for *me*?"

"Why, yes! I could see something in the way that she looked at you. A tenderness... an *affection*."

"Surely that was before she discovered that I had been deceiving her, and before I revealed the depths of the quagmire in which I am trapped at present!" David shook his head. "No... She deserves a respectable gentleman. Not someone whose very name is connected with scandal and suspicion."

"But you apologised. And you have God on your side now. Do not fret, my friend. He will help you."

David frowned. "As He helped me today?"

Isaac's mouth dropped open. "He *did* help you today, David. I saw it with my own eyes."

David raked a hand through his hair in frustration. "He answered my prayer that anxiety would not overwhelm me, but I asked for His help with the main issue, too." He turned his gaze away from Isaac's earnest countenance. "I do not even know if He heard me," he said bitterly.

"Of course He heard you — you said yourself, He eased your anxiety. Besides, He is not some sort of genie, David. He does not exist only to grant our every whim and wish."

"It is hardly a whim to wish to remain alive, Isaac!"

Isaac raised his hands in a calming gesture. "I know that, my friend. But do you not see?" He bit his lip, appearing deep in thought for a moment. "When you have a patient in your care, do they understand everything that you do for them? All of the measurements and prescribed cures, all of the tests you must undertake... Do you always do precisely what they wish you would?"

David sighed. "No, of course not."

"And why is that?"

David set his jaw. He knew where this argument was going.

"Why is that?" Isaac repeated.

"Because I must do that which is best for them."

"Precisely."

Loath as he was to concede to his friend's logic, David's shoulders slumped. He nodded in weary agreement.

Silence stretched through the room.

"How could going to trial be what is best, though? I am not guilty. Yet I continue to be treated as such."

"I do not know..." As he settled himself more comfortably in his chair, Isaac sighed. "Perhaps the delay will allow for more compelling evidence to be gathered, evidence that will more clearly support your case and show beyond a trace of doubt that you are not to blame. Or, perhaps the extra time will permit the Edwards family a chance to rethink taking action against you in the first place."

David shook his head. "How is it that your outlook on everything is always so unswervingly positive?"

Isaac looked down, exhaling abruptly. "I assure you, that is not the case. If you could see the man I was shortly after my sister died, you would hardly recognise me now. It is only time and prayer and holding fast to the truth of Scripture that has enabled me to heal. To find hope again. I have truly seen God do miracles. I never believed that, after Emma died, I would be able to truly *live* again, laugh, enjoy food — simple things that I had always taken for granted. Everything was so bleak. So dark. Nothing made sense anymore. But, the more I reached out for God's help, the more I found it — the more I found *Him*. I shall never forget the night I surrendered to Him, David. What a relief it was to be free from all the guilt and sorrow I had carried around for so long." He shifted in his chair, his countenance animated. "There is a verse — in the Bible — which says that those who trust in Christ become new creations. Entirely new. The old — gone. The *new* has come. That is *exactly* what happened to me that night. I suppose most people might not see it as a miracle, for they could not see how lost and hopeless I was before it. But I could. And, until my last breath, I shall declare it to be so."

David smiled, despite his heavy heart. Isaac's words had woven in the room an atmosphere of such peace and rest that he languorously rested his head against the back of his chair and closed his eyes.

New creations...

He thought back to when he'd prayed on the train, surrendering his own heart and life to Jesus.

Perhaps I have been unjust in my complaint about you, Lord. I am sorry. Please, help me to trust in You. And help me to have peace about the trial, even though I do not understand why everything is not yet resolved. Show me, Lord — why am I so discontent?

With piercing clarity, the answer instantly flashed into his mind.

He had been focusing on the wrong viewpoint entirely. Instead of being grateful for the miracle of forgiveness, as Isaac had spoken of, David had instead been ungrateful that God had not acted in accordance with his own wishes.

How presumptuous he had been, thinking he knew better than God.

David squeezed his already closed eyes even more tightly shut.

Please, forgive me Lord for thinking that I know better. I willingly admit, here and now, that I do not. Help me to be content — no matter my circumstances. No matter the outcome of all that lies ahead.

As he opened his weary eyes, the familiar surroundings seemed a little more welcoming. And, he knew that no matter what lay ahead, there was one thing he could depend upon that would never alter.

God would be with him and would always do what was best.

Even if it wasn't always what he would choose himself.

CHAPTER 47
TO GO

A few days later, Grace had just finished pouring Miss Withers a cup of tea when Higgins entered the drawing room.

"A letter for you, ma'am."

Grace glanced up, alarm draining through her. Could it be from David?

The footman offered Miss Withers the silver tray, and she picked up the letter with an alacrity that Grace was relieved to see returned. Her employer's cold had mostly resolved itself, though a lingering cough still marred the lady's days and nights.

"Thank you, Higgins."

As Higgins left the room, Grace held her breath, praying that Miss Withers would open it immediately and share its contents with her.

"Ah, I believe it is from David. Oh, I do hope everything has been resolved..."

Grace's heart and stomach seemed to flip simultaneously. "What does it say?"

Miss Withers looked up knowingly at her. "Oh, my child... Come, sit by me. Perhaps, you might read it to me. I—" Her words broke off into a cough. She handed the letter to Grace, motioning for her to open it.

Grace's fingers trembled as she broke the seal, pulled the page from its enclosure, and unfolded it.

A swift glance at the bottom of the page confirmed her hopes — and fears.

"It *is* from David."

"Read it, child. Aloud."

Grace drew a deep breath, trying to force some strength into her voice.

Dear Aunt,

I am sorry to say that — "Oh!" — *that my hearing was not successful. We met with a frightfully strict magistrate, who has a long history of insisting upon a full trial for nearly all of the matters which pass into his hands. As a result, my own case is to be tried in a little under two days. My adviser, Mr. Crump, and my lawyer, Mr. Gibbs, have been working together and hold some measure of confidence that I may be found innocent, though, I confess, I do not share their optimism.*

I shall endeavour to write with further news once I have any, or if I am not able to write myself, I shall entrust the task to Mr. Taylor. He has been a true and faithful friend to me, and I fear that I shall never be able to repay him for all the kindness he has shown to me.

I trust that your symptoms did not develop into a cold, or anything more serious. Please do write and let me know how you are. I think of you — and Miss Stratton — daily, and I pray that you are both in good health.

Please, give my greetings to Miss Stratton, and tell her again how sorry I am for hurting her. You are very blessed to have such a loyal and faithful companion, and I know that she is blessed by your company, too. I miss you both, and I only wish that I could have enjoyed your company more fully and honestly while I was there. I am truly sorry for all the confusion and upset that I caused you both.

Thank you for forgiving me, Aunt. I shall always endeavour to be worthy of your kindness.

Your loving nephew,

David Carbury

Grace blinked back the tears that pricked her eyes and swallowed hard, fighting against the lump aching in her throat.

His case was going to trial. And, if the judge declared him guilty, he could be—

She squeezed her eyes shut, her imagination casting horror after horror into her mind's eye.

"Poor David," Miss Withers mused. "I had hoped that it would not come to this. Though, it is encouraging that his advisor and his lawyer believe it will turn out in his favour." She sighed. "We must continue to pray that all shall be resolved well, and soon."

Grace opened her eyes and nodded.

"Oh, Grace, will you not read his letter? It might lend you some comf—"

"I have read it."

Miss Withers's eyebrows lifted. "You have?"

"Yes," Grace croaked.

"And?"

"And he apologised. And he... he declared his feelings toward me."

"Oh, Grace! But that is glad news, is it not?"

"It... It is complicated, Miss Withers."

"But how?"

Grace lowered her head, searching for words to make sense of her conflicting thoughts. She sighed. "I have always wished to marry someone who follows God. Who truly follows Him — not merely out of formality, but out of faith. Genuine faith. David... he does not. I do not believe he had even set foot inside a church since he was a boy until he came here." She drew a deep breath. "I love him, I do... but I cannot go against my conscience on the matter. Nor against Scripture itself. I am praying for him, not only for his legal situation, but also that he will fully surrender to the Lord. In true faith. Only then could I inform him, in good conscience, that I return his affections."

Miss Withers sighed. "I believe you are right about his lack of church attendance. But are you sure that he has no faith? I am old enough to have discovered that not everyone who attends church every week is truly a Christian, nor is everyone who does not attend regularly always entirely without faith."

Grace sighed. "I agree wholeheartedly with the first. I have seen many hypocrites in my father's church — those who attend merely out of tradition, not out of any desire for truth." Grace paused. "I wish he were still here. David, that is. I wish he and I could discuss matters of faith together, that I might gain a better understanding of his beliefs — or indeed, if he has any at all."

"You ought to write to him, perhaps. Begin a dialogue by letter since you cannot do so in person at present."

"I have written to him. Though I suppose I only told him things. I did not ask him anything about his own thoughts and beliefs. I should have." She buried her face in her hands. "Oh, why do I keep doing everything wrong?" She lowered her hands. "Honestly, I have been more and more convicted of late of my *own* shortcomings and follies. I wish to represent God well, but I feel that all I do is appear cold and pointed toward the very people to whom I wish to be compassionate and gracious!"

"There, now — you are being much too hard on yourself, child. You do not appear cold at all. You have been very kind to me."

Grace sighed, grateful for Miss Withers's words yet not remotely comforted by them.

The drawing room door opened, and Beatrice bustled in past the footman and his extended arm.

"Beatrice!"

"Good morning, Grace. Good morning, Miss Withers."

Miss Price followed Beatrice into the room.

As everyone greeted one another, shame coloured Grace's cheeks. She had completely forgotten it was the day that Beatrice and her aunt were due to visit.

A few minutes later, after Beatrice and her aunt had settled into their chairs and Miss Withers and Miss Price were engrossed in a conversation about their ailments, the drawing room door opened again.

Higgins strode across the room, the silver tray in his hand once more. As he approached the small company of friends, he stopped beside Grace and lowered the salver toward her.

She glanced at the envelope, expecting to see the penmanship of her mother or father. She frowned. The handwriting was entirely unfamiliar to her.

"Thank you, Higgins," she said, not hearing Beatrice's chatter as she prised the letter open and hastily unfolded it.

Dear Miss Stratton,

I do hope you will not object to my writing to you, but I feel that I must convey something to you on Dr. Carbury's behalf. Though, I must confess — he knows not that I am writing to you, and I imagine he would try to stop me from doing so if he had any notion that I was planning to do so. However, I feel that it is in his — and your — best interests for me to write. And so, here is what I feel I must say.

Recently, I had the pleasure of sharing the gospel with David, and I am delighted to say that he has genuinely placed his faith in the Lord. Do pray for him, as he is still quite new to it all, but already I can see a great change within him, entirely for the better.

I know that his actions during his time in Lindenfell were very painful for you, and I do not wish to make light of them in any way. I only wish to assure you that he truly regrets his deception, and that his feelings toward you are as constant as any man's could be.

Here we come to the reason for my writing to you. I know that David wrote to you before he left, and I know that it would be a tremendous encouragement to him if you were to write, in turn, to him. I also suspect that you share his affections, and I wish to emphasise the limited time he may have to learn of this fact. His advisors are certain that he will not be convicted, but David's hope is at a low ebb. Even with his newfound faith, the pressure and strain that this whole situation is placing upon him is something he is finding more difficult to navigate than I believe he wishes to admit. As is his hope to be reconciled to you, I believe.

Forgive me if I am rambling, Miss Stratton. Letter-writing is not something with which I have been gifted. I suppose I am sending this because I wish to convey two hopes — one, that you might be assured of David's newly-gained faith, and two, that you be left with no uncertainty that he loves you and is genuinely sorry for hurting you. I wish to share both these assurances, in case either has been a hindrance to you, keeping you from forgiving him or confessing your feelings toward him in return.

If I have written anything offensive, then I implore you to please forgive me, and dispose of this letter as you see fit, in the knowledge that I am truly sorry to have misspoken. But if, however, anything I have written has been helpful to you, then I beg you — please write to David before it may be too late. His trial fast approaches, and while his lawyer believes the outcome will be favourable, there still remains the chance that it may not.

Yours faithfully,

Isaac Taylor

P.S. Please give your friend Miss Beckwith my deepest regards.

"Grace?" Beatrice's voice worked its way into Grace's consciousness. "Is it from your parents?"

Grace gaped at her friend. "He... he has turned to the Lord, Beatrice!"

"Who has?"

"David!"

"David? *He* sent you the letter?"

"No... Mr. Taylor—"

"The letter is from Mr. Taylor? Mr. Taylor wrote to you?" Beatrice's eyes widened.

"Oh, Beatrice, I must tell him... I must."

"Tell him what?"

Grace could hardly breathe. "That I love him!"

"You love Mr. Taylor?"

"No! David!"

"Oh!" Beatrice placed a hand on her chest and heaved a relieved sigh. "Well, then... you ought to write to him." She nodded thoughtfully, still evidently regaining her composure.

A stream of thoughts assailed Grace's mind. Memories and ideas, questions and daring solutions.

Come with me, Cordelia.

The words from Samuel's letter echoed loudly in Grace's ears, magnifying in their scope with each passing second.

Grace stood abruptly, barely aware of the three sets of eyes fixed upon her. "I must go."

Beatrice frowned in confusion. "Go where?"

Grace gulped. "To London. To the trial. To... to David."

"What? You cannot go to London all by yourself! Why, it is not safe!" Miss Price sputtered, her tone aghast.

Grace fixed her eyes on Beatrice. "Come with me. It will be safe enough if the two of us go together."

Beatrice's mouth dropped open, excitement dancing in her eyes.

Grace turned to face Miss Withers, her heart hammering. "If you need me to stay with you, I shall. But, if you will permit me to—"

"Go." Miss Withers nodded slowly. "Do not make the same mistake that I did."

Gratitude surged in Grace's chest as she bent down and embraced Miss Withers. When Grace released her, Miss Withers fixed her with a look, through tear-brimmed eyes, of poignant understanding.

Blinking back her own tears, Grace turned. "Come, Beatrice. We must ready ourselves. We have not a moment to lose!"

Beatrice leaped to her feet with a delighted giggle.

"Beatrice!" Miss Price exclaimed, her tone dripping with disapproval.

"Do not hinder them, Edith. They shall journey together, then meet with David and his friend, who will ensure their continued safety. All will be well."

Grace cast Miss Withers a look of gratitude as she and Beatrice strode toward the door.

Reaching the hallway, Beatrice grinned at Grace. "Oh, it is all so exciting! And so romantic!"

Grace exhaled deeply. Exciting and romantic, yes.

But it was also terrifying.

As she and Beatrice hurried upstairs to pack some of Grace's things, she silently prayed that God would help them find David and Isaac without incident.

And that she would be able to tell David she loved him before it might be too late.

CHAPTER 48
GRACE AND PEACE

The mid-morning rays streamed through the lace curtains, bathing his two advisers in warm light. From his seat on a sofa by the drawing room wall, David squinted as he observed them, somewhat daunted by the array of books and papers spread out before them on the little round table in front of the drawing room window.

"Now, then. Here, I believe, is our strongest piece of evidence," Mr. Gibbs said, shuffling through a substantial stack of paper and thrusting a sheet toward the other man.

"No, no, Mr. Gibbs, the testimonies from the various physicians and surgeons to whom I have spoken — those are surely our strongest hand to play," Mr. Crump retorted, punctuating his sentence with a long, loud nasal breath.

"Hand to play, indeed! This is a highly delicate matter — not a game of cards at some provincial tavern!"

"Gentlemen, gentlemen..." Isaac interjected as he approached them, raising his hands and looking imploringly at Mr. Gibbs and Mr. Crump in turn. "We are all working toward the same goal."

A few more grumbles erupted before the two older men

settled into a more amiable discussion. Isaac watched them for a moment before lowering his hands and approaching David.

As Isaac plopped down beside him, David groaned slightly.

"You still could not sleep?" Isaac asked.

David shook his head, stifling a yawn.

"But, David, it is above a week now since you have had a full night's sleep. And, I mean you no offence by saying this, but you look as though you have not slept in over a year!"

David noticed the hint of alarm that widened his friend's eyes upon seeing him more closely. "I tried. I did." He sighed. "My body wishes to sleep, even now. But my mind... it is like a prison guard — on constant patrol to prevent such a thing from happening." He smiled sardonically.

"Letter for you, sir."

"Thank you, Andrews."

David smiled at his butler, grateful that the man had returned to his station so promptly upon hearing of his return.

Andrews nodded and left the room, glancing with no small interest at Mr. Gibbs and Mr. Crump before doing so.

David had almost become immune to receiving letters from strangers. Most wished to ask him about the case or accuse him of unrelated charges. Some offered their support, and some were vital communications from some figure of authority, conveying what he and his advisors must do or provide at each stage of the proceedings.

As he opened this letter and saw its composition, a thought flashed into his mind. A thought he'd only recently managed to suppress after much inward wrestling.

His eyes darted to the signature at the bottom of the page.

Grace!

She had written to him.

Trembling crept into his hands.

As he read her words, his heart beat faster and faster as he neared their conclusion.

When he reached the end, he paused, then read it all again.

With a sigh, he folded the letter and held it firmly in his hands.

"Good news?" Isaac asked.

"Yes... It is from Grace." David's heartbeat slowly returned to its typical pace.

"It is?" Isaac shifted in his seat to face David more fully. "Well, that is wonderful! What did she say?"

David closed his eyes momentarily as he relished the words. "She forgives me."

"Oh, David, that is splendid!" Isaac hesitated. "Did she say anything... else?"

Sorrow squeezed David's heart. He must be grateful for what she *had* said — not disappointed by what she had not.

It was harder than he'd anticipated. "No..."

Isaac's face fell. He examined David's. "Are you all right?"

David nodded. "I confess, I had hoped that she might... return my affections. But, if she does not, then..." He shrugged, sorrow stealing his words. "I am truly grateful that she has forgiven me, though. That is a comfort. Especially if—"

"Now, David. Mr. Gibbs and Mr. Crump believe that you shall come through this and be vindicated. Do not trouble yourself with thoughts of what most likely will not come to pass."

David nodded, thinking of Grace. His throat seemed to burn, and he could not speak for a long moment. "I wish I could see her again. I truly wish that I could speak with her one last time."

"David!"

"No, I know you believe that all will be well. And, it may be. But it also may not. And if that is the case, I must take comfort in the fact that, though she does not love me, she does not hate me." He nodded slowly. "That is good to know, at least. Another blessing in the midst of... everything else."

Isaac's brows knit together, his expression a blend of pity and determination. "You shall see her again. When this is all over — and you have been vindicated — we shall return to Lindenfell, to Careo House, and you shall celebrate with Miss Stratton, and with your aunt. There is joy ahead, David. I know it."

David forced a smile. Dear Isaac — he was always so encouraging, so optimistic. But he could not allow himself to be distracted by his friend's kind words. He must be practical. Realistic. The truth was that only God knew what lay ahead for him now.

And God would be with him, whatever the outcome might be.

David sighed. He must be grateful for Grace's kind words of forgiveness. But he must not permit any more of his energy or attention to be fixed upon her. He would not see her for some time, if at all. There was much to be done in the meantime — much that was required of him here in London.

Perhaps, he would see Lindenfell once more.

Perhaps, he would not.

Either way, he had the Lord on his side, and despite the disappointment and sorrow that mingled in his heart knowing that Grace did not return his love, he knew that the Lord's peace remained within him and could not be removed.

As Mr. Gibbs and Mr. Crump droned on in the background, David leaned his head back and closed his eyes. Just before he fully drifted into a light doze, he saw, in a dream, a familiar face smiling at him.

Grace...

CHAPTER 49
LONDON

Grace stifled a gasp as she disembarked from the train. The station was enormous — it seemed larger than the whole of Lindenfell.

"I cannot believe we are in London!" Beatrice gushed at her side.

"Nor can I."

This time yesterday, they were at Beatrice's little cottage, packing a suitcase of her belongings after they'd finished packing one for Grace at Careo House. Now, they were standing on the platform of a London station, about to embark on quite a different kind of journey than the one that had brought them there.

"Come, we must find lodgings for the evening. Then, in the morning, we shall travel directly to David's address."

Her voice hid well the nervousness rattling within her heart. Throughout the entirety of the train journey, when Beatrice's happy chattering hadn't held her attention, Grace had rehearsed what she might say to David.

There had been no time to waste — not when his trial was to take place in little over a day. She hadn't even had the time to write, to warn him that she and Beatrice were about to burst upon his and Isaac's company.

She only hoped they would be welcome.

A smile flourished within her. The man had declared his love for her — of course he would welcome her.

Still, anxiety clawed at her stomach.

"Do you have the name of the street that my aunt mentioned?" Beatrice asked.

"Yes. Vine Street. Oh, look — there is a cab. Come, we must see if it can take us there."

A few minutes later, they were clattering over the cobbles inside the carriage, having given the driver the name of the street to which he was to take them.

Beatrice smoothed her skirts. "Do you think... Mr. Taylor will be... pleased... to see me?"

Grace took in the expression of shy hope on her dear friend's face and smiled in encouragement. "I am sure he will."

Beatrice sighed. "At least you are certain of David's affections. I must own that it is terribly disconcerting that..." Her voice trailed off as she frowned and bit her lip. "Oh, Grace, forgive me. I do not mean to be so selfish when there is so much at stake with—"

"You are not being selfish at all." Grace shook her head and waved a hand. "I would feel entirely the same were I in your shoes." She gave a short laugh. "I still find that I am more nervous than I can say at the thought of seeing David, despite knowing what he has said in his letter, and what your Mr. Taylor told me in his."

Beatrice rolled her eyes. "He is not *my* Mr. Taylor." Her lips tugged at the corners.

Grace smiled, despite the anxiety roiling within her. "I believe he will be, before long."

Beatrice lifted her brows. "As I believe you shall be Mrs. Carbury."

Grace's smile faded as she fought off dismal thoughts of what might become of David the next day. "I hope so..."

Beatrice gave her a quick embrace.

The carriage pulled to a stop a little sooner than Grace had expected.

"Vine Street, miss."

"Oh! Well, thank you very much."

The driver helped them both down, and Grace slipped a coin from her purse and handed it to him.

He tipped his hat. "Cheers, miss."

As the cab sprinted away, Grace and Beatrice examined the buildings on the narrow, cobbled street on which they found themselves.

"Number twenty-two, my aunt said?"

"Yes. This one is fourteen, so it must be down this way..."

The two young ladies picked their way carefully through the grime and stench of the little street.

"It smells horrid!" Beatrice exclaimed.

"Yes," Grace said, her nose crinkling. "Oh! Here is number twenty-two."

She wrapped the door with her gloved knuckles and waited, trying desperately not to breathe too deeply.

The door flew open, causing Grace to jump. A skinny, bedraggled man with wildly disarrayed hair and long stubble peered inquiringly at her as he scratched his bare neck.

"Excuse me, but is this number twenty-two?"

It cannot be.

"Yes. Who's asking?" The man spoke with a thick Cockney accent, suspicion audible in his voice.

"Forgive me, but my friend and I are in need of lodgings for the evening. We were told that a Mrs. French lived here and had a room available."

The man scoffed and spat on the ground. "She ain't lived here for years, love. And I ain't got no spare room, even for the jammiest bit of jam like you..." He leered at Grace, repelling her even further.

"Oh. I am sorry to have bothered you, sir."

"Sir," the man chuckled. "Not often I get called sir, I tell ya!"

Grace forced a polite smile before turning away, catching sight of a confused-looking Beatrice a few paces away.

"Hold up, love."

Grace froze, grimacing inwardly as she turned back to face the man. "Yes?"

"If it's rooms what you want, I've seen lodgers come and go from that house there."

Grace turned, following the direction in which the man's finger was now pointing, and saw a house on the other side of the street with a blue front door and a faded wooden sign above it.

She looked back at the Cockney man. "Thank you very much."

He nodded, still watching her as she turned to rejoin Beatrice.

"He said that Mrs. French moved away years ago, but that the house across the street might have a room."

Beatrice's eyes reflected the disappointment and apprehension in Grace's heart, but she simply nodded. Without a word, the two picked their way across the street.

The house was decidedly less shabby than number twenty-two had been, and three relatively clean steps with iron railings at either side led up to a blue front door. The faded wooden sign that Grace had noticed while standing on the pavement opposite was still too obscure to read now that she was closer, but she thought she could discern some mention of ales and pies. Whatever it was, she was certain it was old enough to not have any bearing on its current use.

Grace gripped the iron railing with her lace-gloved hand, the chill of the metal working its way into her fingers with icy persistence. She ascended the steps, then rapped the door knocker with affected confidence.

As she awaited a response, Grace drew a deep, crisp breath. A sudden gust of wind encircled her neck with a cold draught, but the shudder that passed through her had little to do with the weather.

The door opened to reveal a respectable-looking older gentleman. His large stature and twinkling eyes made him seem to Grace like a merry giant. Upon seeing her, he raised his brows in surprise, then grinned warmly.

"Good afternoon, young lady. May I help you?"

The man's voice was deep and rich, and his accent indicated he'd had a more refined upbringing than the man across the street.

"Good afternoon. Yes... My friend and I require lodgings for the night. We had been directed to number twenty-two, to a Mrs. French, but there was a... *gentleman* there who informed us that she had moved away. He suggested that we ask you, instead, as he mentioned that you regularly take lodgers...?"

Her voice trailed off into a question as the seeming hopelessness of their situation grew in her awareness.

"Why, you have arrived at precisely the right moment. I had a short-term lodger who left about two hours ago, so I do, in fact, have one room available."

"Oh, splendid," Grace said, glancing at Beatrice in relief.

"It is only the one night you require it, you say?"

"Well, I imagine it may be for a few nights... I am not entirely sure at present. Is that all right?"

"Of course!" He stepped aside and motioned to Grace and

Beatrice. "Come in, come in, out of that cold. My, the temperature seems to be dropping by the hour! There is a nice warm fire inside — you may rest beside it whilst my housekeeper prepares the room for you."

"Thank you, sir."

The man smiled pleasantly and bowed at each of them in turn as they made their way inside.

He guided them to a parlour with rich red wallpaper and a luxurious, warm rug lining the centre of the floor. Brass and mirrors shimmered in the glow of the firelight and candlelight, and Grace could have happily spent the whole night curled up in one of the inviting armchairs beside the fire.

"What a lovely room," she said to the man.

"Thank you, miss. I shall have Nora bring you both some tea in a moment. Might I just take your name and where it is that you have travelled from?"

The man opened one of the drawers in a bureau to the right of the fireplace and pulled out a brown leather journal. He lifted a quill and swiftly inked it before turning back to Grace and Beatrice. "For my records, you understand."

"Of course..."

Grace hesitated, her mother's warnings coming back into her mind. What she would say if she could see her now — in London, and in a stranger's home.

Grace shook her head, swatting away the unpleasant worries. "Miss Grace Stratton."

"And Miss Beatrice Beckwith. We have travelled from Lindenfell."

The man stared at Grace, his lips parted slightly. He blinked, then fixed his gaze on Beatrice. "Lindenfell, you say?"

"Yes."

Grace's heart raced. Why had he looked at her like that, brief as it had been?

There is nothing to fear, you silly girl. You are here with Beatrice, and this man has a housekeeper and a maid... You are safe enough. Besides, tomorrow you shall be reunited with David, and as Miss Withers said, he will, without question, ensure that no harm will come to either of you.

"Lovely. Well, why don't the two of you make yourselves comfortable, and I shall send Nora in with some tea for you. Warm you up after being out in the cold, eh?"

He flashed a twinkling smile at Beatrice, who thanked him as she returned it.

"And you are? Mr...?" Grace's heart hammered as she awaited his response.

"Oh, how indecorous of me, I am sorry. Mr. Milvern, at your service."

Relief washed through Grace.

Milvern. It is not the same man.

She nodded politely as he bowed at them, then watched him stroll out of the room.

Slowly, she lowered herself onto the armchair facing the one Beatrice had tucked herself into.

"He seems a lovely gentleman," Beatrice said. "What providence to find such a place!"

Grace released the anxious breath she hadn't even realised she'd been holding. "Yes..." She considered Beatrice's words and nodded. "You are right. If the man across the street had not suggested that we try this house, we would never have discovered it on our own, and we might have had to walk all over the place trying to find somewhere to stay." She shuddered. "I am very glad we do not have to do *that*, at least."

Beatrice nodded. "You are thinking of your mother's warnings, of all that you told me on the train?" Her voice was hushed, even though she and Grace were the only two in the room.

"I cannot help it. All my life, she has wished for me to stay as far away from London as possible. I am still amazed she permitted me to come here once, long ago, with my father. She would be terribly worried if she knew I was here again now."

"But that dreadful man is still in prison, surely? And it was a very long time ago."

"Possibly… I do not know. But my mother suffered such cruelty at his hands. She has not spoken to me of half of it, I am sure. I suppose, even though he is either still in prison, or too old now to do anyone harm, he still seems a threat owing to how monstrous he was to her, and for how long."

Beatrice nodded sombrely. "I cannot even imagine..." She shook her head, a mournful expression on her face.

Grace shifted her gaze to the dancing flames in the fireplace. She exhaled quietly, grateful for her mother's rescue, yet feeling guilty that she was in the very town to which she'd been so concerned about her going.

A few moments later, a maid brought in some tea, presenting it to them with such warm smiles that Grace was soon ashamed of her earlier suspicions.

This seemed a safe and pleasant establishment, indeed. Beatrice was right. It was clearly God's providence that had led them here. He was with them, looking after them.

And tomorrow, at the trial, He would look after David, too.

CHAPTER 50
ENCOURAGEMENT

David's butler strode into the drawing room, the small square salver he used to deliver the post raised aloft in his right hand. "A letter for you sir."

"Thank you, Andrews."

David instantly recognised the swoops and flourishes of his aunt's hand. Then, he noticed the postmark across the red stamp, its date indicating that it had only been posted the previous day. Concerned about his aunt's health — and Miss Stratton in general — David tore the envelope open impatiently.

As his eyes scanned the words, a frown gathered on his brow.

"Is something the matter, David?" Isaac stood near the window. Muffled sounds of carriages and conversations drifted up from the street below.

David couldn't help letting a smile creep onto his face. He finished reading and lowered the letter. "She is coming, Isaac!"

"What? Who?"

"Grace... My aunt says that she and Miss Beckwith left

yesterday for London. She enlisted Miss Price's help to post this letter without delay, in order to encourage me by letting me know. They shall be present for my trial." He exhaled in surprise. "She is coming! What do you think that means?"

"Miss Beckwith?" Isaac blinked a few times in rapid succession, then seemed to take in the rest of David's sentence. "What does it mean? Why, it is obvious. Miss Stratton wishes to support you. It shows that... that she cares for you."

David's heart swelled with hope. He laughed abruptly. "I suppose it does... Isaac, I cannot believe it — she is coming!"

For the first time in as long as he could remember, the smile on his face reached all the way inside.

Grace would be there. Supporting him.

Loving him?

No. He must not place his hopes there. Perhaps, she was trying to console him somehow — prove that her forgiveness was genuine. He must not expect anything more, despite how much he wished to.

"And, Miss Beckwith, too?" Isaac settled onto the chair opposite David.

"Yes..." David smiled again, remembering his conversation with Grace in the carriage about secret admirers and the attraction that seemed to be present between Isaac and Beatrice.

"I shall have to do my best to find out."

That's what he'd told her.

"Without telling him about Miss Beckwith, of course?"

He could still remember the earnest entreaty in her eyes as she'd uttered those words in response.

"Of course."

Perhaps that was one thing he could do for her now to prove his own remorse. One way he could keep his word, after the many ways he had broken it.

"Isaac...?"

"Yes?"

"Would I be correct in my assumption that you are... looking forward to Miss Beckwith's arrival?"

Isaac ducked his head, moving his lips in a rapid succession of unspoken speech. "Wh—"

"You care for her, do you not?" David chuckled.

Isaac's features relaxed. "I do." He sighed, a small smile playing on his lips.

"I thought so." David observed his friend, picturing his and Miss Beckwith's engagement, then wedding, then everyday contented married life. All the milestones he had hoped to share with Grace.

He sighed. All that lay before him now was uncertain at best, and—

No. He must not dwell on things that were not in his power to change. Even if the worst outcome came about, it would not matter for very long. God had accepted him, forgiven him. If his time on earth was soon to be over, at least he could face eternity with confidence, owing to the redemption he'd been given that he knew he did not deserve.

"She is always so... joyful," Isaac said, a short chuckle escaping him. "So gentle and friendly. Truly, Miss Beckwith... *Beatrice...* is a delightful young lady. I have admired her for quite some time. Since I first came to Lindenfell and met her, in fact."

David nodded, pushing away his gloomy thoughts like cobwebs in an alleyway. Tomorrow was unavoidable, whatever its outcome. But, today, he still had his freedom, and a friend to whom he was closer than anyone, even though they'd only known one another for a short time.

He silently thanked God for Isaac. He had done so much to help him. Now, it was David's turn.

"Isaac, you ought to tell her."

Isaac's gaze searched the room as he seemed to consider David's words. "I… It would be terribly awkward if I was to do so, only to discover that it was… unwelcome news to her."

"Unwelcome news? Isaac, I have seen how she looks at you. You, and no one else. It is obvious. She regards you with no small measure of affection."

Isaac's eyes widened in hope. "Truly? You believe so?"

"I *know* so." His heart ached as he remembered Grace's unwitting admission of Beatrice's feelings, and how worried she had been about betraying her friend's confidence. "Trust me. She cares for you. A great deal."

A smile of amazement slowly spread across Isaac's face.

"Tell her," David said. "And always be truthful with her."

David turned his gaze to look out of the window, a bitter taste rising at the back of his throat.

If only he could turn back time and take his own advice.

CHAPTER 51

A FRIGHTFUL DELAY

"Oh, we are going to be late, I am sure of it!" Grace rifled frantically through her portmanteau and tugged out her second-best shawl. "Of all the mornings to spill tea on oneself at breakfast!"

"Grace, calm yourself," Beatrice's soothing voice floated through the room. "We have time enough, yet."

They'd passed a cosy and quiet night in their room at Mr. Milvern's boarding house, and the time of David's trial was close at hand.

"But we still have to find a cab and actually travel to the place, and when we were leaving the breakfast room, the clock said—"

"I know what it said. Do not worry. We shall be there on time, I assure you. Now... Is that better?"

Grace finished shuffling the shawl around her shoulders and pinned it in place by affixing the cameo brooch her mother had given her the day she'd left Shiloh Hall. She stroked it absent-mindedly, hoping her parents would have the chance to one day meet David.

"Yes, I am ready."

She wondered for a moment if she had lied.

Ready? She had never been so nervous.

She could hardly imagine how David himself must feel at this moment. Squeezing her eyes shut, she offered a silent prayer.

"Oh! I am sorry — I left my reticule in the breakfast room! I shan't be a moment..."

Beatrice hurried out of the room before Grace could respond. She sighed, holding her face in her hands. They were certain to be late now.

Less than a minute later, the door latch clicked open.

"Beatrice, there truly is no time to del—"

Grace looked up, expecting to see Beatrice. Her stomach flipped.

"Mr. Milvern."

He stepped into the room, closing the door behind him, an intense gaze fixed upon Grace the whole time.

Grace's heart picked up speed. "May I help you?"

Mr. Milvern chuckled — a self-satisfied sound, devoid of humour. "Oh, you already have, my dear."

Grace clenched her jaw to keep it from trembling. "I do not understand your meaning, Mr. Milvern..."

The man grinned.

A horrid, leering grin.

"Oh, you will."

CHAPTER 52

PROCEEDINGS

David clenched his hands as he waited for Isaac's return. The day of his trial had arrived, and he sat with Mr. Gibbs and Mr. Crump in the enormous hall of the court building, which was eerily silent, save for Isaac's approaching footsteps.

And only Isaac's.

David's heart sank as his friend came into view. Alone. "Still no sign of them?"

"No..." Isaac shook his head, his lips pursed in sympathy. "I am sure they have only been held up on their journey here. Delayed on the road, perhaps. They will arrive soon enough, I am sure of it."

David nodded politely, though his heart and mind believed the opposite of Isaac's words.

She wasn't coming.

His aunt had misunderstood, somehow. Perhaps she had written in a fit of delirium — she *had* appeared to have been falling ill the day he left Lindenfell, after all.

It had been folly for him to believe it could be true.

He'd read Grace's letter — the words of her own hand. She hadn't mentioned anything about coming to London.

Hadn't indicated that she had any feelings toward him at all, other than regret for her prolonged silence and initial unforgiveness.

"Time to go in, gentlemen," Mr. Crump said, hauling himself to his feet. "Do not worry, Dr. Carbury — all shall be well."

"He is right. I am sure of it." Isaac's eyebrows rose in affirmation. "The sooner we go in, the sooner you shall be able to lay this whole sorry situation behind you and move forward with your life."

David nodded, though more out of duty to his friend than in agreement with his sentiments.

The three men made their way down the silent corridor. David hesitated, turning back to Isaac after motioning for Mr. Crump to wait a moment. "I am sorry... But might you check one last time?"

Isaac glanced at Mr. Crump, who waved an impatient hand and nodded.

"Quick as you can, boy."

Isaac bolted away from them, his absence seeming somehow to heighten the sense of loneliness that wrapped itself around David's shoulders.

You are not alone. God is with you.

No matter what, He will see you through.

David closed his eyes for a moment as he asked God, for what seemed the hundredth time that morning, to bestow strength and courage upon him.

Footsteps bounded into his awareness.

David opened his eyes, something deep inside him clinging to hope that, this time, Isaac would not return alone.

But as he saw the expression on his dear friend's face, he knew that no one else was about to follow him around the corner.

No one else had come.

Isaac shook his head grimly. "I am sorry, David. I am sure there is a good reason why they are late."

"Come now, we really must proceed!" Mr. Crump said, his pudgy cheeks reddening.

David placed a grateful hand on Isaac's arm, then turned and followed his advisor into the room where his earthly fate would be decided.

By a complete and utter stranger.

CHAPTER 53

TRAPPED

Grace stared in horror at the man towering in front of her, reeling at his unsettling words. What had been a comfortable boarding room mere moments ago now felt like a claustrophobic jail cell.

"You mean, you... you..."

He chuckled, his eyes glinting cruelly. "That is correct. Had you fooled, did I not? Even though the names sound so much the same..."

Blood thundered in Grace's ears.

She had to get away from him.

She had to get as far away from this hateful man as she could, before—

"You look so much like your mother... I could not believe my eyes last evening when you appeared on my doorstep." He chuckled again, the most unnerving laugh Grace had ever heard. "Can you imagine? Why, it is almost as though it is meant to be."

"You deceived me, Mr. Millforte. And I will not stand for it."

"No... I expect not... I expect you had better sit down,

Miss Stratton." Another so-called chuckle that made Grace's skin crawl.

Panic rose within her. She knew some of what he'd done to her mother. Was that what he intended to do with her?

Bile rose in her throat as she glanced around, desperate to find some way out other than the door which was now blocked by his monstrous frame. Even though he was evidently in his seventies now, his expansive stature and agile movements made him seem as strong as an ox and as ready to pounce as a jaguar.

"I must leave," Grace said. "I am late for an appointment. A very important one."

"*Leave*? Oh, but there could be no appointment more important than *ours*... It is about time for us to become better acquainted, don't you think? Ours is a meeting that is well overdue."

Grace grimaced. His sinister tone repelled her. How was she ever to get past him?

Help me, Lord. Oh, please, help me!

Millforte sauntered toward her, and instinctively Grace moved backward.

He grinned, as though it was all some kind of game to him. "Now, Grace... Do you really think you can get away from *me*?" He emphasised the last word of his question with a mocking smile.

Grace glanced from him to the door and back again, hoping she'd done so quickly enough that he wouldn't have noticed.

She darted forward, her eyes fixed on the door, her mind willing her to reach just a little farther—

Vice-like pressure squeezed her arms, flinging her backward.

Pain jolted her as she collided with the wall.

She gasped for breath. "Ah!"

"Oh, no, no... Do not think that you will succeed like your mother did. Her and your prig of a father." Millforte sneered, hissing an oath under his breath.

"My mother and father..." Grace's defence trailed off into violent coughing as pain coursed through her side where it had impacted the wall.

"Do not even speak of them!" Millforte bellowed. "I spent *years* in prison because of them and their little set-up."

"Set-up? You were guilty of far more than that for which you were arrested!" Her strength was returning, the pain growing more tolerable.

Millforte's cold eyes glared at her. "I would wager, young lady, that you do not even know half of what I am capable of."

A chill shot through Grace.

How could she get around him? How—

The door opened, and Beatrice froze as she saw them both at the far side of the room.

"Ah, Miss Beckwith, how lovely to see you this morning. I urgently require a private interview with your friend, though. Perhaps you might—"

"Run, Beatrice! Get help! It is him — it is Millforte!"

Beatrice's expression turned from confusion to consternation. "Grace?"

Millforte moved forward.

"Go, Beatrice! Get help!" Grace screamed. She lunged at Millforte, aiming to knock him off balance, but as she collided with him it was she who lost her footing. The man was as solid and unmoving as the walls that encased them.

He whipped his head around and glared at her.

Grace glanced at the doorway just in time to see Beatrice flee.

Her heart surged with hope, then crashed in terror as Millforte's hand closed around her arm.

"She may return at her leisure, but she will not find you

here, my dear. Oh, no... I have somewhere very special for you."

Weakness washed over Grace. Whatever happened, she must not permit herself to be removed from this room. The city was enormous, and if Beatrice returned with help, there would surely be no hope of anyone finding Grace unless she remained precisely where she was.

Help me, Lord. Show me what to do!

She yanked her arm away from him, desperate to loosen his grasp, but she was trapped.

As trapped as her mother had been all those years.

Pity and sorrow roiled within her.

"Come. We have much to share."

His leering smile and intimate tone made Grace realise that he didn't just mean conversation. There was no doubt he had a very different definition of sharing in his sick, twisted mind.

"No! Please!" In vain, she continued to tug her arm away from him, to no avail.

He laughed, a cruel cackle this time. "Oh, Grace... You really ought to learn from your mother's mistake."

"The only mistake my mother made was trusting you in the first place!"

He growled, tightening his grasp on her arm. He yanked her roughly. "You have no idea what I have in store for you, young lady." He sneered the words close to her ear, his breath cascading across her face and neck.

Grace fought an urge to vomit.

He started pulling her toward the door, and no matter how intensely she dug her boot heels into the floorboards and tried to wrangle her arm away, she was powerless to stop him.

She remembered her great aunt Abigail telling her about

the time Grace's father had been pushed down the stairs by Millforte. He'd almost died. All to protect her mother.

There was no way she had the strength or ability required to have a hope of pushing Millforte down the stairs.

But one thing was clear, whatever else might occur...

She must not leave this room.

CHAPTER 54
AN UNEXPECTED OUTCOME

"Did you see the *look* on Mr. Polkinghorne's face?" Isaac asked a third time, breaking into peals of laughter once again, filling the court building's hall with echoes of mirth.

The trial concluded, David watched his friend as though observing a dream, his mind reeling from all that had occurred within the courtroom.

"Capital result, my boy!" Mr. Crump grasped David's hand and pumped it up and down, breathing noisily through his nose the whole time.

"What stellar timing for the testimony of the Scottish doctor, was it not?" Mr. Gibbs asked. He couldn't have looked more pleased if he'd been the witness himself, David thought.

"Are you all right, David? You have not said a word!"

David allowed himself a tentative smile. "I… I cannot quite believe it. I expected we would be here for hours. But, in less than one, it is all… done."

"And now you can move forward with life, eh?" Isaac smiled warmly.

David shook his head slowly in disbelief, reliving the sequence of events in his mind.

Mr. Edwards's family's legal representative had spoken first, and the more he had, the more evident it had become that their case had no real foundation. The two witnesses whom he had called to the stand, whose testimonies he'd hoped to use to secure a conviction, had been Mr. Edwards's wife, and Augustus.

A chill passed over him as he recalled the man with whom he had once shared a vibrant medical practice glaring unflinchingly at the judge as he'd spouted spurious inaccuracies, all in a vain attempt to further his own career by ensuring that David's would flounder.

But, the few words that Mrs. Edwards had uttered had seemed to contradict the very foundation of the case.

Augustus had begun to look worried.

And, rightly so.

When Mr. Gibbs had taken the stand, he'd read a testimonial he hadn't even mentioned to David during their morning meeting. A respected Edinburgh doctor had written to express his unwavering confidence in both chloroform's safety and necessity, noting that his own practice had been using it continuously for over a year with no fatalities whatsoever. More and more doctors were relying upon it, he'd said, and while a few patients seemed to suffer adverse effects, the majority of reports lauded it as safe and beneficial.

Further, Mr. Gibbs had spoken to a coroner, who had intricately described the post-mortem findings that supported the more likely cause of Mr. Edwards's death as being the cholera, not the chloroform.

The Edwards side had all turned positively pale as the contents of the letter and the coroner's report had been read aloud, and Isaac's theory about them being driven by grief rather than facts seemed to have been validated.

The judge had then given the decedent's family one last

chance to retract their charges, and with drooping shoulders and weary sighs, they had.

Much to Augustus's chagrin. He'd squeezed his hands into fists, flashed a defiant look of scorn at David, then stormed out, pale and piqued.

A myriad of memories and emotions swirled in David's mind like a whirlpool. It was all still too much to take in.

"Gentlemen, a pleasure to see you all," Mr. Gibbs said with a smile, his eyes gleaming with satisfaction. "Though, I do hope that we shall not be required to meet under such circumstances in future, you understand."

"Indeed. Thank you, Mr. Gibbs," David said, extending his hand to the man. After shaking both his and Mr. Crump's hands and thanking them both, he found himself alone with Isaac in the hall which had previously seemed menacing in its sombre enormity. Now, it was merely part of a building, and all that towered over him was grateful relief.

He silently thanked God — again — for the favourable outcome.

They came to the end of the corridor, passed through the main hall, and stepped outside.

"Well, I say we go and find something to eat, and celebrate this wonderful day."

David smiled at his friend's eager words. "That sounds—"

Footsteps and screeches interrupted him, jolting into his awareness with sickening terror. His darting gaze settled on a woman's figure, rushing toward them with an expression of terrified frenzy on her countenance.

"Miss Beckwith!" Isaac exclaimed, darting forward.

David squinted. It couldn't be...

"Help!" she shrieked.

The word, and the distress in which she uttered it, gripped David's heart with fearful urgency. He started forward, glancing about for Grace.

Who was nowhere in sight.

"Miss Beckwith, what is the matter?" Isaac asked, grasping her wrists with care as he caught up to her.

She looked as though she'd been running for her life.

David's throat burned. "Miss Beckwith, what is the matter? Is Miss Stratton with you?"

At the mention of Grace's name, Beatrice's face crumpled in terrified sorrow. "Oh, Mr. Taylor, Dr. Carbury, he *has* her!"

"Has her? What do you mean? Who has her?" Isaac asked, stroking Beatrice's wrists, his brow furrowed in concern.

David held his breath.

Beatrice shook her head as though she hadn't even heard Isaac's questions. "He has her now! Oh, she never should have come to London! Her mother was worried this would happen, and now it has!" Tears poured down her cheeks. "He means to do her harm, I know he does! You must come at once! We must help her, somehow!" She shook as she spoke, her sobs growing hysterical.

David's stomach lurched, his head spinning. "*Who* has her? Where *is* she?"

Please, Lord, keep her safe.

"Where is she?" David repeated, his voice distorted by panic.

Isaac pulled Beatrice toward him, embracing her and speaking gently in an attempt to calm her. He looked at David, a fear in his eyes that intensified David's own.

"Miss Beckwith, please, tell—"

"We took a room last night on Vine Street. We must get back there immediately!" Beatrice gasped out the words between sobs.

"David, hail a growler, or an omnibus. Now."

David blinked at his friend, then launched into a long stride toward the road. Once on the kerb, he tapped his foot impatiently, struggling to stand still as he waited for a carriage-for-hire to roll into view. Isaac and Beatrice caught up to him.

Finally, David spotted a horse-drawn vehicle.

He jumped into the street, waving his arms frantically. "Stop! At once! Please, stop!"

The approaching growler slowed, the bewildered driver eyeing David warily. "Summit the matter, gov'ner?"

"Please — take us to Vine Street. At once!" David turned and waved Isaac and Beatrice over. He launched himself into the carriage, his breathing rapid and erratic.

"Calm down, mate... I'll 'ave you there in no time, don't you worry."

David tapped his foot impatiently, his whole body on edge. Were he somehow able to be transported instantly to Vine Street, he still could not arrive there quickly enough.

Isaac helped Beatrice into the carriage, then climbed aboard himself.

"Go!" David shouted, forcefully punching the roof twice in quick succession, though the driver had already nudged the horses into motion.

"Miss Beckwith, please — who is it that has Grace?" David's throat burned as he spoke, his entire being consumed with anguished impatience.

"The man..." Beatrice's voice faltered. "The man who kept her mother all those years."

David froze, an eerie sensation creeping over him. "*Kept* her *mother*... what do you mean?"

Beatrice wiped her eyes and drew a deep, shaky breath, evidently attempting to compose herself. "Grace's mother... She was kept in a brothel for years by her uncle — a horrid man who treated her more cruelly than we can even imagine. Grace's father rescued her, and the man was sent to prison — we believed he might still be in it." Her face crumpled. "This same man has Grace now."

David's vision clouded over, and he clutched the edge of the seat.

Kept in a brothel. Treated cruelly.

What kind of man could even fathom doing such a thing to a woman?

David's blood ran cold.

The man with whom Grace was presently alone.

CHAPTER 55

DESPERATE MEASURES

"Wait!"

Grace looked frantically around the boarding house's bedchamber, hastily assessing every vase and trinket to ascertain if there was anything heavy she might use to defend herself.

She shuddered at the realisation that she and Beatrice had slept here last night. How trusting — and vulnerable — they had been.

Millforte paid no heed to Grace's frenzied plea. He lunged at her and she ducked under his arm, fear quickening her steps.

"Wait! Look!"

He paused, turning to face her.

She gulped, her mind scrambling to think of some ploy that would buy her some time.

David's face flashed into her mind. Was this the desperation he'd felt? The sense of life-or-death urgency that had compelled him to conceal his true identity?

Anguish echoed within her soul. Had the judge reached the verdict yet?

Were they *both* to lose their freedom this day?

Please, Lord — rescue me from this horrid man, as you rescued my mother. Please help me, Lord.

"What is it, *Grace*?" With a quick motion he grabbed her arm.

Grace stared at the monstrous man as he towered over her, squeezing her arm so tightly that it throbbed.

"Why did you do it?" Her voice was small and hollow.

Millforte shifted impatiently. "Do what?"

"All of it. This life. All the crime, the greed. The... debauchery."

Millforte's eyes glinted with amusement and pride. "Because I do what I like. Don't you?" His grip on her arm loosened ever so slightly.

Grace blinked.

Please, keep him talking, Lord. Make him forget that he is trying to make me leave.

"But why is... all *that*... what you like?"

Millforte chuckled, looking at her as though she were an idiot. "Because it feels *good*." He squeezed her arm again.

"But it is not good."

Millforte rolled his eyes. His grip relaxed a little. "Oh, Grace. Poor, innocent Grace. Your *perfect* father has brainwashed you, no doubt. But you are here now. You will soon find out how *good* it all is." He looked her over salaciously.

Nausea flooded Grace, along with a fresh wave of fear. "But, why?" She could hardly croak the word.

Millforte chuckled. "Pleasure, my darling. What is there to live for, if not pleasure?"

"Everything. And, besides, doing right is not devoid of pleasure. In fact, it is only when we live according to what God has commanded that we can have any hope of true pleasure at all."

He removed his hand from her arm, passing it across his face in exasperation. His teeth clenched more and more tightly the more he spoke. "Spare me the self-righteous diatribe that your mother dared to spout at me!"

Grace remembered. Her mother had told her that she'd spoken of God to Millforte, before Henry and the magistrate had arrived to arrest him. She'd told him about redemption, about the love and freedom that Jesus offered.

A new depth of appreciation for her parents swelled within Grace's heart. They had truly lived out their faith, even when faced with the evil that now stared coldly at her.

"It is true, Mr. Millforte. It is all true."

"We shall see how long it takes for you to change your mind, hmm?" he reached for her arm again, but she skirted out of his way just in time.

"Why, you—"

"No!" she pleaded, darting ceaselessly from one side of the room to the other as she evaded his persistent attempts to seize her again.

"You are only making things worse for yourself — I hope you realise that," Millforte said through gritted teeth as he swiped through the air, grasping for her.

She looked around, searching for something — anything — that would help her defend herself.

Brass glimmered from across the room.

Millforte lunged at her again.

She dashed to the fireplace and seized a large brass candlestick from atop the mantelpiece. Drawing herself up straight, she darted just out of Millforte's reach, then stepped to the side. Gathering all her strength, she raised the heavy metal object high in the air and slammed it into the side of his head with as much force as she could muster.

He staggered sideways.

Her pulse thumping, Grace watched in silent horror as his eyes rolled backward.

He slumped, motionless, to the floor.

CHAPTER 56

FACE TO FACE

As the growler turned off the main street onto a much narrower one, Beatrice began to gesture wildly toward a gleaming house with a clean blue door. "There! That is the house!"

David glanced through the carriage window and thumped the ceiling.

The driver tugged on the reins, and the horses began to slow their steps.

David shouldered the door, opening it while the carriage was still in motion. He stumbled forward as his feet hit the ground.

"David!"

"Oh!"

He barely heard Isaac or Beatrice as he rushed toward the door.

Just as he was about to ram all his weight against it, it swung open and a woman with pale, tear-stained cheeks and dishevelled hair appeared in the doorway.

David lurched forward, throwing his arms around her. "Grace!"

She clung to him in desperation, and he embraced her tightly. He led her down the steps and onto the street, then squeezed her close to himself again. "Grace, are you well? Did he hurt you?"

"I—" Her voice fractured.

Against his own wishes, David moved back, his hands finding Grace's. He squeezed them as he raised their joined hands between them, looking her steadily in the eyes. "Grace, where is the man? Did he hurt you?"

A sinking sensation swept through David's whole body. He'd never seen someone so overcome with trauma.

"Grace—"

"There you are, you wretch!"

Grace yelped, slipping her hands out of David's and darting back from the hulking figure in the doorway.

David stared at the man who had uttered the hateful words. Blood trickled from his left temple. Greying hair crowned a hard face, and his eyes were as cold as a winter's night.

Anger rose in David's chest. This was the man who had tried to capture Grace, having all manner of evil intentions toward her?

How dare he…

Steeling his jaw, David stepped two paces toward the man.

"Don't tell me you are a preacher-man, too?" he sneered, reaching into his frock coat's inner chest pocket and pulling out a pepperbox pistol. He aimed the weapon squarely at David, who froze mid-step, his heart racing.

"No!" Grace screeched, somewhere behind him.

David swallowed hard. He'd seen the damage a gun could do. Had tended to a few patients who'd been injured — or worse — by a bullet ripping through their flesh.

Please, do not let him shoot any of us.

Blood thundered in David's ears. "Set down your weapon and face me as a gentleman!"

A taunting laugh rang out into the crisp air, though the man's features remained stiff with contempt. "Give me back the girl, and you may keep your miserable life."

The man's words hit David like a slap across the face. "*Give* you the *girl*...? I shall *give* no one to you! And she is not a girl, as you say — she is a young lady. A respectable young lady, whom I personally guarantee you shall never see again."

"Oh, no — *really*?" The man chuckled cruelly. "Sounds so much like your father, the sop!" He tilted his head and looked at Grace. "Is he your beau, Grace? Hmm? Like mother, like daughter, eh? Falling for a—"

"Do not dare to address her ever again!" David lunged for the pistol while the man was distracted, clinging to it with all his strength, endeavouring to pull it from his cruel hands.

"How dare you!" Millforte bellowed in his ear, his acrid breath warming David's cheek.

"David!" Grace screeched.

Behind him, all David could hear were two ladies sobbing, and the faint voice of Isaac trying to soothe them.

"Isaac, get them out of here!" David yelled, desperate to look over his shoulder at Grace, but willing himself to keep his gaze fixed on the pistol over which he and Millforte were locked in a terrifying tug of war.

Millforte growled in David's ear. "You shall not win this, boy."

Fresh energy coursed through David's muscles. He tightened his grip on the pistol and threw his shoulder straight into Millforte's chest, sending him crashing into the side of the doorway.

Millforte grunted, then launched himself at David, almost knocking the weapon out of his grasp. David tightened his fingers around the metal and tugged. It didn't budge.

With a frustrated growl, Millforte bashed his shoulder into David with surprising power. David flew backward, landing sideways on the ground.

"All right, boy. Now get out of my way." The brute of a man practically spat the words at him before sprinting down the street.

David glanced in the direction he was headed and saw Isaac, Beatrice and Grace further down the road. Despite their hurry, the cad had already made a considerable gain on them.

"No..."

David scrambled to his feet, half-tripping along the street as he forced his legs into motion in pursuit of Grace's would-be captor.

He'd been fleet of foot once, though it had been a long time since he'd won races as a youth. Surely, even now he could outrun an opponent who was older and heavier than him.

Lord, give me strength.

He focused on the large man in front of him, willing himself to close the gap stretching between them. After a hundred yards he was on his heels.

David launched himself into his back, catching him at just the right moment in his stride to knock him off balance. Millforte's steps faltered, and the pepperbox pistol dropped to the ground.

David scrambled for the weapon, grasping it just as Millforte tried to swipe it from his reach.

"Do not force me to use this!" David heard his voice waver as he straightened up and aimed the pistol at the panting man.

Millforte only smirked — no hint of fear on any of his features. "I doubt that you would."

"I would do *anything* to protect her." David's tone was low, his hands steady.

"Anything? Even something *wrong*?"

The man's taunting words dripped with derision... and delight. Somehow, he was enjoying it all — as though it were some kind of sordid game.

But David wasn't willing to play along.

He stared unflinchingly at Millforte.

"Anything," he repeated.

CHAPTER 57
THE STRUGGLE

David motioned back along the street with the gun. "Over there. Now."

Millforte smirked coldly, seeming to draw out each step for as long as he could.

"Now!" David shouted. He used his left hand to secure his grip of the pistol and straightened his arms as he aimed the weapon at the beast of a man before him.

Millforte grudgingly obeyed, though David's nerves twitched in anticipation, expecting him to strike again at any moment.

For a split-second, David shifted his gaze to glance past Millforte's shoulder, just in time to see Isaac, Beatrice, and Grace disappear around the corner.

Please let me live to see her again.

Millforte launched himself at him and knocked him flying. Still clutching the pistol, David hit the ground. He groaned as pain flashed down his shoulder and back. But he couldn't scramble to his feet before Millforte raised his boot and stamped it firmly down onto David's stomach. The hulking brute sneered and spat at him, then kicked him, and was gone.

David lay in swirling agony, clutching his stomach and rocking from side to side in a hopeless effort to ease the pain.

"Ah... Oh!"

Rolling over, he pushed himself up on his hands and knees and crawled a few inches. A fit of breathless coughing stopped him in his tracks.

"Sir? Are you all right, sir?"

A man's voice came from above him.

"Help..." David rasped.

"Here, sir — can you stand?"

Strong, wiry hands encircled David's shoulders, tugging him up off the ground and onto his feet.

David bent over, his whole abdomen engulfed in hot agony. Slowly, he straightened up.

A man stood before him, eyeing him with surprised concern. "Steady now, guv — you all right?"

"Please... I need your help. The man who did this. Help me catch him."

"Oh, say no more, son. Any mug-hunter that'd leave a gentleman lying in the street in this awful shape ain't welcome around these parts. I tell ya, the neighbourhood's not what it used to be, that's for sure."

David nodded his gratitude as he and the man started down the street, in as long a stride as David could manage. Pain tore through him with each step, but all he cared about was making sure that insolent bully wouldn't get anywhere near Grace ever again.

Turning the corner, David and the man stopped abruptly.

Millforte and Isaac were both rolling on the ground, engaged in a bout of fisticuffs. Grace and Beatrice stood huddled together beside a stout woman in a dusty apron.

"Isaac!" David launched himself toward the struggle. He

glanced at the man who had helped him and pointed at Millforte. "This is the man! Help us!"

"But that looks like... it is! Mr. Milvern?"

At the sound of his alias, Millforte's head jerked around to face the man. "Charlie Wilson — get these ruffians off me at once!"

David and Isaac each pinned one of Millforte's arms to the floor. His legs thrashed and kicked wildly.

"Mr. Milvern?" Charlie glanced from Millforte to David, confusion written all over his face.

"He is not Milvern — he is Millforte! And he is a criminal!" Grace screeched.

Charlie's face paled. "Millforte? That fella what was in prison and all?"

"Yes! And he has not reformed at all!"

Charlie, still wearing an expression of disbelieving dread, moved toward the fray and knelt across Millforte's ankles, pinning them to the ground. "Now what do we do?"

The stout woman put her hands on her hips. "My husband's gone to fetch the constable. He'll be here soon, and he'll sort you all out, see who's telling the truth."

With Millforte a little more subdued, David glanced back at Grace.

She caught his gaze, and the earnest concern he saw in her eyes flooded him with renewed vigour.

He turned back to the man struggling beneath him. "I hope you are ready to spend more time behind bars," David hissed.

Glaring at him, Millforte growled, struggling more furiously against the three men pinning him down.

"What's all this, then?"

David glanced up, relief washing through him as he saw a man in uniform striding toward them.

"Constable!" Beatrice called. "This man tried to kidnap my

friend, and he has a long history of ill treatment toward women — even this young lady's own mother!" Her voice wavered as she delivered her impassioned claim.

The constable grew closer. "Kidnap, eh?"

"And he assaulted me in the street — this man can tell you. He found me in a sorry state and came to my aid," David said, nodding toward the man Millforte had addressed as Charlie Wilson.

"That true, sir?"

"Yeah... And he's a liar to boot! Told me his name was Milvern, he did, but this lot are saying it's Millforte — that fella what the police caught a few decades ago. Big write up about it in the paper, there was. I was just a young lad at the time, but I remember all the fuss. There couldn't have been more talk about him if he'd been Spring-heeled Jack 'imself!"

Isaac pointed to his left, looking up at the policeman. "That's his pistol, too. He drew it on this man," he said, nodding toward David. "I have no doubt he had every intent of using it, until David got the better of him."

A deep chuckle came from beneath them. "I assure you, that pathetic sop could never get the better of *me,*" Millforte said.

"All right, all right. You'd best come with me, Mr. Millforte, down to the station. See what's what."

David frowned. "You cannot release him. You must ensure that he is properly charged and incarcerated. Until he is, he will continue to be a threat to every young lady in London!"

"Leave it with me, son." The policeman raised a brow, and David grew conscious of how dishevelled his appearance must be, and how little his appearance would lend any credibility to his words.

The policeman motioned for the three men to release Millforte.

Reluctantly, one by one, they loosened their grips.

The policeman helped Millforte to his feet, then opened his mouth, but before he could speak, Millforte swung low to the ground.

Like a cat chasing its tail, he drew himself upward again as he circled the rest of the way around, levelling the pepperbox pistol at the paling constable.

"No one moves. Or this man will be the first to die."

CHAPTER 58

NO MORE

Grace froze. She glanced at Beatrice, whose own form was stiff with fright.

Millforte flicked the pistol's barrel upward briefly. "Everyone behind him. Now."

David, Isaac, and Charlie edged toward the policeman, each coming to a stand alongside him.

"I said *behind* him!" Millforte bellowed. He moved the pistol slowly from side to side, pointing it at each of them in turn.

Grace's stomach flipped.

Please do not let him harm any of them, Lord.

"Stay..." Millforte said, as though to a dog learning obedience.

He moved backward, the pistol trained on the small group of men. Changing course slightly, he inched closer, in Grace's direction.

Her throat went dry.

No...

He was closing in, picking his steps with stealth and confidence.

In a blink, he was before her, reaching for her, his gaze still fixed on the men Grace prayed would defeat him.

"Do not touch her!" David yelled, stepping forward.

"Ah, ah, ah!" Millforte said in a sing-song tone, as though scolding a naughty child. "One more step and I pull this trigger."

David's hands twitched by his side.

Millforte seized Grace's arm, and before she knew what was happening, he'd let go of it again. David had launched himself at Millforte, smacking the pistol from his hands.

Millforte punched David in the jaw, knocking him off balance. He grabbed David by his coat lapels and threw him onto the ground.

Millforte knelt over him, placing his enormous hands around David's neck. He clenched his jaw, his face turning red with rage.

David gasped for air as Millforte squeezed his throat.

"No!" Grace screamed.

The two men struggled against one another, rolling and rocking from side to side in each of their efforts to triumph. The other men drew near in search of a way to assist.

A crack split the air, then another.

Suddenly, both men were still.

Millforte slumped down on top of David.

Neither man moved.

"David!" Grace screeched, running toward them.

Who had fired? The others circled the fallen men. The policeman stood chalk white, still aiming his pistol at Millforte's side.

"No..." She turned back to the unmoving bodies and knelt beside them, noticing a red trickle on the ground oozing into a growing puddle.

Blood.

"No! David!"

Grace pushed Millforte as hard as she could, but to no avail.

The policeman and Isaac rushed forward and worked together to drag Millforte's bulky frame off David.

As his form came into view, Grace's heart froze.

Blood stained his waistcoat and surtout, and his face looked horridly pale.

"David? David! Oh!" Grace's whole body trembled as sobs overpowered her. She leaned her head down, listening, waiting for some sign that he was still alive.

She placed her trembling fingers close to his lips.

Breath warmed them.

David's breath.

"He is alive! He is breathing!"

The constable and Charlie rushed over, kneeling beside her. The policeman laid a hand on David's throat while Charlie examined the pool of blood beneath, patting his hands on David's side.

"I don't think that's his blood, miss," Charlie said.

Grace's heart lifted. "No?"

"There is a heartbeat," the policeman said.

David's eyelids flickered. He groaned slightly.

"David!" Grace leaned closer.

He opened his eyes, fixing them on Grace, though seeming to look straight through her. He tried to say something, but a raspy wheeze was all that emerged.

He coughed, clutching his throat.

"David? Can you hear me?"

His eyes found hers again, and this time, gazed right into them. "Grace..." he croaked.

"Are you hurt? Are you injured anywhere?"

David pushed himself up onto his elbows. He paused, then shook his head. "I do not think so... Only my throat a little," he said, breaking off into another cough.

Isaac's voice came from behind them.

"He's dead."

Grace turned to look at him, then followed his gaze to the lifeless Millforte lying a few paces away, staring at the sky with unseeing eyes.

"Oh!" Grace huddled closer to David, shuddering in horror.

Strong arms encircled her, pulling her close into a warm embrace. She rested her head against his shoulder, closing her eyes.

She was safe now. All of them were.

Millforte could do them — and her mother — no more harm.

CHAPTER 59

NO DOUBT

Grace relished the familiar sights of Careo House's drawing room — the lace curtains, the Queen Anne chairs, the marble fireplace. She still found it hard to believe — after all that had happened that morning — that she was really back in Lindenfell.

"Will you not have some more?"

Grace looked up at Beatrice, thanking her as she accepted the cup and saucer of steaming tea from her friend's hands.

Beatrice lifted another one and offered it to David.

"Thank you, Miss Beckwith." His voice still sounded a little scratchy, and deep purple bruises mottled his neck.

The sight of them made Grace shudder. How gracious God had been to preserve him throughout the events of that horrible day.

To preserve them all.

She remembered Millforte's still, silent figure lying in the middle of the street. The blood, the atmosphere, the shock.

She focused on David as he sipped his tea. "How do you feel now?"

"Oh, I am well enough," David said, fixing his caring eyes keenly upon her. "And you?"

Grace released a heavy sigh. "In truth, I am still a little shaken. I cannot believe it all happened. Nor that... *he*... is now dead."

David breathed out a heavy sigh. "Nor I."

"I am very much glad to be back here." She glanced around the room again. Careo House had become so familiar to her in recent times that it was almost like being at home.

After more policeman had arrived and taken all their statements, the shaken company of friends had decided to travel back to Lindenfell by train that afternoon. Grace hadn't wanted to spend another minute in London, and the others had required little persuasion.

A few hours later, they'd found themselves in Miss Withers's drawing room and, having recounted most of the day's events to their host, Grace was only now beginning to breathe more deeply and release some of the tension her weary muscles still held.

Miss Withers had turned so pale upon hearing all that had transpired that Grace had feared a reprisal of her recent illness, but David assured her that his resilient aunt would come to no harm. The aged woman was presently engaged in a cheerful conversation with Beatrice, with a little more colour in her cheeks than when they had first arrived.

David was probably right. She was stronger than she looked.

"Yes, it is a comfort to me, too," David agreed, reclaiming Grace's attention. "Although..." He stared at his teacup.

Grace's heart stuttered. Was he thinking the same thoughts as she? Did this homely place hold bitter memories for him, as well as pleasant ones?

David placed his cup and saucer on the mahogany tea

table in front of them. He looked up at her with wistful eyes. "Miss Stratton... Could I have a word with you? Outside?"

Grace's heart raced. Outside. The place she had learned the devastating truth about all of his lies. She nodded, reminding herself that all was forgiven, and that the sorrowful memories of that day need not lay any claim to her now.

"Oh, Grace?" Miss Withers said, her conversation with Beatrice evidently at an end.

Grace turned to David, lowering her voice. "Excuse me, I ought to see to your aunt first..."

"Of course," he said with a smile, though she could tell by his tensed shoulders that the delay was a disappointing one.

Grace made her way toward Miss Withers, her heart hammering. What did David wish to say?

"Are you well, Miss Withers?" she asked, settling in the seat beside her employer. She glanced at Beatrice, who was now engrossed in a happy conversation with Isaac. The sight warmed her heart.

"Might I be correct in assuming...?" Miss Withers asked, motioning to the chatting pair.

Grace smiled. "I believe the feelings are mutual." She chuckled, then her smile faded a little. "I suppose that is a silver lining to our gloomy day."

Miss Withers shook her head slowly, a sombre look altering her features. "I cannot believe all that you have come through this day, my dear."

Grace sighed. "Nor I, in truth. But you have a very courageous nephew. I do not know where we would be without him. Truly."

Miss Withers smiled as she glanced at David. "Yes. He *is* a good boy." She looked back at Grace. "Have you and he managed to... come to any agreements?"

Grace laughed nervously. "Well, we have been rather occupied today..."

"Oh, I know, my child." Miss Withers patted Grace's arm affectionately. "But... you, yourself, have made peace with everything?"

"Yes." Grace smiled. "I truly have. And I am so thankful. God has shown me, in His word, a lot about what love truly is — and is not." She paused. "I have *you* to thank, too."

"Me?"

"Yes. The Lord was already speaking to my heart... nudging me about forgiving David. Then, Mr. Taylor's letter brought the welcome news about David placing his faith in the Lord... And, *your* letter, or the memory of it, at least... It was what gave me the courage to rush to London. To put my faith and feelings into action."

A sad smile lit Miss Withers's face. "I am glad, my child. Glad, too, that you will not live with the regret of never knowing what might have been." She gave a short, melancholy laugh. "All these years, I might have been Mrs. Millforte... but now, at least, you sha—"

Grace froze. "What did you say?"

"I said, all these years, I might have been Mrs. Millforte. If I *had* run away and married Samuel."

The room seemed to tilt and sway before Grace's eyes. She clutched the arm of the chair, desperate not to show any sign of her horror to Miss Withers. "Samuel's last name was... Millforte?"

"Yes. Why? Do you know someone of that name?"

She thought back to their earlier conversation. None of them had mentioned the man's name to Miss Withers upon telling her of their ordeal in London.

They'd spoken of him only in descriptions.

Not by name.

But...

Horror flooded Grace. It couldn't be the same man. She'd read the letter herself — Samuel was tender and kind, willing to risk everything — for *love,* no less! But Millforte... all he'd cared about was money, and his own pleasure.

No. There *had* to be some other explanation. Surely, the man who had terrorised them all that day was not the same man whom Miss Withers had almost—

"Grace?"

"Oh... I... I... What was he like? Samuel..."

Confusion flickered on Miss Withers's brow for a moment before nostalgia softened her features. "Oh, he was very handsome. He had dark hair and was *so* well spoken. A true gentleman. Though, his frame was anything but delicate. He was tall, with broad shoulders, and twinkling eyes, as blue as the sea."

It was Millforte's description, save for the dark hair. Though, time could have easily transformed it into the greying hair of the man in London.

"He was very close friends with the young man that my father actually *wanted* me to marry — Mr. Milvern."

The room seemed to swim. "Milvern?"

Miss Withers nodded. "Yes. Oh, Samuel knew Milvern had no interest in me, nor I in him, and so, they remained friends. They were so close, in fact, that people often assumed they were brothers!"

Grace forced a smile upon seeing Miss Withers's amusement, even as turmoil roiled within her. She suppressed the overwhelming urge to weep.

Samuel — the man whom Miss Withers had spent her life pining over — was the same man who had stolen her mother's youth and had attempted that very day to ruin her own.

The physical description.

The name Milvern.

There could be no doubt about it...

It was the same man.

CHAPTER 60

A PAINFUL CHOICE

David watched Grace and his aunt speaking, a sense of wary apprehension rising in his chest. He was too far across the room to hear their words, but he was in little doubt that the subject of their discussion was not an agreeable one.

At least, not to Grace.

He strained to hear past Isaac and Beatrice's chatter and laughter, but it was no use.

Something was very wrong. Grace, already wan from their earlier ordeal, had grown even more ashen, and the nervous fluttering of her hands made him want to rush over to ensure that she was all right.

Eventually, his aunt rose from her chair, prompting the gentlemen in the room to do the same.

"Good night, everyone. I must retire now. Have as much more tea as you wish, only do get some rest soon, yourselves. It has been quite an exhausting day for you all." Miss Withers's tone was gentle and sorrowful, and David's heart squeezed with gratitude at her evident concern.

"Good night, Aunt," he said, with a bow. "Sleep well."

She nodded, her lingering look at him filled with tenderness.

"You are sure you do not wish me to help you?" Grace asked, her whole body stiff with unease.

"Quite sure, thank you." Miss Withers cast Grace a loving smile, nodded at Isaac and Beatrice, then strolled regally to the door.

As soon as she had left the room, David rushed to Grace's side.

"Miss Stratton, are you ill? You look—"

"Millforte is Samuel!" Grace half-blurted, half-gasped. "Samuel is Millforte! And she has no idea! Oh... What are we to do? Ought we to *tell* her? But how could we, I—"

"Who is Samuel?" David asked.

"Samuel? The man who wrote her the letter?" Beatrice asked in a wary voice.

Grace turned to face her. "Yes!"

"Impossible!" Beatrice rose to her feet.

"Who?" Isaac stood and took a step nearer Beatrice.

"What letter?" David asked.

Grace drew a deep breath, willing herself to calm down.

"Grace, are you sure? It cannot be!" Beatrice's chest rose and fell rapidly.

"It is! Oh, I wish it was not so, but it is him. There is no doubt."

Grace recounted her conversation with Miss Withers as a sick knot formed in David's stomach. He glanced at Isaac and Beatrice, whose faces revealed the horror that he was certain was apparent on his own.

"You are telling me that... that maniac today is the man with whom my aunt had hoped to share her life?" David asked, knowing the answer yet willing it not to be true.

Grace looked at him, her lips drawn together in disbelieving regret. "Yes."

"I cannot believe it," Beatrice bemoaned, clasping her hands.

"What a blessed escape she had from it all..." Isaac mused.

"But she has pined after him all these years, believing that she made the wrong choice. What should we do? Ought we to tell her? But that would surely be too much for her to bear!" Grace's shoulders drooped.

David sighed. Lies had consequences — he knew that only too well. He fixed his eyes on Grace. "I believe you and I have learned that even a well-intentioned concealment of truth can often be more painful than the alternative. Therefore — even though it will be difficult — I believe we must tell her."

Grace shook her head, looking at him pleadingly. "I cannot..."

"Then I shall. I do not wish for her to mourn that man any longer. Isaac is right — it was a blessing that she escaped him. She must know that. Find comfort in that."

"But it will crush her to know what he... how he turned out..."

"Perhaps, for a time. But think, Grace — you and I know vividly how important it is to be told the truth. And, the Bible says that we are to speak the truth in love, and that the truth will set us free... I have to trust that God will be gracious toward my aunt, and will heal her broken heart properly, upon finding out the truth. Sometimes, when there is a fracture, we must cause more pain initially in order for the bone to set correctly. We could withhold the pain, and leave the patient to recover, but they would bear a permanent weakness or even become crippled as a result. Sometimes, we must do something painful in order to bring about complete and proper healing. It is not pleasant — not at all — but it is necessary. I shall speak with her tomorrow and 'reset the bone' as gently as I can."

Grace sighed wearily, eventually conceding with a gentle nod.

"Do not worry, Miss Stratton," Isaac said. "I believe David is right. And God *will* help her to recover from it all. I know it."

Beatrice looked at Isaac admiringly, and as he turned back to her and caught her gaze, he smiled, dipping his head a little.

David suppressed a smile as he looked at Grace. He flicked his gaze briefly toward Isaac and Beatrice, then looked at her again, raising his eyebrows momentarily.

Grace looked at them, then back at David, and a small smile worked its way onto her lips.

"I have not yet had a chance to tell you that I kept my promise..." David whispered.

Grace observed him, frowning a little. "Promise?"

"Mm. To discover the truth about a certain... secret admirer?"

Recognition flickered in her eyes, then she smiled, appearing the most relaxed he had seen her look all day. "Oh, I see..."

"Yes. I believe it is rather obvious now, and my report is most likely unnecessary, but... It would seem that the affection is most definitely returned."

Grace gave a light laugh. "It would very much seem so."

A sense of awe overtook David as he continued to observe Grace. How precious she had become to him. And how close he had come to losing her — multiple times, now.

He knew he could not endure doing so again.

"Miss Stratton?" His throat was dry. "Might I speak with you for a moment outside?"

Grace nodded, the knowing look in her eyes doing nothing to ease his growing nerves.

He strode toward the patio doors and pulled them open, praying silently for the right words to say.

The words he'd been longing to say for weeks.

CHAPTER 61

TRUE LOVE

As Grace stepped outside behind David, she closed her eyes, relishing the breeze as it washed over her face. The country air smelled heavy with peace and sunlight, though the shadows lengthened all around them.

Opening her eyes, she couldn't help smiling at David's expression. He was observing her with a shy earnestness, his hands and fingers twitching in a nervous dance.

David cleared his throat. "Miss Stratton... I wish to ask you something. Something I could not ask before, as two enormous obstacles stood in my way. The first, as you know, was my deception. And the second, was the matter of my future — or, indeed, whether I was to have one at all. But, those two things being resolved..." He stepped closer to her, his gaze now fixing steadily upon her. "Miss Stratton... Grace..." He smiled, his grey eyes sparkling. "Will you... marry me?"

Delight flooded Grace, and she couldn't hold back the huge smile that spread across her face. She looked at the man she had once known as John, the man she'd believed she would never speak with again... the man who had come so close to losing his life twice that very day — once for his profession, and once for her. "Yes," she said, exhaling an overjoyed laugh. "Yes, I will marry you."

Surprised joy animated David's features, and he pulled her toward him in a glad embrace. "I promise I shall always be honest with you. I would give my life to make sure that you are safe."

Grace pulled back from his arms, catching his gaze. "I know... You almost did, today."

David said nothing, only shook his head slightly and grasped her hands, stroking them gently. "I love you, Grace..."

Gratitude burned in her chest. "I love you, too. And I am so glad that no real harm came to you. I was so afraid. Yet, so grateful. You rushed toward me, to protect me."

"I would gladly do so again."

Just then, the final piece of the puzzle that had seemed to be missing from her life clicked into place, revealing the whole picture. "Just as the Lord did for us—"

"Yes." David smiled, unmistakable peace in his eyes. "And I am so glad He did."

They embraced again as the sun slipped out of sight, plunging the air around them into a cool dusk.

Grace closed her eyes and smiled as she nuzzled her ear against David's chest, listening to the steady rhythm of his heart.

Sure and steady... that's what love was. Real love.

Like the love that God had for her. Like the love that He had blessed she and David with.

Whatever the future might hold — events large or small, good or bad — she was not facing it alone.

She never had been.

God had been with her — guiding her, preserving her.

And now, David would be, too.

All because of love.

WHAT DID YOU THINK?

I really hope you enjoyed reading this book
as much as I enjoyed writing it for you.

If you did, please consider leaving a rating or review on
Amazon, BookBub or Goodreads.

A review doesn't have to be a long, in-depth critique — just a line or two about what you liked about the book would make my day and help other readers find my stories.

Reviews really are so helpful and encouraging for authors, and your feedback on *The Letter* (no matter how short!) would be so very much appreciated.

Thank you.

READING RESOURCES

Want to read and discuss this novel with your book club?

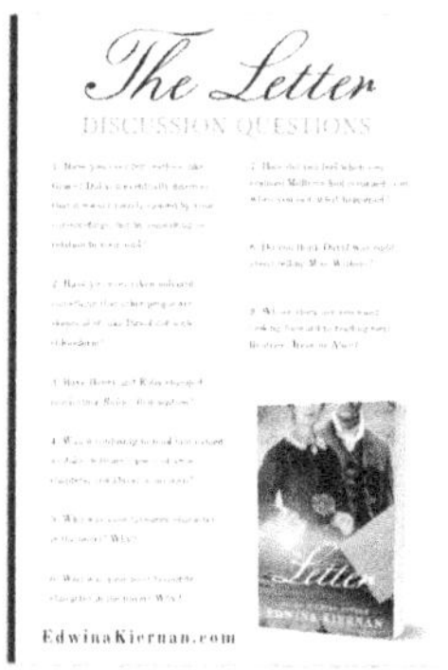

Visit **edwinakiernan.com/reading**
to download your discussion questions for
The Letter and my other books.

ACKNOWLEDGEMENTS

This novel would not be what it is without:

Lynne Tagawa —

I am so thankful that God answered my prayers with such a knowledgeable and delightful editor.

You have taught me so much, and working with you has been such a joy.

Thank you for going above and beyond to meet my deadlines and for all of your feedback that helped me set a richer atmosphere throughout the story, scene by scene.

Lord-willing, I can't wait to work with you again on the next one.

The K Team —

Rachel Knowles and Philippa Jane Keyworth —

You're not only my *Hearts of the Hall* co-authors, but two of my dearest friends.

Thank you for all of your support and understanding throughout such a hectic schedule!

I truly cherish both of you, and appreciate your enthusiasm, encouragement and all-round epicness as we continue to travel the author path together.

Let's go back to Duriel Hall soon!

AND A HUGE, SPECIAL THANK YOU TO:

My husband, Paul, and son, Luke —

Truly, you are the two most magnificent earthly blessings I have ever been given.

Thank you both for all of your love, encouragement, joy, laughter and for showing me daily that life and love are such precious gifts.

I cannot even begin to describe how thankful I am that the Lord has given us to each other. I love you both, far much more than I can say.

I thank my God in all my remembrance of you, always offering prayer with joy in my every prayer for you all

Philippians 1:3-4

ABOUT THE AUTHOR

Edwina Kiernan is the Christian author of the award-winning novel *Ruby's Redemption*.

An enthusiast of classic novels and history, Edwina combines her faith, imagination and research in hope-infused tales set in times past.

She is a committed follower of Jesus (the Living Word), and endeavours to use her pen to point others to Him.

When she's not writing, Edwina loves spending time with her dashing husband and lively little son, reading and studying the Bible, getting lost in a captivating novel and drinking more types of tea than most people realize even exist.

Join her mailing list for free gifts, updates, regular giveaways and lots of classic and historical fiction goodness.

Subscribe at: **EdwinaKiernan.com**

amazon.com/author/edwinakiernan
bookbub.com/profile/edwina-kiernan
goodreads.com/edwinakiernan
x.com/EdwinaKiernanHQ
instagram.com/edwinakiernan
facebook.com/edwinakiernan

RUBY'S REDEMPTION

2021 READERS' FAVOURITE AWARD WINNER

IN CHRISTIAN HISTORICAL ROMANCE

Book 1 in the Gems of Grace series

A gentle clergyman. A broken prostitute.

A blossoming love that will endanger both their lives...

Forced into depravity by her tyrannous guardian after her parents' death, Ruby's life is one of vile deeds and violence. Unable to remember much of life outside the brothel's walls, years of despair and abuse have crushed all hope of ever breaking free from her captor's iron grip.

Until an unlikely encounter with Henry, a gentle country clergyman, sets an escape in motion that will change both their lives. But when Ruby's worst fears are realised, the uncommon pair will face more devastation than either thought possible.

As the dawning of a new life of peace and love is ripped from her grasp, Ruby discovers that true freedom has a high cost... but who will have to pay?

Available in Paperback, eBook and Kindle Unlimited at

edwinakiernan.com/ruby

PEARL'S PROMISE

2022 READERS' FAVOURITE AWARD WINNER

IN CHRISTIAN HISTORICAL ROMANCE

Book 2 in the Gems of Grace series

A duty-bound heir. A dejected spinster.

A love that could ruin both their families' demands for their futures...

Pearl Acton's worst fear is coming true: she'll be trapped in a loveless marriage—just like her parents—as her family seeks to quickly marry her off to a wealthy stranger. Until an encounter with a gentle heir sparks a fragile hope that somehow Pearl might aid her family *and* marry for love.

Nicholas Dalton has always been a disappointment to his father, with his poetic soul and disorganised nature. In London for the season, Nicholas finds an instant connection with Pearl, but it would seem her future is promised to another. Isn't it?

Pressures soon mount, compelling Pearl and Nicholas to uphold their family duties. Is it too late to escape their crushing obligations and forge a new path - together?

Available in Paperback, eBook and Kindle Unlimited at

edwinakiernan.com/pearl

BERYL'S BLESSING

2023 READERS' FAVOURITE BRONZE MEDAL

AWARD WINNER IN CHRISTIAN HISTORICAL ROMANCE

Book 3 in the Gems of Grace series

She's used to being alone.

He can't get away from his guilty conscience.

Will an arranged marriage help them heal, or force them to confront long-hidden truths and new depths of despair?

Five years ago, Beryl Haywood was crippled in an accident that claimed two lives. Since then, reading and painting have been the only companions to/in her long, lonely days.

Frederick Sinclair is struggling to adapt to normality after returning from the French battlefields. A hefty weight of guilt and regret weighs on him, taunting him that he'll never be free from it.

As the newlyweds begin to wonder if love might lie ahead, a startling discovery shakes them each to the core, threatening to snatch away the future they'd begun to hope they might share...

Available in Paperback, eBook and Kindle Unlimited at

edwinakiernan.com/beryl

GEMS OF GRACE BOXSET (EBOOK ONLY)

All three *Gems of Grace* novels — *Ruby's Redemption, Pearl's Promise,* and *Beryl's Blessing* in one eBook volume!

Read now:

edwinakiernan.com/gems

RESTORING MISS HASTINGS

Penniless and alone… A stranger takes her in.

But will her presence ruin his chance to restore all he's lost?

heartsofthehall.com/restoringmisshastings

THE LAMP (Victorian Virtues, Book 2)

Will God hear their cries and grant them a future together, or will deadly occurrences tear them apart forever?

England, 1849. Beatrice Beckwith is an orphaned young lady living with her aunt. On the brink of her deepest wish coming true, her plans unexpectedly collapse. Then, a startling discovery and an outbreak of cholera set in motion a series of catastrophic events, plunging her into even bleaker darkness.

Isaac Taylor is forced to leave Miss Beckwith just as he's arranged a meeting to propose. His deceased great-uncle's derelict house needs restoration. But dust is not his only enemy, and a web of secrets soon entangles him.

As they each face their darkest moments, they'll endure more devastation than ever before. Can joy once again be found, or will dangerous circumstances extinguish its light—and their very lives?

Available in Paperback, eBook and Kindle Unlimited.

A VANISHING ACT

(Ever After Mysteries, Book 11)

On screen they're a darling duo, but it's a whole different story behind the scenes...

Hollywood legend Kent Selwood isn't happy sharing the limelight with rising star Stella Sanders. Tired of her diva drama, Kent makes it clear—he wants Stella gone.

Seamstress Bonnie Roseland is practically invisible to everyone at the studio, except for slick actor, Jerry Jackson — the one man she wishes would leave her alone. Her deep-rooted faith helps her see beyond the glitz and glamor to the broken realities and dysfunctional atmosphere at the studio.

When the studio receives blackmail letters, Kent's attitude makes him the prime suspect, and he's swiftly banished from the lot, despite insisting that he's been framed. Only Bonnie believes him — and she's confident she knows who the real culprit is.

But when a ransom note arrives after Stella goes missing and evidence is discovered that clearly implicates Kent, will Bonnie help him uncover the truth in time to save his career... and Stella's life?

Available in Paperback, eBook and Kindle Unlimited.

edwinakiernan.com/vanishing

HEART OF INTEGRITY

(Hearts of the West, Book 2)

Not all fault lines are hidden in the earth...

Ifor Morgan and his father have traveled far from their home in Wales to settle in the small mining town of Lone Pine, California—driven by a need to escape the shame and sorrow of his brother's fatal scandal.

Susan Kelly is starting over, too. Miles from her home in Ireland, she's determined to build a life for herself in Lone Pine that doesn't involve any of the deception she was caught up in back home.

As Ifor and Susan forge a cautious connection, people from Susan's past show up in town, entangling her in a fresh web of illegal activity.

And when a devastating earthquake throws the town into a state of upheaval, secrets soon shake those least expecting to uncover them...

Available in Paperback, eBook and Kindle Unlimited.

edwinakiernan.com/integrity

AUDIOBOOKS

RUBY'S REDEMPTION AUDIOBOOK

Narrated by ***Sophie Linfield***

Listen now:

edwinakiernan.com/rubyaudio

(Visit the link above to listen for FREE with a 30-day Audible trial!)

PEARL'S PROMISE AUDIOBOOK

Narrated by ***Alexandra Lee Smith***

Listen now:

edwinakiernan.com/pearlaudio

(Visit the link above to listen for FREE with a 30-day Audible trial!)

Other titles will be available in audiobook format soon.

WANT A FREE BOOK?

Get a free copy of my Victorian novella, *Restoring Miss Hastings,* as a thank you for signing up for my weekly email newsletter.

You're free to subscribe at any time, but if you stick around you'll get updates, freebies, recommendations and exclusive giveaways, plus encouragement and lots of historical fiction fun!

Sign up here:

EdwinaKiernan.com/FreeBook

Made in the USA
Coppell, TX
16 August 2024

36069869R00198